FALLEN STAR

A PROJECT GAUNTLET MISSION

RICHARD TURNER

Copyright 2018© Richard Turner

All rights reserved. No part of this publication may be reproduced or distributed in any form or by any means, electronic or mechanical, including photocopying, recording, or by any information storage or retrieval system, without the prior written consent of the authors.

ISBN: 1545339686

ISBN-13: 9781545339688

FALLEN STAR

A PROJECT GAUNTLET MISSION

1

July 9, 1947

Northwest of Roswell, New Mexico

Lieutenant Colonel Raymond Lloyd turned the wheel of his blue 1947 Chevrolet Aerosedan over in his callused hands and drove off the empty highway onto a dirt track. A coyote running alongside the trail saw the car coming and stopped to watch as it passed by. Lloyd rubbed the back of his neck with his right hand. The muscles were as tight as steel. He grimaced. If Lloyd didn't get some good news, a full-blown tension headache was only minutes away. Lloyd looked out over the desolate landscape and wondered how everything had gotten out of hand so quickly. Since the end of the war things in his office had been relatively quiet, and that was just the way he liked it.

Lloyd was a career soldier, who had served as a pilot in the U.S. Army Air Force in the skies over Europe. Under a pair of sunglasses, his weary brown eyes were bloodshot. Lloyd's chestnut hair was almost gone from the top of his head. His round face was tanned from having been outside under the hot New Mexico sun for the past couple of days. Lloyd wasn't wearing his usual army uniform. Instead, he wore a pair of brown slacks and a tan-colored shirt.

He could see a farm just up ahead. Lloyd slowed down and approached the front gate, where a couple of military policemen dressed as farm hands stood guard. Lloyd fished out his identification and flashed it to one of the MPs. The man quickly checked his ID and opened the gate. Lloyd drove toward an old, white, wooden house with three vehicles parked in front of it. He parked his car and got out. Right away, the dry, scorching, late-afternoon heat struck him. It was like walking into an oven.

The front door to the house opened. A man in his early thirties with thick blond hair waved at Lloyd. "Good afternoon, sir," said the man. "How was the drive?"

"Long and hot," Lloyd replied gruffly. He had been on the road for close to eight hours and was looking forward to a shower and a cool beer or two after he concluded his business at the farm. "Is the rest of the team here?"

"Yes, sir. Major Gordon and Captain Thurman arrived a couple of hours ago."

Lloyd followed the man inside and smiled when he saw a full pitcher of iced lemonade sitting on the table.

"Here, let me pour you a glass," said the blond-haired man.

Lloyd took the glass and drained it in one gulp. "Another one, please, Captain Jones." Although there was a fan in the corner running at full power, the temperature inside the house was stifling.

"Certainly, sir."

Besides Lloyd and Jones, there were two other men sitting at a round table in the small kitchen. Both were dressed in casual attire. Major Gordon had thinning black hair, while Captain Thurman was bald and wore silver-rimmed glasses on his pudgy nose.

"Okay, gents, fill me in on what we know," said Lloyd as he took a seat.

Major Gordon spoke first. "Sir, as you are aware, the public affairs officer at the Roswell Army Airfield issued a statement to the press yesterday indicating that a flying disc had been found and recovered by personnel from the base."

"Yes, the damn fool caused quite an unneeded panic in the

Pentagon," said Lloyd, wiping his sweat-covered brow with a red-and-white checkered handkerchief. "He'll be lucky to find work as a janitor after that monumental screw up. Wasn't he aware of the Fallen Star Protocols?"

"Apparently not. The orders were locked away in the base commander's safe, and by the looks of things had yet to be read by anyone on the base."

"Goddammit. It's a priority-one document. It should have been read the day it was received." Lloyd shook his head. "When I get back home I'll speak with the ops staff at the Army Air Force Headquarters and make sure the word gets out for everyone to read the protocols immediately before we have another one of these incidents."

"Yes, sir," said Captain Thurman. "A new statement was given by the base's commanding officer to the press earlier today refuting the initial claim of a flying disc being discovered."

"What was the new cover story?" asked Lloyd.

"A weather balloon, sir."

Lloyd chuckled. "Inventive, yet highly plausible. Has this gone out on the newswire?"

Thurman nodded.

"Have they done anything to reinforce their story?"

"Yes, sir," said Gordon. "An old weather balloon that crashed in the desert late last year was shown to the press. Afterward, it was loaded up into a C-54 transport plane and flown to Los Alamos for further examination. Once the crash team at Los Alamos sees the wreckage, they'll issue another press release confirming the weather balloon narrative."

"Very good. This should put this incident to bed quite nicely." Lloyd emptied his glass and wiped his parched lips with the back of his hand. He looked around the cluttered farmhouse. "Say, who owns this place?"

"It belongs to a man called Fred Deckard," replied Jones.

"Is he trustworthy? I don't want this falling apart because

someone couldn't keep their damned lips shut."

"Sir, don't worry, Mr. Deckard is very reliable. He fought in the First World War with the Marines and is a true patriot. When we asked him if we could rent the place for a week to test some equipment, he never batted an eye. He even refused to take any money from me and insisted it was his national duty to help us out."

"Where is he now?"

"In town with his only daughter and her three kids."

"Where's her husband?"

"He died during the war. At Okinawa, I think."

Lloyd turned his head away for a moment before standing up. He had lost a younger brother and two cousins in the war. He knew the pain of dealing with the loss of a loved one all too well. Lloyd looked at the men in the room with him. "Okay, let's not drag this out any longer than we have to. Where is it?"

"It's in the barn behind the house," explained Gordon.

Together, the four men walked to the barn. A man with an army-issued M1 rifle stood guard outside. Thurman opened the side door and held it while everyone else walked inside.

Lloyd had barely stepped inside when he stopped in his tracks. His eyes widened the second he saw the large silver disc sitting on the back of a vehicle trailer. It was about twenty meters in circumference with what looked like a cockpit for two pilots in the middle of the craft. The front of the ship was damaged from where the disc had struck the ground. He walked toward the ship and placed his hand on the outer shell. It was smooth and cool to the touch.

Lloyd shook his head. "Can you believe it? This is the third one of these to crash in as many months."

"Sir, when it gets dark we're going to cover the craft with a tarp and drive it to Los Alamos where it will be flown to Wright-Patterson Air Base in Dayton," explained Jones.

"Will you three be accompanying it all the way to Ohio?"

"Yes, sir."

Lloyd let out a sigh and ran a hand over his unshaven chin. "I suppose there's only one thing left to do. Where are they being held?"

"I can show you. If you'll follow me, sir," said Gordon, motioning back to the door.

The two men walked out of the barn and to a silver trailer parked next to a decrepit-looking stable.

Lloyd stopped at the door and looked at his colleague. "How are they doing?"

"Fine, sir. They haven't said a word but seem to be in remarkably good health considering how hard the disc hit the ground when it crashed."

"Okay, wait outside while I talk to them." Lloyd opened the door and stepped into the air-conditioned trailer. The instant he saw the two occupants sitting at a table sipping water, he shook his head. "For the love of God, I should have known it would be you two!"

One of the pilots flashed a pearly-white smile at Lloyd and said, *"Guten tag, Herr Colonel."*

2

Iraq – present day

Coalition Special Forces Training Camp – North of Al Kut

Captain David Grant walked out of his tent, and stopped to look up at the night sky before heading to the showers when something made him glance upward. Because there were no major towns around to create light pollution, it was easy to see the beauty of the heavens. Millions of stars twinkled overhead. He stood and watched as a shooting star streaked above the base before burning out. Grant had just come from the gym, where he and a friend had pumped iron for over an hour. With some reluctance, he turned back toward the showers. His recent weightlifting session had turned into an hour long bench-press competition with one of his friends. Now, he was tired and sore. And to rub salt into the wound, he'd lost by just one kilo.

They'd have to see what happened in the rematch scheduled later in the week.

Grant pulled open the door to the shower tent and walked in. The place was deserted. He removed his sweat-stained clothes and hung them up before stepping under a shower faucet. Grant turned the water on, lowered his head, and let the hot water massage his tired and aching shoulder muscles. After soaping and washing himself off, he reached over and turned off the taps. Grant ran a hand over his face to wipe away the water before grabbing his towel and drying off his taut body.

His mind drifted back to the last conversation he'd had with his father. Grant had just turned thirty and was facing what his grandfather used to call 'that inevitable fork in the road.' Grant's ailing father had once more asked him to leave the army and move back home to take over the family business. Grant had joined the army to get away from home in the first place. As far back as he could remember, he had always wanted to see the world and serve his country. He hoped to have at least a twenty-year career in the army before moving back home to run his family's vineyard. To further muddy the waters, Grant was waiting on word from his commanding officer to see if he was going to be promoted to major later in the year. The only thing Grant knew for certain was that he didn't know what to tell his father the next time they spoke.

After pulling on some clean shorts and a tan army T-shirt, Grant walked over to a row of sinks along the wall of the tent and stopped to look in a mirror. Although his hair was already cut short, Grant couldn't decide if he should get a trim in the morning. What little hair he had on his head was light brown, and his sharp eyes were sky-blue. He stood just under two meters tall, and was, without a doubt, in the best shape of his life. After one last look at himself, Grant grabbed his laundry, pushed open the door, and stepped outside into the cool night air.

Camp Bayonet was a coalition Special Forces training establishment where American, British, Canadian, and Australian soldiers taught Iraqi special operators how to be squad and platoon leaders. Normally, the camp would be home to over three hundred Iraqi soldiers and civilians, but now it was almost empty. The last batch of recruits had graduated two days ago, and the next crew wouldn't arrive for another week. The quiet time allowed the coalition staff to conduct a personnel rotation of their own. Half of the training staff assigned for the year would soon be replaced by fresh instructors.

Grant welcomed the peace and quiet. It gave him a chance to

catch up on the mountains of paperwork, which seemed to pile up on his desk daily. His job in the camp was that of a company mentor, who helped guide his Iraqi counterpart through the training of his new squad leaders. After ten months in theater, Grant was looking forward to rotating back home to the States. Where he was going to next was still up in the air, but he had asked to be posted back home to the 82nd Airborne Division. Grant walked back to his tent, dropped off his dirty clothes, put a pair of old runners on his feet, and then retrieved his M4 carbine, which he slung over his back.

Outside, the Muslim evening call to prayer played over the camp's speakers. Grant had heard the pre-recorded calls five times a day for months and was now mostly oblivious to them. He stepped out of his tent and watched as a handful of Iraqi security personnel accompanied by some of the camp's civilian staff made their way to a small mosque built at the other end of the base. He wanted to forget the last conversation he had with his dad and watch a movie on his computer, but a nagging voice in the back of his mind told him to do an hour of work at his desk before calling it a night.

He was halfway between his quarters and his office when the camp plunged into darkness. Grant stopped in his tracks and looked around. Every light in the camp was out. An uneasy feeling swept over him when he couldn't hear the base's power generators running. He brought his watch up to check the time. He was surprised to see that, like everything else, it had ceased to work. The only light came from the full moon high above the camp.

"Hey, does anyone know what the hell is going on?" called out a man with a strong Australian accent.

Grant turned toward a shadowed figure standing outside of a tent. He walked over and recognized Sergeant James Maclean from the Australian Army training team.

Maclean held up a satellite phone. "I was chatting with my sister back home in Sydney when the bloody phone died on me."

"Odd, isn't it?" said Grant. "Everything in the camp with an electrical circuit has switched off. Even my watch has stopped working."

Maclean checked his wristwatch and swore. "Mine's not working, either."

Several more men walked out of their tents and looked around the darkened camp.

"Someone must have forgotten to pay the bill," called out a man, eliciting a few nervous laughs.

"I wonder how far this blackout extends?" said Grant to Maclean.

"Only a small portion of the camp is on the Iraqi electrical grid," explained Maclean. "Most of our power comes from our portable generators. Besides, what could have caused our watches to stop working?"

"I once read that an electromagnetic pulse could cause everything using electricity to stop working. But it would take a fair bit of power to knock out all the electrical circuits in the camp."

"Okay, I'll buy that, Captain. But what could have caused an EMP out here in the middle of nowhere?"

Grant shrugged. "Perhaps it was from a massive solar flare striking the atmosphere somewhere above us?"

"Maybe, but I'm not sure that's the answer. I've never read about something happening quite like this anyplace else in the world."

"There's got to be a first time for everything, Sergeant. Come on, let's climb the nearest tower and see if the local villages are affected as well."

At the top of the tower, they found two Iraqi security guards sitting on the floor and smoking cigarettes.

"On your bloody feet," said Maclean, grabbing one of the men by the collar and hauling him up.

Grant looked out toward the horizon. It was the same

everywhere he looked. The countryside was pitch black. "Whatever happened, it's big. It knocked out everything around us for kilometers."

"Sir, we should let Colonel Rodriguez know what has happened, so he can organize some form of security with the local Iraqi police until the power comes back on," suggested Maclean.

"Yeah, good idea."

They had taken fewer than a half-dozen steps from the bottom of the tower when a dark shadow flew across the base.

Grant looked up and blinked. He was sure he had just seen something resembling a helicopter, but this one didn't make a sound. A fraction of a second later, the ground where the other allied soldiers had congregated seemed to boil as thousands of tiny projectiles tore the hapless soldiers to shreds.

Maclean grabbed Grant's arm. "Come on, sir, we've got to take cover."

"Where?" asked Grant, watching the last of the doomed soldiers drop to the ground.

"There," said Maclean, pointing at one of the camp's mobile generators.

With his heart pounding away in his ears, Grant followed Maclean. They ran toward a nearby generator bolted onto on the back of a vehicle trailer. The two soldiers came to a sliding halt underneath the trailer.

"Why the hell did we take cover under here?" whispered Grant.

"Don't say another word or move a muscle, sir," warned Maclean.

Grant glanced over and saw his colleague staring at the Hesco bastion wall just off to their right. He froze in place and watched as two figures crawled over the wall and down onto the ground. In the silvery light of the moon, Grant could see the intruders were wearing skintight outfits that covered their entire bodies. Even their faces were hidden behind a blackened glass faceplate. Each one carried a short rifle with what looked to be a silencer built onto the muzzle. The two men moved with cat-like stealth from body to body, checking to see if they were still alive.

Throughout the camp the flimsy tents and office trailers were systematically shot to pieces by the circling helicopter. Anyone caught out in the open was killed within seconds.

"Buggers," muttered Maclean when the intruders shot and killed a wounded man trying to crawl away from them.

The attackers took one last look around for survivors before moving out of sight.

"I don't understand; why didn't they see us?" whispered Grant.

"Because whoever is attacking the camp is undoubtedly using thermal imaging to target our people," replied Maclean. "If we had stayed out in the open, it wouldn't take them long to see the heat coming from our bodies and pump a couple hundred rounds into us. I was praying that the heat from the generator would mask our bodies from observation. Anyone looking in the direction of the generator would only have seen a white-hot blob and not us."

Grant slid his M4 from his back and flipped off the safety. His mouth was dry with fear. He had been in combat on a number of occasions in Afghanistan, but nothing he had done in the past compared to what he had just witnessed. Grant took a couple deep breaths to calm his speeding heart and shifted his weight, intending to poke his head out from under the generator and look around.

"Don't, sir," Maclean whispered harshly. "We don't know how many of them there are in the camp. If you fire your rifle, they'll hear it and come running. No matter what, we need to stay alive to report what happened here tonight."

Grant lowered his rifle and looked over at Maclean. "Who the hell were those bastards? I didn't recognize a single piece of equipment on either of them."

"I don't know, sir, but we can eliminate ISIS as the attacker. They don't have that kind of equipment or training. One thing's for sure: whoever they are, they mean business."

"But why attack us? We're just a training establishment. We're not a threat to anyone."

"Captain, someone out there doesn't agree with you."

Grant clenched his carbine tight in his hands and listened to the absolute silence surrounding them. "Well, I don't hear them anymore, and I, for one, am not going to sit here and wait for someone to come and help us. There were over one hundred people in the camp before the attack. I need to know why we were targeted for extermination."

"Okay, but I need a weapon," said Maclean. "Mine's still in my quarters."

"There's one," said Grant, pointing at a dead Iraqi's AKM lying on the ground.

Maclean crawled out from underneath the trailer, crept over to the dead body, and picked up the assault rifle. He made sure it was loaded before making his way back to Grant. "I say we climb back up in the tower and see what we can see."

Grant nodded.

As silently as possible, the two men made their way to the tower. At the top, they found the guards' bodies. Both had been shot with a single round to the side of the head.

Grant got up on his knees and peered out into the darkness but couldn't see a thing.

"Here, try using these," said Maclean, handing him a pair of binoculars taken from one of the dead guards.

Grant brought the binoculars up to his eyes and looked around. Although nowhere near as good as a pair of night vision goggles, binoculars were the next best thing. The camp was deathly quiet. Grant ground his teeth together when he saw the unknown attackers had not only murdered every human being in the vicinity, but also the camp's guard dogs.

"Sir, I thought I saw something," whispered Maclean. "Take a look northeast."

Grant turned around and adjusted his binoculars. In the silvery light of the moon, he saw a group of men dressed like the intruders standing out in the open. One of the men pointed at a dry riverbed which ran behind the camp. As one, the assailants nodded and ran toward the wadi.

"Sir, you gotta take a look at this," said Maclean.

Grant lowered his glasses and turned around. He froze as a large, dark shape flew over the camp. Like the other craft, it had been modified to barely make any noise. Instead of a thunderous sound from the rotor blades slicing through the air, the helicopter was no louder than a finely-tuned car's engine. It slowed down and then descended to the ground. Dust and debris kicked up by the helicopter's powerful rotor blades swirled up and around the ship as it landed.

"That looks like a Russian Mi-26 heavy transport helicopter to me," said Grant. "But I've never heard of one that can fly nearly silent." He handed back the binoculars. "Here, take a look."

Maclean adjusted the eyepieces. "Yeah, it's a Mi-26. But why the hell would the Russians attack us?"

"I don't know. Lots of other countries own Mi-26s, so it might not be the Russians."

"Hey, sir, look! They're offloading a couple of backhoes."

Grant shook his head. "Say again?"

"Whoever they are, they're going to dig something up."

Grant took back the binoculars and watched as the two digging machines were led over to the top of the riverbed before driving out of sight.

"None of this makes any sense," said Grant. "I have to see what they're after."

"Yeah, me too," agreed Maclean. "There's an old goat path that runs by the eastern wall. We should be able to use that to sneak our way over to the wadi without being seen."

Grant nodded. "Lead on."

Like a pair of ghosts in the night, the two soldiers used the shadows to hide in as they crept through the camp. There were dead bodies everywhere they looked. Most had died right outside of their tents. Grant fought to block the images of his friends lying facedown on the sand from his mind. He silently swore when they had to step over the dead body of their commanding officer. *Payback is going to be a bitch*, he thought.

They slipped outside of the camp and waited a moment to make sure they weren't being followed before pushing on. Maclean pointed at a trail which led past an old abandoned home. Grant trailed behind the Aussie. It was when he stepped on a sharp rock that he remembered he was dressed in shorts, runners, and a T-shirt, hardly the best attire to wear when sneaking around in the dark, but he didn't have much of a choice in the matter.

Maclean stopped in his tracks and raised a hand.

Grant froze and held his breath. *Had they been spotted?*

A couple seconds later, Maclean lowered his hand and carried on to the edge of the wadi.

Grant let out his breath. Both men climbed down onto the dry, rock-strewn riverbed. The sound of the backhoes' excavators clawing at the ground filled the air.

"Thankfully, that noise will drown out everything else," said Maclean over his shoulder. "It should help us get real close to whoever these bastards are."

Grant nodded. "I agree. Let's see what they're up to."

Just as they were about to move, an ear-shattering explosion tore through the night. Less than fifty meters away, rocks and dirt shot straight up into the night sky. Grant and Maclean dove for cover as debris began to rain to the ground. A rock as large as a volleyball struck the sand right next to Grant's head, startling him.

"I guess they're in a bit of a hurry," said Maclean, standing up from behind a tall boulder. He brushed the dirt off his uniform and looked down the riverbed. "The coast looks clear."

With the sound of the blast still ringing in his ears, Grant flipped his weapon's safety off and brought it up to his shoulder. As quiet as a pair of mice, they crept forward until they could see the backhoes. The two soldiers took cover behind a jagged boulder that jutted out from the ground.

To Grant, it looked like the intruders were busy digging out what appeared to be a crashed airplane. He could only see half of it sticking up out of the sand, but it was unlike any plane he had seen before. Instead of being long and narrow like most craft, this one appeared to be circular and had what Grant took to be its cockpit in the center of the craft. Grant's fear subsided somewhat and gave way to curiosity. As the backhoes removed more earth from the craft, it was clear the plane, or whatever it was, was still in good condition.

"Ever see anything like that before in your life?" Grant whispered.

"No, sir, not unless you include the movies," replied Maclean. "Looks like they're going to lift it out of here using the chopper."

Grant brought up the binos and examined the craft. The backhoes pulled back as several men crawled up onto the ship and attached steel cables to it. The heavy transport chopper took off and maneuvered itself over the top of the craft and slowly descended until one of the men fed a heavy metal hook attached to the cables into a sturdy shackle on the belly of the helicopter. The man jumped down and waved over at another man standing at the top of the wadi. Right away, the chopper began to take up the slack. As soon as the line went taut, the helicopter pilot applied more power to help lift the craft out of the ground. For a few seconds nothing happened, and then ever so slowly, the ship began to move. It didn't take long for the rest of the craft to escape its resting place. The pilot brought the helicopter and its cargo high in the sky before banking east toward the Iranian border.

Grant popped his head up and watched as the rest of the intruders crawled out of the wadi and ran to a smaller helicopter waiting for them in the open field. Within seconds, the darkened craft lifted into the air and flew after the larger helicopter.

"If I hadn't seen what had just happened with my own eyes, I wouldn't have believed it," said Maclean.

Grant nodded. "I doubt those bastards will be back. It looks like they've got what they came for. Sergeant, we've got to get back to the camp and look for survivors."

"Yes, sir. I'm with you. The scent of blood carried on these winds will bring the wild dogs down from the hills, and I'll be damned if any of them are getting near any of our mates. We can build a couple of really big bonfires near the camp's entrances. That should keep them at bay until the sun comes up, or help arrives."

With that, the two soldiers jogged back to their devastated camp, lost in their thoughts about what had just happened and what was to follow.

3

Ali Al Salem Air Base – Kuwait

Grant pushed the plate of food away from himself, stared up at the clock on the wall, and saw that time was creeping by slowly. He let out a dejected sigh and drummed his fingers on the table. The thought of yet another pointless interview with some nameless individual in a dark suit had driven away his meager appetite.

It had been a week since the attack. They had been found the next day by a U.S. Army Special Forces team, who arrived to look for survivors. The two soldiers had been flown directly from Iraq to the sprawling allied air base in Kuwait, where they were summarily locked up in an old maintenance hangar far away from the rest of the station's personnel. All their dirty clothes had been taken from them the moment they landed at the base by soldiers in full decontamination gear. After showering they were examined by a team of doctors before being separated and interviewed by a seemingly never-ending stream of experts. Some of them were in uniform and some not, but all of them asked the same question: what happened that night out in the desert? Grant had not seen or heard from Sergeant Maclean for over four days and was beginning to wonder if he had been released to the Australian authorities on the base.

The door to the room opened, and Maclean stepped inside. Like Grant, he was wearing a set of tan coveralls. The man didn't look any worse for wear. He stood as tall as Grant but had broad muscular shoulders. His blond hair was cut short. He had bluish-green eyes and a nose slightly askew from the numerous fights he'd had in his youth as a private in the Australian Army.

"Good afternoon, sir," said Maclean, looking at his wrist where his watch usually sat, forgetting it wasn't on his wrist, then checking the time on the clock hanging on the wall.

"Afternoon, Sergeant," replied Grant, nodding.

Maclean took a seat at the table. "I don't know why, but I always feel naked without my watch."

Grant chuckled. "I know how you feel. I thought they'd let you go."

"No such luck. I guess they're tired of talking to us separately. You gonna eat that?" said Maclean, pointing at Grant's uneaten BLT sandwich.

"No. Help yourself."

Maclean picked up the sandwich and took a bite. "Have you been interviewed yet by the slender woman with short, black hair and a porcelain complexion?"

"Yes. She came in dressed in a dark suit, so I asked to see her ID."

"And?"

"She smiled and said I didn't need to see it."

"Same thing happened to me. I don't know why, but that woman creeped me out." Maclean devoured the rest of the sandwich.

"Sergeant, I was wondering, have you been in contact with anyone from your armed forces?"

Maclean shook his head. "No, not a one."

"Don't you think that's a bit odd? There were over a dozen Australian officers and NCOs in the camp when it was attacked. You'd think your government would want to hear what happened there. Especially from one of their own people."

"Yeah, I thought about that, too. But I assumed your government was keeping mine in the loop. At least, I hope they are."

The door swung open. A military policeman stood to one side as a small man with curly red hair walked in carrying a stack of file folders in his arms. He looked to be in his mid-thirties and wore a rumpled blue suit with a white shirt and a red bowtie. Freckles covered his round face. He placed his folders down on the table and removed his glasses so he could clean them with a handkerchief.

"Good afternoon, gentlemen," said the man with a strong English accent. "My name is Doctor Jeremy Hayes, and I work for the British Ministry of Defense."

"Have they run out of Americans to interview us?" quipped Maclean.

Hayes shook his head. "Sorry? I don't follow what you're saying. I'm here as a representative of Her Majesty's government. To save time, I'm going to debrief the two of you together."

Maclean let an exasperated sigh. "For the love of God! Haven't the Americans shared the information we've already provided with you people?"

"Oh yes, very much so," replied Hayes, lifting his pile of folders. "That's why I'm here. May I sit down?"

Grant smiled and pointed to the nearest chair. "If it'll speed things along, please join us at the table."

Hayes sat. "I've read all of your testimonial evidence and only have one or two questions for the two of you."

"What would you like to know?"

Hayes opened two files, pulled out two pieces of paper, and placed both down on the table. "These are the drawings you both made of the object that was extracted from the riverbed in Iraq."

Grant glanced down at his picture and nodded, as did Maclean.

"They're remarkably similar," said Hayes. "You both captured the scale of the unidentified object with impressive detail."

"It was hard to miss hanging underneath the modified Mi-26 helicopter," said Maclean.

"Yes, of course. Now, when asked to identify the type of craft you think you saw, you had startlingly different answers. Captain Grant, you wrote that you believed it was either a Russian or Iranian experimental stealth UAV, which had inadvertently crossed into Iraqi airspace before crashing. Sergeant Maclean, however, wrote that he thought it could possibly be a UFO."

Grant looked at his colleague and shook his head. "Really, Sergeant, a UFO?"

"Hey, why not?" replied Maclean. "I've never seen a UAV that's disc-shaped. Have you, Captain?"

"Just because you haven't seen one doesn't mean they don't exist," said Hayes. "There are dozens of highly experimental prototypes of aircraft and drones being flown and tested by the NATO powers that the public has no knowledge of. It only stands to reason if we're doing it, so are the Russians, Iranians, Chinese…etc."

"Yeah, but they had to dig it out of the ground," countered Maclean. "If it were some type of experimental drone it would have crashed recently and would surely have been found by the farmers living around the base. No, sir, this plane, or whatever you want people to call it, crashed there a long time ago. A bloody long time ago."

Grant saw the logic in Maclean's argument and began to re-evaluate his opinion. He decided to push Hayes a little. "I have to agree; Sergeant Maclean could be onto something."

"Gentlemen, I feared this might happen," said Hayes, putting the two pictures away. "In the MOD, I work for the advanced propulsion workshop, and I can assure you that the craft you saw was a drone, and not some kind of UFO from outer space."

"Then why did the locals never spot it, and more importantly, why did the people who slaughtered our friends have to blast it out of the ground?" said Maclean.

"I can't say why the Iraqi farmers never came across the drone," said Hayes. "There was a powerful sandstorm in your region a week before the attack. Perhaps that's when the UAV was lost. The blowing sand could have easily covered the drone lying at the bottom of the riverbed. And the reason they had to use explosives to free it was because when it crashed it jammed itself tightly into the rocks."

Grant and Maclean looked at one another and shook their heads. They weren't buying Hayes' explanations.

The professor placed his hands palm down on the table and smiled patronizingly. "Gentlemen, just because you can't identify something doesn't make it an extraterrestrial craft. For that to occur, you would need some form of proof, and you have none. In fact, there has never been an alleged alien crash site that has held up to scientific scrutiny. Trust me when I say that there are no UFOs or alien bodies being held by anyone inside or outside of the U.S., nor any other allied nations' governments. No extraterrestrial culture or technology has ever been uncovered by anyone anywhere in the world. You have to face facts. To date, there has been no irrefutable evidence found connecting UFOs to extraterrestrials. If you want the truth, you have to realize that what you saw was a man-made craft and not some downed alien disc."

"Well, if you put it that way, I guess I may have been mistaken," said Maclean.

"It happens. A few years back I thought I saw a UFO, but it turned out just to be some flares dropped by a C-130 during a training exercise on the Brecon Beacons in Wales."

"Is there anything else you would like to discuss, Doc?" asked Grant.

"No, I think I'm done," replied Hayes, scooping up his folders and standing. "Good day, gentlemen." He turned and exited the room.

The second the door closed, Maclean jumped out of his seat. "That man's full of crap. His job was to come in here and convince us that we didn't see what we both saw."

Grant sat back and linked his hands behind his head. "Agreed, but we're not really sure what we saw. Now are we?"

Maclean shrugged. "No, I suppose not, but I'm not convinced that what I saw was a UAV. Doesn't it strike you as odd that since the first day we arrived here, these so-called experts haven't asked us a question about our dead mates?"

"Yeah, but I thought they had all they needed from us."

Maclean grew agitated. "The craft is all these bloody people care about. Not you, not me, not our dead friends."

The door opened and a tall African-American U.S. Air Force Colonel with a shaved head walked inside and closed the door behind him. He had a black leather briefcase in his right hand, which he placed on the floor by his feet.

Both soldiers respectfully came to attention.

"Please take a seat, gentlemen," said the colonel, pulling out a chair at the other end of the table.

Grant and Maclean resumed sitting.

"I'm sure by now you're both sick and tired of talking to people, so I'll keep this short. My name is Colonel Oliver Andrews, and I have been brought in to conduct this investigation."

Grant raised a hand. "Sir, I'm not trying to be disrespectful, but why is the Air Force investigating the attack of Camp Bayonet? Shouldn't the army be doing that?"

"That investigation is already over, Captain," replied Andrews. "It has been determined that ISIS sympathizers infiltrated the camp dressed as Iraqi security personnel and waited until it was quiet before attacking and killing everyone there."

"That's a load of bull, and you know it, sir," said Maclean. His voice grew loud. "It wasn't ISIS. It was someone else who killed all my mates. I was supposed to be going home on leave in a month with Sergeant Adams. He was going to get married, and I was supposed to be his best man. Someone's going to answer for his death."

"That may be so, Sergeant, but as far as the U.S. and Australian forces are concerned, what I told you is the official story."

Grant leaned forward in his chair. "What about the two stealth helicopters that we saw? How do you explain those, Colonel?"

Andrews fixed his dark brown eyes on Grant. "They weren't there. In fact, it would be in your best interest to never say a word to anyone about what you believe you saw one week ago."

Grant shook his head. "Colonel, over the past few days we've told more than a dozen people about what happened in Iraq. They have our sworn statements, and now you want us to pretend that it never went down the way it did?"

"Correct, Captain."

Grant sat back and crossed his arms. "May I ask why, sir?"

Andrews reached down and lifted his briefcase onto the table. He opened it and placed a photograph in front of the two soldiers. It showed the burnt hulk of a Mi-26 helicopter sitting in the desert. "This was taken by a military surveillance satellite over Iran the day after the attack on the camp. As you can see, whoever was behind the attack flew north of the City of Dehloran and landed. They then transferred the craft you saw dug out of the ground onto a waiting plane. Since they didn't have any further need of the Mi-26 anymore, they set it on fire. Intelligence analysts believe the tire marks on the ground next to the wreckage belong to a Russian-built An-12 transport aircraft."

"Damn. So, it was the Russians who did this," said Maclean. "Those bastards! Why would they do something so stupid as to risk a war with NATO to retrieve a crashed experimental drone?"

"First off, there is no direct evidence connecting this to the Russian government or their armed forces," said Andrews. "Secondly, the craft you believe you saw doesn't correspond with any known Russian aircraft or drones."

"So, whose was it then?" asked Grant.

"We don't know. That's why I've been brought in." Andrews reached into his case and brought out two pieces of paper, which he slid across the table to Grant and Maclean. "Gents, before I say another word, these are your non-disclosure agreements. If you wish to leave this base before you grow old and die, I suggest that you sign them without delay."

Grant picked his up and read it. He raised an eyebrow and looked over at Andrews. "This non-disclosure form is for the rest of our natural lives."

"Yes, I know," replied Andrews as he placed a fountain pen on the table.

"Hey, I don't work for you or your armed forces," protested Maclean. "Before I sign this, I want to speak with one of my own officers."

"I thought you'd say that." Andrews stood and opened the door. A Royal Australian Air Force officer got out of a chair in the hallway and nodded at Andrews. "Wing Commander Wallace will be more than happy to fill you in on your government's position regarding this investigation, Sergeant."

"Yes, sir," said Maclean getting to his feet.

When they were alone, Grant placed his paper down on the table. "Colonel, if I sign this, then what? Are we free to go?"

Andrews shook his head. "Not yet. As you two are the only people to have seen the crashed craft and the men who took it, I need your help with my investigation."

Maclean strode back into the room, picked up the pen, and signed his name. His face was pale. He looked at Grant. "I'd sign it if I were you, Captain."

"Why?"

"Have you ever heard of a place called Diyarbakir prison?"

"No."

"I'm not surprised. It's in Turkey, and I've been reliably told that it's a nasty place to be locked up in for the rest of your life."

"So? What does that have to do with us?"

"Because, sir, I've been told that Amnesty International declared it one of the most brutal prisons in the world. My people told me to sign on the dotted line or we'd both end up in a secret military installation somewhere in the Indian Ocean that makes

Diyarbakir look like a holiday spot."

Grant looked at Andrews and saw he was smiling. A shiver ran down his spine. He was being boxed into a corner with no recourse. Grant pursed his lips, took the pen, and signed his name on the paper.

Andrews took both forms and slid them into his briefcase. "Now that that's out of the way, there are a couple more people you will need to see before we leave."

Grant's head was swimming. "Leave? Where are we going, Colonel?"

"To Batumi, Georgia," replied Andrews. "That's where the An-12 landed."

"Sir, before we have any more discussions or board a plane to Georgia, can we at least speak with our families to let them know we're still alive?" asked Grant, knowing his parents would be worried sick wondering if he was still alive or not.

Andrews sat back and ran a hand over his smooth head. "Unfortunately, no."

"Why not?"

"Because both of your families have been told that you were severely injured in the attack and are in the hospital recuperating from your wounds. You have my word that you can speak with them when this is all tidied up."

"Sir, you won't be able to keep this a secret forever. The truth is bound to get out."

"You'd be surprised what has been kept secret from the public over the past few decades. Besides, if the truth somehow leaked out about what happened, it would only be because one of you two said something you shouldn't have. Any breach of the non-disclosure agreements that you both signed will result in hard jail time for the rest of your lives. As for Camp Bayonet, the world's media is already reporting this as the worst incident of ISIS infiltration into the Iraqi security forces since we re-deployed our forces into Iraq. Trust me, the message is being carefully controlled. Hell, even ISIS has gleefully taken responsibility for the attack, even though they had nothing to do with it."

"I see you've thought of everything, sir," said Grant.

"That's why I work in the Special Investigations Branch in the Pentagon. Now if you'll excuse me, I need to make a few calls before we depart."

"And when might that be?" asked Maclean.

Andrews looked at his watch. "In precisely two hours and thirty-one minutes."

Both men respectfully stood as Andrews.

"What a bunch of horse crap," said Maclean. "My God, they're laying it on pretty thick. I can see it in his eyes. That colonel is deliberately not telling us the whole story." He stood and pushed his chair across the room with his right foot. "I honestly don't give a damn about that alleged UAV. All I want to know is who killed my mates, and how I get my hands on them."

"In a matter of hours, Sergeant, I think you're going to get your chance," said Grant. "If there is a secret drone sitting in the back of a plane in Batumi, you know it's going to be guarded, and I'm willing to bet it'll be the same bastards who attacked our camp."

Maclean clenched his right hand into a fist until his knuckles turned white. "God, I hope so. It's high time somebody paid for what happened."

4

A white Learjet entered Georgian airspace at an altitude of ten thousand meters and flew straight toward the coastal city. Built on the shores of the Black Sea on the remains of an ancient Greek colony, the picturesque Batumi was the second largest city in Georgia.

Grant and Maclean sat in the passenger compartment, accompanied by Colonel Andrews and Professor Hayes. The two soldiers had traded their tan coveralls for some of their civilian clothes recovered from the camp and some new ones bought on the base in Kuwait.

Hayes opened his briefcase and produced a handful of photographs, which he handed to Grant. "Captain, this is the An-12 we believe was used to transport the downed UAV from Iran to Georgia."

"How can you be sure this is the same jet?" asked Grant as he studied the pictures showing the transport plane parked inside a spacious hangar.

"We have our sources," Andrews curtly replied.

"If this drone is so important, why is it still there?" asked Maclean. "It's been over a week since the attack. Why haven't they moved it?"

"We don't know why," said Hayes. "Hopefully, you can determine that for us once you find a way inside the hangar and positively identify the craft you claim to have seen being dug out of the sand in Iraq."

Maclean leaned forward, and like a jackhammer, he jammed his right index finger into Hayes' chest. "Listen here, Doc, I know what I saw. The captain and I aren't making this stuff up for kicks."

Hayes' eyes widened. He sat back, trying to get out of reach of the Australian sergeant.

"Sergeant, calm down and sit back in your seat," warned Andrews. "Before we boarded this plane, your armed forces posted you to my office, so until you're told otherwise, I am your new commanding officer. Learn to control that temper of yours."

Grant looked at his colleague and nodded.

Maclean let out an infuriated sigh and stood up. He walked to the back of the aircraft and poured himself a glass of water.

"I take it I'm also posted to your office?" said Grant to Andrews.

"That is correct," responded the colonel. "It's only temporary. When this investigation is wrapped up, you'll both be sent back to your respective organizations."

Grant smiled thinly. He wasn't sure if he believed Colonel Andrews or not.

"Sergeant, please take your seat," said Andrews.

Maclean walked back and sat down.

"Before we land, there are a couple of things we need to go over," said Andrews. "First off, quit using each other's rank. First names only from now on."

"I don't even know your first name, Captain," said Maclean.

"It's David," replied Grant. "But you can call me Dave, all my friends do."

"And I'm Jim. Only my sister calls me James. It's going to take some getting used to, calling an officer by his first name."

"Now that that's out of the way, here are a couple of surveillance devices we need you to wear," said Andrews. He nodded at Hayes, who opened his briefcase and gave the two soldiers two small boxes each.

Grant opened one and saw there was a contact lens case inside of it. "I don't get it. I don't wear contacts."

"Those aren't ordinary contact lenses," explained Hayes. "Inside you will find a lens with a built-in camera."

"You've got to be kidding," blurted out Maclean as he checked out the lens.

"There's no need to put them on now. You can slip them over your right eyes just before we land."

"And what's in the other box?" asked Grant.

"Near-invisible hearing aids," explained Hayes. "We'll be able to hear everything you say. We can also speak to you via the device."

Maclean chuckled as he looked at Hayes. "If you work for the advanced propulsion workshop at the British MOD, then I'm a male underwear model."

Hayes shrugged and turned to look out the window.

"Sir, will there be someone there to meet us when we land?" Grant asked Andrews.

"Yes. I have an asset on the ground who has been watching the An-12 ever since it landed," said Andrews.

"Has this person had any luck getting near the plane?"

"No. My orders to her were to observe and do nothing else. She's the one who secretly took the pictures of the plane in the hangar."

"Colonel, what if we can't get close enough to the plane to see what's inside?"

"Be creative. I need to know if the UAV is still there. If it's not, we could be in a world of hurt."

Grant found the last statement to be strange, but let it go. He sat back and closed his eyes. He let the enormity of everything that had and was about to happen sink in.

The Learjet landed smoothly and taxied to a building used for private airport customs and reception. The front door of the jet opened, and the stairs were lowered by the co-pilot. Almost right away, a heavy man in an ill-fitting, dark blue uniform boarded the plane.

"Passports, please," said the man in English.

The co-pilot handed over everyone's passports. The man smiled and stamped the books without reading the passports. The last book, the co-pilot's, held the usual two-thousand-dollar bribe.

"Please enjoy your stay in Georgia," said the customs agent before leaving.

"That's it?" said Grant.

"For now," replied Andrews.

"Hello in there," called out a woman's voice. Her English was good despite her Georgian accent. "Permission to come on board?"

"Permission granted, Tatiana," replied Andrews, smiling.

A slender woman in her mid-fifties with salt-and-pepper hair walked up the stairs and into the plane. She was wearing a blue jacket over a short dress. In her left hand was a shopping bag. A pin on her jacket identified her as a member of the Georgian Customs Agency.

"Gentlemen, I'd like to introduce you to Tatiana," said Andrews. "She is my best asset here in Georgia."

"You flatter me, sir," said Tatiana.

"I'd like you to meet Misters Gray and Black," said Andrews, indicating with his hand to Grant and Maclean.

Grant held out his hand. "Pleased to meet you, Tatiana."

"It's not my real name, but the pleasure is all mine, Mr. Gray."

"Evening," said Maclean.

"Oh, Mr. Black is handsome, and, judging by his accent, he is from Australia," said Tatiana, smiling. "I do like a man with an accent. Do you think you could leave him here with me for a few days after we finish our job?"

"I don't see why not," said Andrews.

"Hey, I'm standing right here, you two," protested Maclean. "How about we get to work?"

"He's all business," said Tatiana, pouting. "Such a shame." Tatiana placed her shopping bag on the carpeted floor. "Here are the coveralls you asked for, Colonel, along with the necessary identification badges."

"Get changed," ordered Andrews.

Grant and Maclean nodded and pulled on the dirty white coveralls.

"It fits perfectly," said Grant. "I'm impressed."

"Da, I had your sizes forwarded to me," explained Tatiana.

"Along with our photos," said Maclean, admiring the fake ID.

"Okay, gentlemen, I will lead you to the hangar where the plane is parked," said Tatiana. "I have a young mechanic who is quite enamored with me waiting to let you in via a back door. He'll go with you as far as the plane, but he's been told not to step inside."

"Armed backup?" asked Maclean.

"None; you're on your own," replied Andrews. "I can't afford to risk the life of my only agent in Batumi."

"But we're expendable?"

Andrews shrugged. "Try not to get caught, and this should be over in the next thirty minutes or so."

Grant slipped on his contact lens and blinked a couple of times to get it in place.

"It's working," announced Hayes, looking up from his laptop.

Maclean slid on his lens.

"Got you, as well," said Hayes. "Now let's check your hearing aids."

"Can you hear me?" said Grant.

"Loud and clear," replied Hayes in Grant's earpiece.

"Keep the engines running while we're gone," said Maclean. "I don't want to spend twenty years to life in a squalid Georgian military prison."

Hayes raised a thumb. "Got him, too."

Andrews placed a hand on Grant's shoulder. "Captain, I have no doubt that you think I'm acting in haste and possibly throwing you two to the wolves."

"The thought had occurred to me, sir," responded Grant.

"Trust me, if there had been another way, I would have used it. You two are the only people who have seen this drone, and time is of the essence. All I need you to do is get inside and confirm that it is still there, and then get the hell out."

"Colonel, what's going to happen after we confirm the UAV is the one we saw and is still on the plane?"

"We'll depart right away, and another team will take possession of the plane."

"What other team?" asked Maclean.

"That's on a need-to-know basis, and right now, you two gentlemen don't need to know," said Andrews. "Now, please follow Tatiana to the hangar and do your job."

Grant looked over at Maclean. "Come on, Mr. Black. Let's tempt fate for the second time in just over a week."

5

The night air was hot and sticky.

Grant and Maclean walked behind Tatiana as she headed toward the closest of three hangars in a row at the end of the airstrip. Her high heels echoed off the walls as they walked to the back of the building.

Grant was surprised to see that there weren't any security guards visible. Grant had expected to see several armed men walking back and forth outside the hangar. He tapped Tatiana on the shoulder. "Where are the guards?"

"What guards?"

"Do you mean to tell me the entire time the plane has been parked here that there haven't been any guards to stop people from nosing around?"

"For the first day or two, there were a couple of men, but after that…none."

"This stinks," said Maclean. "I smell an ambush."

"Quit speaking English," admonished Andrews in the men's earpieces.

As they walked past a parked forklift, Tatiana said, "Stay here while I make sure Luka is waiting for us."

Grant and Maclean faded into the shadows as Tatiana carried on walking.

"Sure wish we were armed," whispered Maclean.

"So do I," replied Grant, peering into the night for Tatiana.

The sound of her heels hitting the tarmac heralded her return.

The two soldiers slipped out of the dark to meet her.

"He's waiting for you two at the back door," explained Tatiana. "He speaks good English, but I told him not to speak to you unless spoken to."

"Okay, thanks," said Grant.

"Good luck, gentlemen. Hopefully, our paths will cross again in the future," she replied. Her eyes lingered on Maclean for a few seconds longer.

Maclean nudged his comrade. "Come on, time's a-wasting."

They walked to the back door. In the dim light, they could see a thin, young man with scraggly, shoulder-length black hair. He waved at the men, inserted a key into the lock, and turned it. He stepped aside as he pulled the door open.

Grant stopped at the entrance and took a quick look inside the well-lit hangar. He could see the tail section of the transport plane and nothing else. "Looks quiet inside," he said over his shoulder.

"Yeah, but be careful," said Maclean.

Grant's heart was racing in his chest. He took a deep breath to calm his nerves as he stepped inside and looked around. The An-12 was parked in the middle of the hangar with its ramp down. The place was as quiet as a tomb.

Maclean and the Georgian joined Grant. "Where is everyone?" said Maclean.

"I'm not sure I want to know," replied Grant. He turned and looked at the lovelorn Georgian. "Wait by the door."

The young man nodded and moved back.

"I guess there's no time like the present," said Maclean.

Grant nodded. He saw a clipboard on the wall and grabbed it. They strode toward the plane as if they belonged there. The feeling they were being watched gnawed at Grant's innards. At the back of the aircraft they slowed down, half expecting a platoon of soldiers to be waiting for them. They peered inside. Like the rest of the hangar, there wasn't a soul to be seen on the plane. With Grant leading, they walked up the ramp and stopped dead in their tracks.

Strapped to the belly of the plane was the disc-shaped UAV.

"Is that the same drone?" asked Hayes.

"It looks likes it," replied Grant. "But I can't be completely sure."

"You don't need to be, Captain. I'm convinced it's the genuine article. Get out of there and head right back here," said a man's voice that Grant didn't recognize.

"I don't know who I'm speaking to, but give me a couple more seconds," said Grant, staring at the disc. "Something doesn't feel right."

"Now, Captain."

Grant ignored the voice and walked to the craft. He looked at the ship and marveled at its simplicity. The craft was smooth and looked to be made from one piece of metal. Grant couldn't see any welds or rivets anywhere on the disc.

"Come on, sir, you heard the man, it's time to go," said Maclean.

"Grant, I gave you an order," barked the man.

Grant reached out and slowly placed his head on the surface of the craft. In an instant, he pulled his hand back and spun around. "It's fake. The damned thing is made of wood!"

The sound of combat boots echoed faintly outside of the hangar.

"Time to leave," said Maclean, running down the plane's ramp.

Grant sprinted after his friend toward the exit just as the lovestruck mechanic was shoved out of the way, and a dozen well-armed men wearing black uniforms and balaclavas ran inside, yelling in Russian.

Maclean came to a sliding halt and threw his hands up in the air, as did Grant, a split second later.

Most of the Russians formed a cordon around the two soldiers, while a couple of men ran to the back of the An-12 and inside the plane.

"Who are you, and what are you doing here?" demanded a man in Russian.

"Sorry, I don't speak Russian," replied Grant.

The man lowered his AK and repeated the question in flawless English.

Grant knew there was no point in lying. "Sir, we're a pair of NATO soldiers looking for the men who attacked our camp a few nights ago in Iraq. We were told they were hiding in here. Unfortunately, the information turned out to be false."

One of the men who had run in the plane jumped down from the ramp and called out in Russian to the team leader. The officer shook his head and took in a deep breath through his nostrils. "What can you tell me about the wooden craft inside the An-12?"

"Nothing," responded Grant. "I didn't know we would find a mock-up, or whatever it is, on the plane."

The Russian officer stepped close. "Don't lie to me, Captain Grant. What happened to the original disc that was found near your camp in Iraq?"

"Bloody hell, how do you know his name?" blurted out Maclean.

"I know yours, too, Sergeant Maclean," replied the Russian. "I wouldn't be any good at my job if I didn't know that there were two survivors from the attack on Camp Bayonet."

Grant stood there, attempting to maintain an outward calm, but inside, it was as if a hurricane was racing through his mind. *Who were these soldiers, and how did they know so much?*

"Get down," said Andrews through Grant and Maclean's earpieces.

Both men looked at one another not sure what to do.

"Now!" ordered Andrews.

The two soldiers threw themselves to the ground just as the hangar's front doors flew off their hinges. Before the sound of the blast had faded away, another group of armed men ran inside and formed a line facing the Russians.

Grant looked up. The tension in the air was palpable. Both teams of men in black uniforms faced each other with their weapons at the ready.

"Captain Grant, Sergeant Maclean, are you all right?" asked one of the new arrivals, a short man with a smooth head, a thick, salt-and-pepper goatee, and a strong Texan accent.

Grant nodded.

The Russian officer lowered his rifle and pulled off his balaclava. "Major Wright, it would appear once again that our respective intelligence services are, as you Americans like to say, a day late and a dollar short. I hate to say it, but we have both arrived too late to catch the prize. There is nothing of value in the back of that plane."

Grant and Maclean got to their feet, unsure of what was going on.

"Are you sure, Yuri?" asked Wright. "Because my people were certain this time around that we'd find something."

"Sir, he's telling the truth," said Grant. "The craft in the back of the plane is a fake. It's made of wood."

"Goddammit," said Wright. He looked at his men. "Lower your weapons."

Yuri motioned for his men to do the same thing.

"Okay, I'm really lost," said Maclean. "Can someone tell me what is going on around here?"

"Sorry, Sergeant, but I'm not at liberty to tell you," replied Wright.

"Nor I," said the Russian team leader.

In the blink of an eye, the power to the hangar was cut, plunging it into darkness. Grant dropped to one knee and instinctively reached for a pistol on his hip that wasn't there. The bone-chilling sound of silencers firing all around him made Grant drop to the floor. He could hear men as they fell to the ground all around him. Terror took hold as the two teams fought together against an invisible assailant. Men fired blindly, trying to hit whatever it was killing them. A hand reached out and grabbed Grant's arm.

It was Maclean who said, "It's a setup. Run!"

Grant didn't need to be told twice. Like a sprinter hearing the starter pistol firing, he was on his feet and running for the front doors that had been blown open. Less than a meter from freedom, a darkened shape stepped in front of him and tried to bring his weapon up to fire. With a cry on his lips, Grant hit the man with his shoulder and sent him flying outside onto the hard tarmac. He came to a halt and saw the man was dressed from head to toe in a suit identical to the ones worn by the men who had attacked their camp.

The assailant's face was hidden behind a darkened glass faceplate. The stunned man reached for his rifle but was a second too slow as Maclean scooped it up and turned it on the attacker. "Don't move!" he warned. "I've fired this kind of weapon before. It is a modified German G11, which fires caseless ammo."

Grant went to grab the unknown assailant by the arm. Instead, the man lashed out with his foot, hitting Grant in the groin. Stars flashed before his eyes. With a muffled moan, he doubled over.

Maclean never hesitated. He pulled the trigger, but nothing happened. The weapon refused to fire.

The assailant leaped to his feet, grabbed hold of the G11, and tried to yank it from Maclean's hands. When it wouldn't budge, he released the weapon and shot his right foot out at Maclean's left leg, sweeping him off his feet.

Maclean hadn't seen the move coming and hit the ground hard, knocking the wind from his lungs.

With pain radiating like fire from his groin, Grant gritted his teeth and stood up. He saw Maclean fall and the attacker dive to the ground for the G11. The man rolled over on his shoulder and came up with the rifle tight in his shoulder. He spun around and aimed the weapon at Grant.

A shot rang out. Grant broke out in a cold sweat. He looked down, expecting there to be a hole in his chest. Instead, the assailant tumbled backward to the ground, dead.

"Are you okay?" asked Tatiana, stepping out from the shadows.

In her shaking hand was a pistol. As she looked down at the lifeless body, her face turned white. "I've never killed a man before."

Maclean got to his feet. "Better him than us."

The firing in the hangar abruptly stopped.

"That's our cue to leave, sir," said Maclean as he handed Grant the G11, bent down, and then threw the dead man's body over his shoulder.

"Gents, for God's sake, hurry back to the plane," said Hayes.

Grant took Tatiana by the hand and began to run. If the extra weight on Maclean's shoulder bothered him, he didn't let it show. Maclean ran as fast as his colleague as they tried to put as much distance as they could between themselves and the charnel house inside the hangar.

"Run!" yelled Andrews from the top of their plane's stairs. The engines were already running.

Grant helped Tatiana climb aboard before turning to assist Maclean with the corpse.

"Why the hell did you bring that?" asked Andrews.

"Because I want to know who these SOBs are, that's why," replied Maclean, laying the body down on the floor of the plane.

Andrews hauled up the stairs and closed the door. He looked toward the cockpit and yelled, "We're all here. Now let's get the hell out of here before it's too late."

Grant sat down beside Tatiana and buckled her in. She sat in her seat shaking like a leaf. "It's okay. We're all alive, and that's what counts," said Grant as he wrapped his arms around her. "You did the right thing back there."

Tatiana nodded and fought back her tears.

The plane started down the runway and began to pick up speed. The nose of the Learjet rose up and a second later, they were airborne.

"Ten seconds," said Hayes to Andrews.

"What's happening in ten seconds?" asked Maclean.

"We can't leave any evidence behind," said Andrews, looking out of his window.

Maclean turned to look out of his window. Below them, they could see the airport. Like flaming arrows in the night, a pair of Hellfire missiles, fired by a stealth UAV, struck the hangar and exploded. The warheads combined with the fuel in the An-12 tore the hangar to pieces. An orange-and-red fireball shot up into the night. A sea of flaming debris rained down onto the tarmac.

"Jesus! What about your people who were still in that bloody hangar?" asked Maclean.

Hayes shook his head. "They were all dead seconds after the attack began."

Grant gently let go of Tatiana and stood up. He looked down at Andrews, his cheeks burning with anger. He was tired of being told half-truths. "Colonel, before we land, I want to know just what the hell is going on, and I don't want any of your need-to-know B.S., either. I don't believe for one second that you're from the Special Investigations Branch of the Pentagon. I'm scared, and I'm tired of being strung along. I think by now Jim and I have earned the right to know who you are and what you're up to."

Andrews sat back and glanced over at Hayes. The professor shrugged and closed his laptop.

"Okay, Captain, you win," said the colonel. "I guess you're in too deep now not to know what it is we do. But not here. Not now."

"Where, then?" said Grant.

"Your new home, Captain. That's where."

6

The Bahamas

Peter Roth looked out the window of his red-and-white EC-155 helicopter and smiled to himself. Up ahead, moving slowly on a brilliant blue sea was his yacht, *Asteria*. He decreased the power to his helicopter's powerful twin turboshaft engines, lined up his craft right behind the *Asteria*, and flew directly above the ship's wake.

He keyed his helmet microphone and said in Spanish, "*Asteria*, this is *Alpha-One*, I am less than two kilometers out, please prepare for my arrival."

"Roger that, sir," said a man through the speaker in Roth's headset.

Roth slowed his helicopter down, lowered the landing wheels, and brought it over the top of *Asteria's* landing pad. He watched as a crewman holding two orange paddles in his outstretched arms guided him down onto the pad. The instant the wheels touched down, Roth reached up and switched off the power to the engines. He waited a few seconds for the rotor blades to stop spinning before unbuckling himself from his seat and opening the door.

A sailor in a naval-style white shirt and blue trousers ran over and held the door.

Roth picked up his briefcase, got out of the chopper, and stepped onto the landing pad. "Thank you, Diego," said Roth to the crewman.

"My pleasure, sir," replied Diego.

"My bags are in the back."

Diego nodded. "I'll bring down your luggage right away."

"No hurry. I'd like some time to myself. How about you bring them to my cabin an hour from now?"

Diego saluted. "As you wish, sir."

Roth walked off the pad, down a flight of stairs, and onto the upper deck. The *Asteria* was one of the most expensive private yachts ever built. At the cost of over three hundred million dollars, the ship was one hundred and twenty meters in length and could accommodate twenty guests in opulent luxury, along with a crew of fifty ex-naval personnel. Roth headed straight for his private cabin on the main deck. His valet, Adrian, a slim man in his fifties, dressed in a black uniform with a long-tailed jacket, was waiting for him outside his door. He held a silver serving tray in his left hand. On it was a flute of champagne.

"Good day, Adrian," said Roth, smiling when he saw the drink.

"Welcome back, sir," replied Adrian dryly. He handed Roth the champagne before opening the door to his cabin.

Roth took a sip. "Ah, a Krug 2000. A fine choice, my good man."

"Yes, sir. The rest of the bottle is on ice in your room."

"Thanks, Adrian. That will be all for now."

Adrian bowed slightly. "Very good, sir. I'll be in my quarters should you need me."

Roth stepped inside his spacious cabin and walked straight to a desk against the far wall. The highly polished oak table shone in the light of the room. The antique had once belonged to José Carrera, the first commander-in-chief of the Chilean Army after its independence from Spain. Roth opened his laptop and turned it on. While he waited for his encrypted computer to boot up, Roth topped up his flute of champagne.

At fifty-two years of age, Roth was South America's wealthiest man, and its most eligible bachelor. He had wavy blond hair, piercing blue eyes, and a weathered face from years of outdoor living. Roth was fit for a man of his age and tried to run or swim several kilometers every day. He had taken his late father's modest aerospace company and turned it into a multi-billion-dollar corporation. Roth had recently diversified his holdings by buying into rocket and satellite technology, along with the ever-growing South American oil and gas industry. His latest oil rig off the coast of Ecuador was performing beyond his wildest expectations.

Roth's computer chimed, letting him know it was ready to use. He took his seat at his desk and typed in his password. The image of a man came up on the screen. His eyes were bloodshot. It was evident that the man had not shaved in days.

"Good morning, Max, how are you doing?" asked Roth in German.

"I've had better days, brother," replied Max, Peter Roth's younger brother.

"I've seen the reports on the news. The Georgian authorities have issued a press statement calling the explosion at the Batumi airport an unfortunate accident."

"Yes, they claim there was a fire during the refueling of the An-12 which caused the catastrophic explosion that engulfed the hangar and everyone in it."

Roth took a sip of his champagne. "So, brother, what really happened?"

"The plan to lure the American and Russian Special Forces teams to the plane worked perfectly. Both groups were eliminated within seconds. Unfortunately, one of my men went missing during the fight. I fear he may have been in the hangar when it exploded."

"Who was it?"

"Bulow."

Roth shook his head. "That is too bad. He was a good man. I will see to it that his family is properly compensated for their loss."

"Thank you." Max hesitated for a moment.

"What is it? Did something else go wrong?"

"We didn't have time to blow up the hangar. It was the Americans who flattened it."

"An unforecasted outcome, but not an unwelcome one, either. How did they do it?"

"They hit the building with two missiles. I think the warheads were thermobaric. The Georgian police found nothing of the bodies we had left behind other than the melted remains of the weapons the Americans and Russians had been carrying on them."

Roth raised an eyebrow. "Ingenious. Where is the real craft now?"

"It was airdropped over Armenia and picked up by some of my people there. It was then flown on to Romania, where the disc is now safely stored in our underground facility in the Carpathian Mountains."

Roth smiled. Their facility was an old Cold War bunker, hidden deep inside the mountains. Years of hard work and planning had paid off handsomely. His heart began to race. He licked his lips. "Have you spoken with Professor Cordovan since it arrived there?"

Max shook his head. "No, I haven't had the time."

"Of course. I'm sorry, Max. I'm just so excited. I'll call him later."

Max ran a hand through his thinning blond hair. "Peter, my men and I are at a safe house in Baku, Azerbaijan. We'll lay low here for another twenty-four hours before taking a flight to Romania."

"A wise idea. I shan't contact you again until you are safely in Romania."

Max's leaned forward. His face filled the screen. "We have done it, brother. Father would be proud of us."

"Yes, he would. Take care, and I'll speak to you two days from now."

Max terminated the conversation from his end. The laptop screen turned dark. Roth closed the lid and sat back in his chair. He looked over at a portrait of his late parents hanging on the wall. He was the spitting image of his father, while his brother had their mother's aristocratic looks. Roth raised his flute of champagne and toasted his parents. "You may have taken grandfather's technology as far as it could go. But Max and I will take it beyond your wildest dreams as we reach for the stars and our future."

7

The Atlantic Ocean

No matter how hard he tried, David Grant couldn't get the man in the shadows to stop nudging him. With an exasperated huff, he rolled over and opened his eyes. It was hard to see in the dimmed cabin.

"Hey, glad you could come back to the land of the living," said Maclean, standing in the aisle.

Grant rubbed his tired eyes and looked around. "What's up? Is something wrong?"

"No, not at all. I've convinced Professor Hayes to let us check out the dead body. Want to see who our friend is?"

Grant sat up. Tatiana was fast asleep in the seat next to him. He carefully got out of his seat and walked to the back of the plane. The corpse lay on the floor, covered by a couple of blankets.

Hayes got down on his knees and pulled the bloodstained covers off the body. In the dim light, Grant could see the man's unusual uniform was a grayish-green color. Hayes moved his hands over the fabric and stopped when he got to the man's glass faceplate. He studied it for a few seconds before unlatching the clasps under the chin and lifting off the glass.

Grant and Maclean leaned forward so they could see the face of their attacker. The man's green eyes were open. He looked to be about thirty-five, had a tanned visage, and appeared to be European.

"This outfit is quite interesting," said Hayes. "It's called a stealth suit, and it is designed to mask a person's body heat. If you were to look at him through a thermal scope while he was still alive, the best you would see would be a blur. He'd probably look like a ghost moving across the ground. There's a power pack on his belt which keeps the suit cool." Hayes looked at the faceplate and grinned gleefully. "My word, whoever built this knew what they were doing. There's a heads-up display projector built into the bottom of the faceplate. I bet their team leader could see where his men were at all times."

"Doc, do you think you will you be able to identify who he is by his fingerprints?" asked Maclean.

"I don't know. He may never have had his fingerprints taken by the authorities."

Maclean picked up the dead man's rifle. "What can you tell us about this? I'm sure it's a modified German G11 assault rifle. I tried to fire it, but it wouldn't work for me."

Hayes hefted the rifle in his hands. "It's heavy. I'd wouldn't be any good in the army."

"It's not for everyone. Can you tell me why it wouldn't fire, and who modified it?"

"These weapons went out of production in the early 1990s. I don't think more than one thousand of them were ever made. I'll get the MOD to contact the German Bundeswehr in the morning and see if they sold them, or the weapon's design patent, to anyone. As for why it wouldn't fire, Sergeant, it's because the gun is coded to the assailant's hand. Only he and he alone could fire the rifle. We tinkered with signature guns for a few years but gave up. It was too expensive, and the technology required to make it work has yet to be perfected."

"Evidently, someone else has perfected it," observed Grant.

"Yes, it would appear so."

"Do we have stealth suits like this?" asked Maclean.

Hayes nodded. "Most NATO countries have a similar suit,

which is worn by their Tier One Special Forces units."

"Have you seen one like this before?" queried Grant.

"No, this is truly state of the art. I'd love to meet the people who made this."

Grant patted Hayes on the shoulder. "No, you don't, Doc. Trust me, these are the kind of people you don't ever want to bump into in a darkened alley."

Hayes covered the corpse and took a seat with Grant and Maclean.

"If this suit isn't from a NATO power, could this man be Russian?" asked Maclean.

Hayes shrugged. "He could be, but a medical doctor will need to examine the corpse first, to help determine where this man comes from."

"If he's not Russian, then who else has the technology to pull this off?" said Grant. "Think about it for a minute: they first had to find the downed craft, and then they had to set off a device which caused an electromagnetic pulse that blackened out twenty to thirty kilometers of the Iraqi countryside. They had advanced stealth helicopters and suits. This operation would have cost someone a small fortune to finance."

Hayes scrunched up his face while he thought. "You know, it's not inconceivable that a private corporation instead of a nation state could be behind all of this. If you can find a city lost in the Amazon rainforest for centuries using a satellite, you could just as easily find a downed craft if you knew what you were looking for. As for the EMP bomb, it's quite easy to put together a device capable of rendering everything with an electrical circuit useless in its wake. The U.S. Air Force has already tested a counter-electronics missile and is now paring down the technology to fit it inside cruise missiles. As for the stealth helicopters and suits, the technology is out there. All a person has to do is find someone willing to sell him the designs, and he can build it on his own without anyone knowing what he…or she…is up to."

"Surely you people keep track of these kinds of illegal business deals?" said Maclean.

Hayes smiled grimly. "Each year the world's powers spend trillions of dollars on surveillance technology, and for all the money expended, they're lucky to catch five percent of what is going on out there. We can make inquiries when we land, but don't hold your breath that we'll find whoever was behind the attack on your camp any time soon."

"Swell," muttered Maclean.

"I suppose the question right now isn't who is behind the attack as much as why," said Maclean. "Who's after this technology, and what do they plan to do with it?"

Hayes sat back and clasped his hands together. "Those very questions quite often keep me from getting a decent night's sleep, Captain. Welcome to my nightmare."

8

Peterson Air Force Base

Colorado Springs, Colorado

The whine from the Learjet's engines grew quiet as the plane taxied to a halt inside an expansive hangar.

Grant looked out his window and saw an ambulance accompanied by two military police cars waiting off to one side.

"When we get off the plane, stay close to me, and don't say a word to anyone," said Andrews to the plane's passengers.

"What about the stiff?" asked Maclean.

"Don't worry about him, that's why there's an ambulance," replied Andrews.

"And the G11?"

"Leave it on the plane next to the body, but make sure it's unloaded."

Maclean ejected the magazine and cocked the weapon twice to ensure there weren't any bullets left in the chamber.

The plane came to a halt. The co-pilot walked out of the cockpit, opened the front door, and lowered the stairs. Everyone stood and followed Andrews down onto the hangar floor. He flashed his identification at the military police and kept on walking.

"How are you doing?" Grant asked Tatiana.

"Tired, and more than a little bit confused," she wearily replied.

"That makes two of us."

Andrews led them out a side door. An Air Force van was sitting there with its engine running. "All aboard," said Andrews as he opened the passenger-side door and got in. The driver waited until everyone was seated before driving away. They drove across the base until they came to an old two-story building.

"Everyone out," announced Andrews.

"Where are we?" asked Maclean.

"We're at Peterson Air Force Base in Colorado. The base is home to the 302nd Airlift Wing, as well as the headquarters for NORAD, and several other important armed forces commands."

Grant read the sign on the front of the building. "Base Archival Records."

"My organization isn't very large, Captain," said Andrews. "We have to share the building." The colonel shepherded everyone inside.

They walked up a flight of stairs and opened a closed door. A woman in her early sixties with short, gray hair and silver glasses on her nose sat at her desk reading over a file. She looked up and smiled. "Good afternoon, Colonel Andrews. Was your trip successful?"

"Partially," he replied. "Miss Young, I have two new team members with me, and one person who needs to be cleansed."

Tatiana furrowed her brow. "What does *cleansed* mean?"

"I assure you it's nothing sinister," said Andrews. "You can't go back to Georgia. Not after what happened. If the authorities don't arrest you, the people who ambushed the Special Forces team will undoubtedly kill you for what you know. For your years of service to this nation, you're going to be given a new identity and a new life here in the States. I'm sorry, but this is it. You can't go any farther than this office."

"I guess this is goodbye," said Grant squeezing one of Tatiana's hands.

"Well, this has been a couple of days I'll never forget," said

Tatiana. "Goodbye, gentlemen. Perhaps our paths will cross sometime in the future?"

"Maybe."

"Please take a seat, and I'll look after you," said Miss Young to Tatiana.

Andrews stepped past Young's desk and opened a door leading to a hallway. At the end was another closed door. They stopped while Andrews opened his briefcase to look for his ID.

"What's in there?" asked Grant when he didn't see a sign over the door.

"Project Gauntlet," replied Andrews.

"I've never heard of it."

"I'd be shocked if you had. Have you heard of Project Sign or Project Grudge?"

Grant shook his head.

"What about Project Blue Book?"

"Hey, I've at least heard of that," said Maclean.

"I'm glad one of us has. What is it?" asked Grant.

"I read a book about it. It was a U.S. Air Force study about UFOs in the sixties."

"To be precise, it was operational from 1952 to 1970," interjected Hayes.

"So, what does Gauntlet have to do with Blue Book?" asked Grant.

"Gauntlet is the Air Force's top-secret successor to Blue Book," explained Andrews.

"I'm getting confused. I thought you two were in the business of retrieving downed UAVs and planes?" said Maclean.

"It's a little more complicated than that," replied Andrews as he slid his ID into a control panel next to the door. With a loud click, the door popped open. Andrews put his ID away and motioned for his guests to walk through the open door.

"I wonder if we should make a run for it while we can?" joked Maclean.

"Then I'd be forced to order one of my people to shoot you," said Andrews, completely deadpan.

"Well, when you put it like that, Colonel, I guess we'll just follow you."

The two soldiers stepped inside and stopped. In front of them was a room set up as a command center. There were half a dozen computer workstations occupied by Air Force personnel, all busily working away. On the walls were four massive flat-screen monitors, showing images coming from drones and satellites flying over countries all around the world.

"This way, gents," said Andrews, motioning for them to join him. "I hope you both slept well on the plane, as you're about to get a crash course on who we are and what we do. And more importantly, where you fit into the organization and why I think you're still needed."

They walked down a short corridor until they came to a briefing room. "Please make yourselves comfortable while I fetch Elena," said Andrews.

"Colonel, do you have to?" groused Hayes.

"Just because you two don't agree on things doesn't automatically make her wrong," said Andrews.

"My body clock tells me it's well past my bedtime. Could we get some coffee?" asked Maclean.

"Sounds like a good idea. I'll see if I can find us a pot," said Hayes.

Grant and Maclean walked into the room and took a seat at a long, wooden table. Pictures of Peterson Air Force Base from its founding in the 1940s until the present covered the walls.

Grant stretched his arms, interlocked his hands together, and cracked his knuckles. "You know, the more time I spend around those two, the less I know about what is going on."

"I hear you," said Maclean. "In Iraq, Hayes said there was no such thing as UFOs and now, here we are in an office of a building masquerading as the base's archives. But whose real role is to investigate UFO sightings."

Grant raised a hand. "That's not quite correct. Hayes said there is no proof that they have ever visited Earth."

"That is what I said, Captain," said Hayes as he walked in with a sleeve of cups and a pot of freshly brewed coffee in his hands.

Maclean poured himself and Grant a cup of black coffee.

"Doc, if you don't believe we have been, or are being, visited by extraterrestrial beings, why are you working here?" asked Grant.

"Because there is an arms race going on out there that isn't just confined to nation states," replied Hayes. "Multinational corporations all around the world are busy gathering intelligence on their business rivals. It won't be long before they start to use advanced technology, currently restricted to the military, to spy on the competition. Don't even get me started on the threat posed by today's terrorist organizations. Can you imagine a mini nuke flown into downtown Tel Aviv inside a stealth drone? The whole Middle East, if not the world, would go up in flames."

"Ah, Jeremy, the eternal pessimist," said a Hispanic woman as she entered the room.

Grant and Maclean stood up to greet her. She was in her forties, her shiny black hair, which was cut short above her ears, framed her slender face. Her gray pantsuit fit her lithe body perfectly.

"Gents, I'd like you to meet Doctor Elena Leon," said Andrews.

"She's not a real doctor," moaned Hayes.

"Please, not this again," said Andrews. "You should know by now that I value both of your opinions."

Elena held out her hand in greeting. Grant smiled and shook it. "Good afternoon, ma'am, my name is Captain David Grant, and this fellow is Sergeant James Maclean."

"My pleasure," said Elena.

Andrews closed the door and waited for everyone to take a seat. "For the newest members of the team, this briefing, naturally, is top secret special access, and anything that is discussed here today can never be repeated to anyone outside of this organization."

"Colonel, I'm not sure what my security clearance is these days, but I'm guessing it's not anywhere near your military's version of TSSA," said Maclean.

"You needn't worry," said Andrews. "The forms you signed in Iraq are all I need. Besides, you wouldn't be in the Australian SAS if you were untrustworthy. Now, to put what you're about to hear into perspective, I guess you should learn more about Project Gauntlet. When Project Blue Book officially closed in 1970, the armed forces decided to keep the investigation into unidentified flying objects going, albeit at a much more reduced level. For close to thirty years, Gauntlet was run by a long-in-the-tooth Air Force captain and his assistant, a technical sergeant. A lot of what they did, however, was focused on the business of misinformation."

"Why would they do that?" Maclean asked.

"If one of our top secret experimental aircraft was sighted or photographed by a member of the public, they would visit them in the guise of fellow UFO enthusiasts and encourage them to report it as a craft from outer space. Both the B-2 bomber and the F-117 fighter were erroneously reported as UFOs for years before the truth came out."

"What happened to make the government enlarge the project?" asked Grant.

"In January of 2000, President Clinton was briefed by his national security team about the proliferation of UAV technology and the impact it was going to have on future wars. It was decided to enlarge Project Gauntlet, and its main focus became the recovery of downed unidentified craft from anywhere in the world. As luck would have it, a week later, people in eastern Finland reported seeing a UFO flying over their homes. In fact, it was a wayward Russian drone, which eventually ran out of fuel and crashed in the forests outside of the city of Kouvola. Gauntlet sent people there disguised as UFO enthusiasts and found the drone partially submerged in a lake. An Air Force recovery team was on standby in Norway and flew straight to the crash site. We had the drone whisked out of the country before the Finns or the Russians ever knew what had happened."

"The recovery of this drone helped NATO understand just how far the Russians had progressed with their UAV technology since the collapse of the Soviet Union," explained Hayes.

"Okay, that makes sense to me, but why even bother to keep looking into alleged UFO sightings if they don't exist?" said Grant.

"Perhaps I should answer this question," suggested Elena.

"Be my guest," said, Andrews, taking a seat.

Elena looked over at Grant and Maclean. "Gentlemen, my job here is to advise Colonel Andrews on all matters relating to Ufology."

"See, I told you she wasn't a real doctor," blurted out Hayes.

"Hey, there's no need to be rude," said Maclean. "Let the lady speak."

"So, what exactly is Ufology?" asked Grant.

"It is the study of all things related to UFOs," replied Elena. "It has been called a pseudoscience by people such as my esteemed colleague, Doctor Hayes, but it has been around for decades, and is in no danger of going away any time soon as a field of study."

"Do you believe that the Earth has been visited by people from another planet?"

"With all my heart."

"But you can't prove it," interrupted Hayes.

"No. Not yet, but I will," Elena replied.

"Doctor, what makes you so certain that extraterrestrials have come to Earth?" asked Grant.

"Because there have been sightings going back to the beginning of recorded time."

Hayes sat forward in his chair. "Yes, and let's take a look at these sightings. In ancient Rome, they wrote about something resembling a clay pot descending from the clouds. In Japan, it was something made out of wood resembling a ship. Here in the United States, in the late 1890s, we had a rash of sightings of mystery ships that were reported to look like balloons."

Elena sat back and crossed her arms across her chest. "And what's your point?"

"The point being is that when confronted with something people can't readily identify, they see what they want to see, using the technology of the day to makes sense of it all."

"What about all of those sightings made during and after the Second World War?" asked Maclean.

"Have you ever heard of Operation Paperclip?" said Hayes.

"No."

"At the close of the war, the allied and Soviet forces rushed to get their hands on Nazi technology and the scientists behind it. Paperclip was the name the U.S. forces gave to their efforts. Let's face it. Without Wernher von Braun and his rocketry experts, it's doubtful the American space program would have been as successful as it was."

"Are you saying that the UFOs reported in the late 1940s are attributable to these Nazi scientists?" asked Grant.

"Most definitely, I am. The Nazis successfully tested flying discs in 1944 and 1945. First in Prague, in the former Czechoslovakia, and later at Peenemunde on the German coast. When your forces captured SS General Kammler, he provided them with the plans and the skills to recreate these discs back home in the States. He wasn't the only Nazi with intimate knowledge of their flying disc program to be captured. Test pilots, engineers, and design specialists were rounded up and sent to secret test facilities spread out all across the country."

"Were these early flying saucers any good?" asked Grant.

"Not really," replied Hayes. "The technology was still in its infancy, and there were numerous crashes in the early days."

Maclean snapped his fingers. "Roswell! Say, didn't a real UFO crash there, and your government covered it up?"

Hayes shook his head. "Sorry, no. The initial reports of a crashed disc were correct, but it wasn't from outer space, it was one of the army air corps' top secret, experimental flying discs that had crashed in the New Mexico desert. The men who flew the craft were a pair of former German Luftwaffe pilots. Unfortunately, they died a couple of months later when their disc crashed into the side of a mountain."

"What happened to these discs?" said Grant.

"The program was scrapped in the mid-1950s. It wasn't worth the money or the cost in test pilots' lives."

"Did the Soviets have a program like the Americans?" asked Maclean.

Hayes nodded. "Naturally. That is where some of the UFO sightings in Alaska and the American Northwest in the late 1940s and 1950s come from. They probed our airspace, and we did the same to theirs. The discs on both sides were soon superseded by more reliable spy planes and then by satellites."

Maclean shook his head. "Man, this puts everything I've ever read or seen on the television about UFOs in a different light."

"What Doctor Hayes is forgetting is that those are but a fraction of the sightings that have occurred over the past century," countered Elena.

"Agreed, but let's look at how the sightings are reported," said Hayes. "Radar and eyewitnesses are the two means by which UFOs get reported. If it's spotted on radar, it has to be man-made. You can't disagree that the number of reported radar sightings dropped dramatically when stealth technology began to be used by the Air Force."

"Yes, you are correct."

"Now, let's look at eyewitnesses. Studies have shown that the people most likely to report a UFO sighting are those whose incomes are at the lower level of society. And by people who have status-related anxiety disorders, or by people who crave attention and hope to get it by reporting a UFO."

"Even you have to agree that some of the best and most credible sightings have come from pilots, military officers, and government officials," countered Elena.

"Those people represent a tiny fraction of the reports cataloged each year in the country, and even they can make a mistake."

"Okay, Professor Hayes, what about all those reports of abductions by UFOs?" said Maclean.

"Sergeant, these so-called abductions are just as easily explained away," replied Hayes. "The typical abductee claims to have been captured and taken on board an alien spaceship for testing of some sort, and then returned to where they are taken from. The problem is that many of these people only remember what happened to them when placed under hypnosis, and this has proven to be a less-than-credible means of obtaining the truth. Some psychologists associated with the abductee phenomenon have been accused of planting memories in their patients' subconscious."

"What about the reports of tracking devices implanted in the abductees?"

"Good grief, Jim, you have seen way too much crap on television," said Grant, shaking his head.

Maclean shrugged. "What can I say? I read and watch a lot of science fiction."

"To date, there hasn't been a single implant found that wasn't man-made," said Hayes. "I'm sorry, but there's no way anyone can convince me that UFOs aren't just misidentified natural phenomena, or the accidental sighting of an experimental drone or airplane."

Elena let out an exasperated sigh and fixed her eyes on Grant. "Captain, you seem to have already made up your mind on the veracity, or lack thereof, of extraterrestrial visitation. I have one question for you. I read your report. Why would a UAV need a cockpit? By design, it is an unmanned aerial vehicle."

Maclean tapped his colleague on the arm. "Hey, she's got you there."

Grant ran a hand over his chin while he hemmed and hawed for a few seconds. "I might have misidentified something on the drone and thought I was looking at a cockpit."

"Yeah, but even the mock-up had a cockpit on it," said Maclean. "We both saw it. So why make one on the drone if it wasn't needed?"

Grant shrugged. "I'll have to think about that one for a while."

"Now you can see why I have these two experts to help guide my thoughts," said Andrews. "While I tend to lean toward Professor Hayes' conclusions, there is always that one or two percent of reports that even he cannot explain away. Besides, if a real UFO were to crash and we could get to it first, just imagine the technological advances that could be made."

Elena stood. "Sir, if I'm not needed anymore, I'd like to read the reports sitting on my desk before it gets too late in the day."

All the men stood as Andrews walked to the door and opened it. "Elena, please swing by my office before you leave today. I'd like your views on why there seems to be an upswing of reported UFO sightings near missile silos here in the States, Russia, and the UK."

"My pleasure, Colonel."

A soon as Elena was gone, Maclean spun around and gave Hayes an evil look. "Hey, Doc, you may be a bright man, but there was no need to be so rude to Ms. Leon."

Andrews stepped between the men. "Sergeant, you're new here. This is how they always speak to one another. Come tomorrow, she'll be on the attack and Hayes will be the one on the defensive."

"Yeah, but I'm always right," said Hayes.

Andrews chuckled. "All I can say is, God help you if you ever get it wrong." He turned his attention to Grant and Maclean. "I bet you two gentlemen will want to get settled in the base's transient quarters before getting down to work."

"And what might that be, sir?" asked Maclean.

"I want you two to find and retrieve the craft that was taken in the Iraqi desert. A dozen good men, along with your colleagues, died because of it. Like you, I want those responsible to pay for what they did."

"We'd be happy to," said Grant. "Which one of your people is responsible for that part of the world?"

"Captain Jones is. She's quite good and is as angry as you are about what happened."

"I doubt that," said Maclean.

"I wouldn't. Her cousin was First Sergeant Long, who died when your camp was overrun."

A pang of guilt hit Grant in the chest. He had met Long a couple of times but hadn't had much of a chance to get to know the sergeant.

"Well, that proves I can still say the most inappropriate thing at the worst possible time," said Maclean.

"It's okay," said Andrews. "You didn't know."

"I sure as hell do now."

"I'll have Technical Sergeant Takei guide you through the process of your administrative in-clearance. Just remember, you're both here as civilian workers for the base's archival staff. Sergeant Takei is waiting to present you with your new ID cards."

"Administration duties!" croaked Maclean. "Somebody please put me out of my misery."

9

The Caribbean Sea

A dark thunderstorm was brewing inside Peter Roth's head. He sat at his desk in his dimly lit room, massaging his temples. The word he had just received from Professor Cordovan in Romania was soul crushing. The disc they had recovered in Iraq was useless. Aside from being packed with sand and rocks, there was nothing inside of it. Sometime long ago, the occupants must have realized the ship was damaged beyond repair and set off a device that had melted the interior of the vessel.

Roth reached into a desk drawer and pulled out a bottle of pills, popped a couple in his mouth, and chased them down with some whiskey. Billions of dollars had been spent getting them this far, and now he had nothing to show for it.

His laptop chimed. Roth glanced at his gold Rolex and saw it was time. He took a moment to compose himself before using a remote to turn up the lights in the room. Roth lifted the screen, pressed the enter button, and waited for the four other members of the Aurora Group to appear. Like Roth, each member of the group was a wealthy entrepreneur. The familiar faces of three men and one woman appeared on his screen.

"So, what can you tell us, Peter?" asked a Russian man with straw-blond hair.

Roth took in a long breath. "The word is not good, Maksim. It would appear the craft we recovered was damaged so badly that nothing can be salvaged from it."

"Nothing?" said the woman. Her voice was tinged with a New York accent.

"I'm afraid not."

"This is most disconcerting," said Maksim.

"I'm sorry, but the ship had been buried in the sand for close to six thousand years. It's amazing that the hull of the ship was still in such good shape."

"We had pinned all of our hopes on this find," said a man with a well-trimmed, white beard and a strong Arabic accent.

"Has anything of value been discovered by your satellite overflights of South America?" asked a Brazilian man with thick glasses on his round face.

"Nothing so far, but I am hopeful," responded Roth.

"Where is your brother, and his men?" asked the woman.

"They're safe, Diane," said Roth.

"That is good. I see the press doesn't seem too interested in the story coming out of Georgia."

"By tomorrow no one will remember anything about an explosion in a hangar in Batumi. People today have incredibly short attention spans. They'd rather read what happened to their favorite celebrities while they were on vacation than real news."

"Very well, Peter. Today has not turned out as I had hoped," said Maksim. "Yet, tomorrow is another day. You and your brother are to be commended for your work to date, and your loyalty to the Aurora Group is beyond reproach."

"The ridiculously easy destruction of both the American and the Russian Special Forces teams has sent a message to their respective governments that they are facing people who possess technology far more advanced than their own and are not afraid to use it," said the Brazilian man.

"Let us hope they keep their noses out of our business from now on," added Diane.

"If there is nothing new to pass on, I must be going," said the

Arabic man. "I have my granddaughter's birthday to attend."

"No, Hamid, I do not believe there is anything left to discuss," said Roth.

One by one, Roth's fellow conspirators left the screen. He reached for his whiskey glass and finished what was left in it before standing and stretching his hands over his head. He was tired. Perhaps Maksim was right, tomorrow was another day, and maybe with the light of a new dawn, his luck would change. If not tomorrow, then in a few days' time.

10

Peterson Air Force Base

With a loud annoying buzz, David Grant's cell phone sprang to life. To him, it sounded like a swarm of bees trying to escape from the confines of his cellphone. He rolled over, opened his tired eyes, saw it was a call from Project Gauntlet's operations center, and answered it.

"Grant here." His mouth felt as dry as the Mojave Desert. After a night of far too many drinks while watching a World Cup soccer game with Maclean, he was in no mood to be woken from his slumber.

"Sir, it's Staff Sergeant Vega. Sorry for waking you, but you and Mr. Maclean are to report immediately to the duty center."

Grant shook his groggy head trying to recall what Vega looked like. "Why? What's up?"

"I'm not at liberty to say. Colonel Andrews will brief you personally when you arrive here. A vehicle has been dispatched to pick you both up."

"Okay, see you in a few minutes." Grant ended the call and flicked on the light on his nightstand. Right away, his eyes felt as if they were on fire. With his head pounding away like a jackhammer, Grant took some headache pills and drank down a full glass of water before walking across the hall and banging on Maclean's door.

"I'm up already!" yelled Maclean. "They phoned me, too."

"Sorry. Just making sure." Grant turned about and went in search of some clean clothes to wear.

A short time later, a nondescript van pulled up outside the building. The driver handed each man a cup of coffee. "I was told to bring these with me," said the young airman.

"Someone's a lifesaver," mumbled Maclean as he grabbed ahold of a cup.

"Captain Jones is the duty officer tonight," said the airman. "She thought you could use them."

Both men slid into the back of the van for the short drive to the ops center. It had been eight days since they had arrived at the base. So far, their attempts to discover where the disc had gone after it was loaded onto the An-12 in Iran had gone nowhere. Each tentative lead was soon met by a brick wall. It was as if it had vanished off the face of the planet.

The mood in the operations room was tense. Some of the people had rushed in from home and were dressed in a mix of civilian and military attire. All eyes were on a screen of live feed coming from NORAD Headquarters, showing the Alaskan airspace.

Grant spotted Jones and walked to her side. "Thanks for the coffee, Erica."

"I heard you two talking about having a few beers when you left work, so I thought I'd help ensure you were both alive when the boss gets in," she replied. Jones was an African-American woman in her mid-twenties with a trim build.

"Cheers," said Maclean, toasting Jones with his coffee.

Grant looked up at the screen. "So, what's going on?"

"At precisely 2338 hours last night, NORAD began tracking what appeared to be an unrecorded meteorite coming through Earth's atmosphere directly above the North Pole," she said. "Within minutes, it was over Alaskan airspace and losing altitude fast."

"So why the three-alarm fire for a meteorite? It's not going to crash into a city or something, is it?"

"No. However, at 2343 hours, it began to slow down and went down near the town of Robertson's Mine, Alaska."

"I've never heard of it. Is it a small community?"

Jones nodded. "It's east of Valdez, near the Canadian border, and is fairly isolated. It has a population of just over six hundred people, most of whom are native Alaskans."

"If it's down, why is everyone being recalled back to work?"

Jones brought up the satellite feed from NORAD on her laptop computer. "Here's the problem."

Grant leaned forward to study the screen. For one hundred kilometers around the town, there wasn't single light on. The whole area was pitch black. "Is there something wrong with the feed?"

"I wondered the same thing, so I spoke with the duty officer at NORAD, and he assured me in no uncertain words that there is nothing wrong with their satellite. Someone or something caused all the power to turn off in the region around Robertson's Mine."

Grant checked his watch. It had been forty-one minutes since the object had gone down. "Could there be something on the meteor that caused this blackout?"

"Not a chance," said Hayes as he walked into the room. "If this had happened while the meteor was still in orbit, I would have said maybe, and that's a big maybe. But the power didn't turn off until the object was directly over the top of Robertson's Mine."

"This sounds too much like what happened to us in Iraq," said Maclean, shaking his head.

"Yes, it does," replied Grant.

"Wait, there's more," said Jones. "When I was speaking with the duty officer at NORAD, I asked him if they could identify where the meteor went down by its heat signature. Have a guess what he told me?"

Grant shrugged. "I have no idea. What did he tell you?"

"They couldn't detect a single heat signature inside the blacked-out area. It was as if the satellite was being deliberately jammed."

"Most interesting," said Hayes.

Grant raised an eyebrow. "If you say so, Doc."

"My skin's crawling," said Maclean. "Something's going on up there that ain't right."

Andrews walked into the duty center dressed in a pair of old Air Force sweats. "Okay, I'd like the duty officer, Doctors Hayes and Leon, along with Captain Grant and Sergeant Maclean to meet me in the briefing room right away."

"Why us?" said Maclean to Grant.

"Beats me. I guess we'll find out soon enough."

As Elena Leon lived the farthest from the base, she was the last to arrive. The second she walked in the room, Elena looked over at Jones. Her eyes shone with excitement. "Is it true? Have we just had an NL-CE1 over Alaska?"

"It appears that way, ma'am," replied Jones.

"Jeez, I thought the Australian Army was bad for acronyms," said Maclean. "Can someone translate that Air Force gobbledygook for me?"

"NL means nocturnal lights, and CE1 is short for a close encounter of the first kind," explained Elena.

"That's great," said Grant. "But now I'm lost."

"Captain, when talking about UFOs, there are four different levels of close encounters. The first is a strange object being observed. The second is physical evidence, such as imprints being left on the ground. The third level is a visual sighting of a craft's occupants, and the fourth, which Professor Hayes says is unfounded, are abductions."

"And I'd be right to call these alleged abductions pure balderdash," added Hayes.

"Doctors, thank you for your observations," said Andrews. His tone told them to let it go for the moment.

The briefing began with a review of what had happened to date by Captain Jones. Andrews thanked her and asked Jones to keep an eye on the situation as it developed while the remainder of the staff talked in private.

"Okay, folks, half an hour ago I received a call from General McLeod, C-in-C of NORAD, and have been told to put a team together ASAP for an on-site investigation," said Andrews.

"Sir, with all due respect, an investigation of what?" asked Grant. "I thought it was a meteor that crashed near the town."

"I'll get to that in a couple of minutes, Captain. The problem is that I don't have people sitting around here waiting for the phone ring. I think you've already noticed that this isn't a very robust organization. Everyone has a job, and they do it to the best of their capabilities. If the General wants us to put boots on the ground, I'm going to have to make a reconnaissance team based on you four people. If you find something up there, I can ask General McLeod to send some people to secure whatever it is until a retrieval team arrives to take it away."

"Sir, you're not coming with us?" asked Hayes.

"No. I've been called back to Washington to testify at a closed-door hearing of the Senate Subcommittee on Defense. I have to explain how twelve men died during what should have been a relatively straightforward recovery mission."

Grant shook his head. "Colonel, can't General McLeod get you out of this hearing? This really isn't the best time for you to be away from your people."

"He tried and failed. I have to go, or we could conceivably lose the funding needed to keep this project running."

"If you're not going, who will be in charge of the mission?" asked Hayes, fidgeting back and forth in his chair.

"Captain Grant will be," replied Andrews.

Hayes frowned at the news. "Sir, please! Captain Grant has only been with us for less than two weeks and barely knows our operating procedures."

"Professor Hayes, if you think I'm going to put a civilian in charge of military personnel, you're barking up the wrong tree. Yes, you have far more time here than Captain Grant, as is Doctor

Leon, but you don't think like a soldier does. You tend to be analytical and cautious, whereas Grant, from what I've observed, is more than capable of thinking on his two feet when things turn deadly. You'll be there to give him advice and to help him, should he need it."

"Colonel, I don't have a problem working with Captain Grant," said Elena. "I guess my ego isn't as large as Jeremy's."

Hayes' face turned beet red. He opened his mouth to say something but decided to close it instead.

Grant looked over at the tongue-tied professor. "Doc, trust me, I'd prefer that the colonel led the mission. But as he can't, I suggest we all try to get along. I have no doubt that I'll be leaning on you quite heavily for advice."

"Sir, I'm still at a loss. What exactly do you wish us to do in Alaska?" asked Maclean.

"Your mission is very simple. I want you to discreetly determine what caused the power blackout, and if there is an anomaly there, I want you to locate it until a retrieval team can arrive. That means I want the four of you to gather up what you think you may need right now and depart no later than 0300 hours," said Andrews. "There's a plane parked on the airstrip for you to use. Captain Jones will have you driven to the plane when it's time to leave. The flight to Elmendorf Air Force Base, Alaska will take about six and a half hours. So, get what sleep you can on the plane, as I suspect you're going to be busy over the next couple of days. From Elmendorf, you'll be flown to Robertson's Mine. There'll be two old government vehicles waiting for you when you get there."

"I take it we're going in undercover. So, what's our cover story?" asked Grant.

"Usually, we go disguised as members of The North American UFO Investigation Society," explained Elena.

"I've never heard of it."

"That's not surprising. It's not as large as some of the other better-funded civilian UFO organizations, but we do have people spread across North America who act as first responders when a suspected UFO sighting has occurred. They travel to the site and interview the people who claim to have seen a UFO. If the sighting is deemed worthy of further investigation, our people let us know, and we are brought in to examine the case in greater detail."

"Who are these people you're talking about?" asked Maclean.

"They're all retired military personnel, mostly Canadian and American, who have worked here in the past. They supplement their pensions by continuing to work covertly for us."

Grant chuckled. "Clever, your people hide in plain sight."

"How many of these alleged sightings have you had to investigate further?" queried Maclean.

"In the five years I have been with Project Gauntlet I have personally investigated thirteen sightings," said Elena.

"All of which, I don't mind telling you, turned out to be misidentifications or outright hoaxes," said Hayes. "The only unknown vehicle we have not been able to explain adequately was the one found outside of your base in Iraq."

Andrews looked up at a clock on the wall. "People, you're wasting valuable time. You can talk all you want on the plane."

Maclean smiled at Hayes. "So, Professor, what toys do have lying about the base that we could bring with us?"

11

The Super Yacht *Asteria*

Peter Roth leaped out of bed, ran to his computer, and turned it on. His heart was racing in his chest. He had just received a secure call from the senior vice-president in charge of his satellite company that there had been an incident in Alaska.

Roth brought up the satellite image of Robertson's Mine on his computer and smiled. There could only be one reason for the perfectly symmetrical power blackout. He had never dared to dream that one day he might have the chance to get his hands on a functioning craft. Roth had long ago resigned himself to searching the world for the crashed remains of ancient vessels. He reached for his phone and called his brother.

"Yes," said Max.

"Max, I think we may have stumbled onto a working ship," said Roth. His voice quivered with exhilaration.

"Where?"

"Alaska."

"When did it arrive?"

"About an hour ago. It looks like it may have crashed on the outskirts of a small town called Robertson's Mine."

"Do you want me to investigate this incident?"

"Yes, of course. But be aware that the Americans are undoubtedly going to send some of their people to check this out."

"Bah, they're nothing to be worried about." Max's tone was

dripping with disdain. "I'll get a team together and head out as soon as I can arrange the flights."

"I want you to be careful, Max. Use only ex-American Special Forces operators during your preliminary search of the town."

"Peter, please, as if I hadn't already thought of that. I know my job."

"Sorry, it's just that I want nothing to go awry this time around."

"It won't. I'll send four of my best men to the town while the rest of the team waits for word in Anchorage."

"Good thinking. If this does turn out to be a real extraterrestrial craft, we could leap hundreds, if not thousands of years, ahead of our competitors."

"Rules of engagement, brother?"

"If there is a ship, I want it. Kill anyone who gets in your way."

"Very well, I'll make my preparations to leave."

Roth hung up and grinned like a child on Christmas morning. He pushed a button on his desk and waited. A few seconds later a steward opened the door to his cabin.

"Yes, sir?" said the steward.

"I know it's early, but I feel like celebrating," said Roth. "Have a bottle of champagne along with some caviar sent up right away."

"Very good, sir," said the man.

Roth looked back down at the image on his laptop and let the excitement of the moment, like a warm wave on a sun-drenched beach, wash over him. The risks were astronomically high, but the payoff would be incalculable. Roth walked to the nearest porthole and looked out at the ink-black waters of the Caribbean. When the sun came up in a matter of hours, he knew his life would never be the same again.

12

Robertson's Mine – Alaska

That's odd, thought Robin Black as she stared at the flashing red light on her bedroom alarm clock. She brought her wristwatch close to her eyes, saw the time, and cursed up a storm as she pulled off her duvet. Black ran a hand through her short, black hair and stood up. She reached for her housecoat and pulled it on over her pajamas. Ginger, her tabby cat, jumped off the bed and followed her down the hallway until Black stopped outside of her son's bedroom.

"Hey, sleepyhead, wake up," said Black as she wrapped her knuckles on the door.

"Why? What time is it?" called out a sleepy voice.

"It's after seven already. The power must have gone out during the night. Get up and meet me downstairs for some breakfast."

"Okay, Mom," replied her son, Samuel.

Black paid a quick visit to the bathroom before shuffling downstairs to throw a pot of coffee on to brew. At thirty-eight years of age, Robin Black was the recently re-elected Sheriff for the quiet town of Robertson's Mine. With her deputy away for two weeks on vacation in Hawaii, Black found herself busy looking after the day-to-day affairs of the town's six-person police force. She was of average height and kept in decent shape by riding her horse when she wasn't on duty. Black was a native Alaskan, who had lived in and around Robertson's Mine her entire life.

Samuel walked into the kitchen, scratching his belly. Sam towered over his mother and was already being scouted by several major colleges for a basketball scholarship. He poured himself a bowl of cereal and sat down at the dinner table. "You know, Mom, I think that's the first time the power has gone out since that really bad storm we had two summers ago."

"I think you're right," said Black, taking a sip of her coffee.

"Mom, just to let you know, I'm planning on staying after school to work on my throws with Coach Barnum."

"That's fine, but make sure you don't stay too late. You have plenty of chores to do around here, mister."

"I'll make sure they get done."

"I've heard that before. Now eat up and get ready for school. You won't earn a scholarship by being late."

Sam wolfed down what was left of his cereal and bolted upstairs to shower and change.

Black smiled. Her son was growing so fast. In a year he would be gone, and her home would be empty. She hadn't thought what she would do then. Maybe take in a lodger? Her husband had died far too young of pancreatic cancer when their son was still a child. She had been in a couple of relationships over the past few years but had never seriously thought of remarrying. For the time being, her son and her job were the only things that mattered in her life. She brushed aside such thoughts for another day and popped two slices of brown bread into the toaster.

Ten minutes later, her son was rushing out the door. He jumped on his dirt bike, started the engine, and drove down the driveway. Black knew as soon as he was out of sight, Sam would speed up and race all the way to school.

She put her blue police uniform on, fed the cat, and locked up before getting into her blue-and-white Chevrolet Suburban and drove to work. The town's police station was located downtown, next to a small café and a hardware store.

"Morning Sheriff," said a man with white hair and deep crow's feet on his aged face as she got out of her car.

"Morning to you, too, Edgar," responded Black with a friendly smile.

"Did you see the light show last night?" asked Edgar.

"No. I was really tired when I got home, so I went to bed around ten. Were the Northern Lights dancing across the heavens again?"

Edgar scrunched up his wrinkled face. "I don't think it was the Northern Lights. I only saw a bright orange light streak across the sky until it disappeared somewhere north of the town."

Black smiled. "You saw a meteor. That's considered an omen of good luck in some cultures."

"If it is supposed to be good luck, then why did all the power go out in the town after it fell from the sky?"

"Are you sure that's what happened? Perhaps you imagined it?" Black knew Edgar had a history of drinking far too much after the sun went down.

Edgar raised his right hand. "I swear, I'm telling you the truth, Sheriff Black."

"Okay, I believe you. Now if you'll please excuse me, Edgar, I have police work to attend to."

"Sure thing, Sheriff." Edgar turned and walked into the café.

Black walked into the station and waved good morning to Sheryl, the police force's long-serving receptionist.

"Sheriff, Fred Cartwright called a few minutes ago and said he was going to be late coming in this morning," explained Sheryl.

"It's not the end of the world. We've gone this long without a working photocopier. What's a few more hours?" said Black. "Is anyone else in?"

"Yes. Bill and Sean are here. I think they're out back getting ready to take a drive up to Mary Olds' home."

"Why? What's going on?"

"That pesky black bear is back. They're going to try and scare it off with some flash-bang grenades. If that doesn't work, I'm afraid they may have to shoot it."

Black was opposed to killing any animal if another way could be found. But the bear had been relocated once already. If it wouldn't leave, she knew it would have to be destroyed. "Okay, tell them to keep me in the picture."

"Will do."

The aroma of fresh coffee reached Black's nose, and she poured herself a mugful. She entered her office and turned on her computer. The first thing she read was the news to see how large the blackout was. She was surprised to read it had affected a radius of one-hundred-kilometers around town; the power had gone out at precisely eleven forty-three in the evening and hadn't returned for close to three hours. She made a mental note to herself to call the nearest Air National Guard station later in the morning to see if the military had been testing anything in the local area. It wouldn't be the first time that strange things had happened while the armed forces were experimenting on a new piece of equipment. Late last year, there had been a string of UFO reports coming into the station. Black had been unofficially assured by a close friend of hers in the military that the sightings were related to a new triangular-shaped stealth plane being flown in and out of Eielson Air Force Base.

The phone on her desk rang. Black picked it up. "Good morning, Sheriff Black speaking. How may I be of service?"

"Robin, thank God you're in," said a frightened-sounding woman. "It's me, Ellen Marshall. Both of my dogs have gone missing."

Black had been up to Ellen's place a couple of times over the years. She had a pair of loveable Great Danes. "Are you sure they're missing? Perhaps they saw a deer in the woods and chased after it? Give them some time and they'll come home."

"I don't know; this isn't like them. They've been gone all morning."

"How about I have a couple of my officers swing by your place and see if they can help you find your dogs?"

"Thanks, Robin, I'd really appreciate that."

"Not a problem, that's what we're here for." Black hung up the phone and shook her head. She was happy that the level of crime in the town of Robertson's Mine was very low compared with some of the larger cities in Alaska, but chasing off bears and looking for missing dogs wasn't why she got into policing. Still, she couldn't complain. There hadn't been a recorded murder in close to eleven years, and she hoped it would stay that way for years to come.

13

Air Force Learjet heading for Alaska

Grant tried to get as comfortable as he could in his chair while he studied several pictures taken from the internet of Robertson's Mine. The town was nestled next to the snowcapped Wrangell Mountains. A couple of rivers ran through the land surrounding the small community. According to one of the files he had read, the Air Force had operated a radar station there in the 1950s and 60s but closed it down when a larger base was built in Fairbanks. There were several stores and restaurants in the small downtown core, along with a school, post office, and a church, which had been built in the early 1920s. The town got its name from a long-abandoned copper mine, which was slowly being converted into a tourist attraction. By the looks of things, most of the town's population lived in small farms and single dwellings on either side of the long gravel road that acted as the town's highway.

"I can't sleep," announced Elena to the rest of the people in the passenger cabin. "I'm just too excited to put my head down."

"Me too," said Maclean. "I can't believe we're going to look for a real-life UFO."

Elena looked quizzically over at Grant and Maclean. "To be honest, I don't know that much about you two."

"Okay, Doc, what would you like to know?" asked Grant, sitting up in his chair.

"Where you're from, if you're married, how long you've been

in the army. You know, that kind of stuff."

"I'll go first," said Maclean. "As you already know, my name is James Maclean, but you can call me Jim. I come from Newcastle, which is north of Sydney. I've been in the Australian Army for eleven years. I started with the Royal Australian Regiment and subsequently tried out for selection with our Special Air Service Regiment when I was a corporal. I've been with the SAS for the past five years and have served in East Timor, Afghanistan and Iraq. I've never been married and considering how much time I've spent overseas, it's probably a good thing. Regrettably, both my parents died in a traffic accident a couple of years back. But I still have a darling younger sister who lives in Sydney with her husband. I think that's all there is to know about me in a nutshell."

"Okay, my turn," said Grant. "My name is David Grant, but only my mother calls me that. Everyone else calls me Dave. I was born in Spokane, Washington. I've been with the U.S. Army for twelve years, and, like my friend, I'm also a paratrooper. I'm single and plan to stay that way for a few more years. I was once head over heels in love while I was at West Point, but she dumped me for some spoiled rich guy whose parents were multi-millionaires. Not that I'm bitter or anything like that about what happened. My parents are both alive. I have a twin brother in the navy who is currently serving on the *U.S.S. California*. My dad would love for me to pull the plug and leave the service to take over the family business. I haven't the heart to tell him that I don't see that happening anytime soon."

"I guess you'd like to know all about me," said Elena. "I'm forty-something and have worked for the U.S. government ever since I received my doctorate in Mesoamerican Folklore. It was, however, my love of UFOs that brought me to the attention of the Air Force. I was married but have been divorced for nearly ten years now. Aside from a sweet old grandmother in Austin, Texas, I have no immediate family."

Grant nudged Hayes. "Your turn, Doc."

Hayes looked over his glasses. "Do I have to?"

"Yeah, you do," replied Maclean gruffly.

Hayes sat up, ran a hand through his curly hair and adjusted his glasses perched on his nose. "If you must know, I was born in Nottingham, England and received my doctorate in physics when I was seventeen years old. I was recruited the day I left university by the Ministry of Defense and have been there ever since. I was working in our version of Project Gauntlet when I was seconded to your armed forces. Unlike Elena, I'm not the slightest bit worked up about this assignment. You'll see, forty-eight hours from now we'll be packing our bags to come home after agreeing that it was only a meteor that crashed somewhere near Robertson's Mine."

"While I think Professor Hayes may be right," said Grant, "I'm willing to keep an open mind."

"Do as you please, Captain, but you'll see that I'm right." With that, Hayes rolled over and pulled a blanket over his shoulders.

"Spoilsport," said Maclean. He looked over at Elena. "Since you can't sleep, would you mind answering a few questions I have floating around in my head?"

"I'll give it a shot," she replied.

"Do you think aliens are behind the pyramids of Egypt, or the lines of Nazca?"

Hayes sat back up. "Oh, this ought to be good."

Elena ignored Hayes. "No, I don't think they are responsible for all of the marvels of the ancient world. Our ancestors were far brighter and more industrious than we give them credit for."

"At last, something we can agree on," blurted out Hayes.

"Please, let Elena talk," said Grant.

Elena smiled and continued. "I do, however, believe that we have been visited in the past by extraterrestrials. Folklore all over the world are full of tales of alien visitation."

"They were simply stories made up to help explain things people couldn't understand," said Hayes.

"Some, yes, but certainly not all of them."

"Okay, what about some of the things you see on TV, like those men in black coming to your door after you report a UFO sighting?" asked Maclean.

"That is nothing but an urban legend," replied Elena. "It is a fact that the federal government in the 1940s was interested in speaking to people who had allegedly witnessed a UFO. I personally think the story got started when two men dressed in black suits showed up at a person's door to question an eyewitness. Which, to be honest, black suits were common fashion back then for men. The alleged eyewitness told someone who then told someone else about strange men in black coming to his door, and that's how the legend began."

"Damn, I was hoping to get my hands on one of those memory eraser thingies you see in the movies."

Grant shook his head. "Jim, you need to watch less television and read some military history books."

"If there are aliens coming to Earth…who or what are they?" asked Maclean.

"In my studies, I have come to believe there are four distinct types of alien species that have visited Earth," explained Elena.

"Not this theory again." moaned Hayes.

Grant raised a hand. "Doc, please, you may not agree with her, but I really want to hear this."

Elena took a sip of water. "By far, the majority of reported alien contacts have been with a species known as the Grays. They are described as being no taller than a child and have smooth, gray skin. Their heads are quite large, and they have shiny black eyes. There have been sightings of taller Grays, but most contacts have involved the shorter of the species. It is the Grays who are reputed to be the ones carrying out medical examinations on the abductees."

"Why are they taking people to be examined?" asked Grant.

"I, and many others, believe that they are trying to breed alien-human hybrids, using eggs taken from women during their abductions."

"Why do they need to create hybrids?" said Maclean.

"We believe their race is at risk of dying out, and they need us to help sustain their ever-decreasing population."

Hayes shook his head and rolled his eyes.

"What of the other races?" said Grant.

"The next most reported group are known as the Nordic Aliens. They stand about two meters tall, have long blonde hair, fair skin, and ice blue eyes. People who have met these aliens say they are friendly and compassionate."

"Do they abduct people?"

"No. People describe their encounters as cordial, and never recall being examined by the Nordics."

"So, what's their interest in Earth?' asked Maclean.

"They are watching over us to make sure we don't blow ourselves up or doing something else catastrophic, which would render the planet uninhabitable."

"So, they may be nice, but they're keeping an eye on a potentially new piece of real estate somewhere in the galaxy in case they need it."

"I don't share your cynicism, Sergeant, but you may be right."

"That's two. What is the next species?" asked Grant.

"They are called the Reptilians," replied Elena.

Hayes chortled. "Reptiles…really?"

"Yes, reptiles. They are described at being anywhere from two to three meters tall, with green, scaly skin."

"And what's their interest in Earth?" asked Grant.

"Like the Grays, they have been known to abduct people to perform medical procedures on them."

"They're not trying to interbreed with us, are they?" said Maclean, scrunching up his face.

"Not at all. They're just being curious."

"Elena, tell them what many leaders in the field of ufology believe about the Reptilians," said Hayes.

Elena cleared her throat. "Some people think the Reptilians are shapeshifters and have already infiltrated many powerful positions throughout the world."

"My God, Elena, that's putting it lightly. These people actually believe the current President of the United States is a Reptilian, as is the Queen of England."

"What do you think?" asked Maclean, looking at Elena.

"No, I don't think they have replaced our world leaders, nor do I believe in shapeshifting. It's only a small fringe of UFO enthusiasts who keep this patently absurd notion alive to sell their books and DVDs."

"Okay, that's three," said Grant. "Who or what is the last species visiting Earth?"

"They are an intelligent species of insects."

"Lord, I hope not," said Maclean. "I can't abide creepy-crawlies. Australia's full of them and most of them are poisonous."

Elena smiled. "Not much is known about them other than they appear to look like a giant mantis. With a large head and shiny, black eyes."

"Have they been involved in abductions?" asked Grant.

"I've never read about anyone being abducted by them. They seem to be more interested in gathering samples of water, plants, and the occasional farm animal for study."

"Great, another species coming here to kick the tires and see if they should buy the planet," joked Maclean.

"This is too much. I've heard enough. Please answer this one simple question," said Hayes to Elena. "How did they get here? Space, in case you missed it, is a mighty big place, and the nearest star system is over four light years away. Most exoplanets with habitable Earth-like conditions are located even farther away."

"The simplest answer is wormholes," replied Elena without batting an eye.

"They're theoretical, not real."

"To us they're theoretical, but to a more advanced species it is entirely possible that they have figured out how to make stable wormholes from their planet to ours."

"Okay, I'm lost again. What is a wormhole?" asked Grant.

"It's a theoretical passage through space," explained Hayes. "If you could build a stable wormhole, you could cover enormous distances in a fraction of the time it would take you to travel normally from one point to another."

"Einstein believed they were possible," said Elena.

"Yes, but it has never been conclusively proven that you can warp space-time to allow you to travel through a wormhole between two different planets. Even if an advanced civilization has worked out how to make a wormhole, the power required to keep it open while a craft transited it would be enormous."

"Professor Hayes, do you believe there is advanced intelligent life out there in the universe?" asked Grant.

"Yes, I do. Have they visited Earth? Most definitely not."

"Well, at least you two have agreed that there is intelligent life out there."

Hayes raised a hand. "Gentlemen, for just a minute, look at things from a purely scientific point of view. Sightings of UFOs took off in the 1950s and 60s and carried on until today. Why do you suppose that happened?"

Maclean shrugged. "You guys were building and testing disc-shaped craft?"

"Yes, there's that and there's also the flood of science fiction films at the theaters. People saw the aliens on the movie screens and when confronted with something they couldn't explain their minds reached back and pulled out the image of a short, bug-eyed alien for them. These alleged sightings Elena is going on about are the product of Hollywood's imagination, not outer space."

Maclean tapped Grant on the arm. "I hate to say it, but I'm beginning to wonder if we should have stayed locked up for the rest of our lives."

Grant chuckled. "It's all just folklore and legends. Professor

Hayes is probably right. Two days from now all of the excitement will be gone, and we'll be heading home with nothing more than a good story about an alleged UFO sighting and a wayward meteorite."

14

Robertson's Mine - Alaska

Patrolman Bill Scott turned off the highway and drove down a dirt road full of water-filled potholes until Ellen Marshall's old log cabin came into view. His partner, Sean McCartney, sat beside him stewing.

"Jesus, Sean, I told you to let it go," said Scott. "It's not worth getting upset about."

"I just don't get why the FBI turned me down again," groused McCartney.

"For the same reason as last time, your education isn't good enough. I told you to ask the boss for some time off to upgrade your marks, but you wouldn't do it. You've no one but yourself to blame for failing to get into the FBI."

"I know...I know. But it still pisses me off."

"Drop it this second and get a grip on yourself. You need to look and act professional while we see what Mrs. Marshall's problem is."

"Didn't dispatch tell us her dogs have gone missing? Ten to one they tried taking on a hungry black bear and lost the fight."

Scott parked their car and got out.

Ellen Marshall was already on the front steps of her home waiting to meet the two officers. "Morning, officers," she said in greeting.

Scott noticed that Mrs. Marshall was wearing an old green

housecoat, with red slippers on her feet. She had pink curlers in her white hair. A smoldering cigarette hung from her lips. "Morning, Mrs. Marshall, what appears to be the problem this morning?"

"It's my dogs, they've gone missing," she replied. "They woke me up around four this morning, barking and howling to be let outside, so I got out of bed and opened the front door. The next thing I knew they took off as if they had the scent of a deer."

"Have you try looking for them, ma'am?" asked McCartney.

"No. My feet aren't as good as they used to be," Mrs. Marshall replied. "They've taken off before but always come back an hour or two later, looking for their breakfast."

"You have a pair of Great Danes, don't you, ma'am?" asked Scott.

"Yes. Their names are Beau and Stanley."

"Okay, we'll take a look around, but I wouldn't be surprised if they're over at your neighbor's house waiting for you to come pick them up."

"I tried calling Ronald earlier this morning, but the phone wasn't working."

"We had some problems earlier with our phones, too," said McCartney. "But everything seems to be working just fine now. Why don't you give him a call, while we take a look behind your home?"

Mrs. Marshall nodded and shuffled her way back inside her house.

"No point dragging this out any longer than we have to," said Scott to his partner.

They walked to the back of the house and looked around for tracks.

"Here," said McCartney, pointing at the dirt. "These paw prints look new."

Scott examined the tracks and saw they led into the forest. "Let's see where these lead."

The narrow trail through the woods meandered back and forth

until it came to a shallow creek, which ran through the middle of Ellen Marshall's land.

McCartney swatted a black fly that had landed on his arm. "Man, I swear these things get bigger and hang around longer every year."

"Your skin's just getting thinner," said Scott.

"I can't see which way the tracks went... can you?"

Scott knelt and pushed some ferns aside. "They turned south toward Ronald Deering's place."

"You called it, Bill. He probably fed them some fresh venison for breakfast, and now they don't want to leave."

"His place isn't that far from here. Let's carry on and see if the dogs are with him."

They had gone less than fifty meters when the two men spotted droplets of blood splattered on the undergrowth.

The hair on Scott's arms stood on end. He instinctively placed a hand on his pistol but didn't draw it from its holster.

"What the hell?" muttered McCartney when he stepped in a puddle filled with blood.

Scott scanned the area, noting several shattered tree branches covered in blood. At the base of the tree, the grass and brush were flat as if trodden upon by something very heavy. He took a step toward the tree and froze. Lying just a few meters away were the mutilated carcasses of the two dogs. Flies and other insects swarmed over the bloody remains. What was left of their bodies looked as if they had been fed through a shredding machine.

"What the hell could have done that?" said McCartney.

"I don't know," replied his partner. "Let's spread out and look for tracks."

Scott kept his hand on his pistol as he walked forward. He had grown up in Alaska and had served in the army before coming back home to be a police officer. An accomplished hunter and tracker, Scott had never seen anything like what had happened to the dogs in his entire life.

"Bill, over here," called out McCartney.

Scott ran to his partner's side. "What is it?"

"Check these tracks out," said McCartney, pointing at a paw print in the muddy ground.

Scott bent down to examine the imprint. His eyes widened when he saw the size of the track. It was almost three times the size of a normal grizzly bear's paw print. By the depth of the track, the animal must have weighed more than one thousand kilograms.

"I've never seen bear tracks that large. I bet this bastard is as long as a truck and is as tall as a man when it's walking on all fours," said McCartney.

"We're going to have to call in the State Wildlife Troopers to go looking for this animal," said Scott. "It's clearly not afraid of dogs, and it won't be long before it bumps into someone living around here."

"What are we going to do about the dogs? We can't just leave them out here."

"I know. Let's go back to the car. You can call this in while I break the news to Mrs. Marshall. After that, we'll come back for the remains."

"Sounds like a plan." McCartney hesitated for a moment. "Bill, do you think we should bring the shotguns with us next time?"

Scott nodded, and then turned around to walk back.

In the woods, a pair of large brown eyes watched the two men leave. It lifted its head, sniffed the air, and took in the men's scent. They smelled different than the other creatures it had just killed. It waited until the officers were out of sight before turning its head and looking down the creek. Its stomach growled. It had just eaten but was hungry again. A new smell wafted on the wind. The animal began to salivate. The only thought in its mind was food. It turned away from the mangled corpses of the dogs and began to walk slowly in the direction of the new find.

15

David Grant brought his eight-year-old, ex-U.S. Air Force, blue Ford Mustang to a halt outside of the police station at Robertson's Mine. Maclean pulled over in an identical-looking vehicle and parked it in the next open spot. They had broken into two teams, each with a military and a civilian member. To ensure a lively exchange of ideas, Grant chose Elena to ride with him, while Hayes and Maclean rode together. Maclean quickly coined the two groups as Team USA vs Team Commonwealth.

While everyone else wore blue jeans and loose-fitting tan or gray shirts, Hayes had insisted on wearing slacks and a white shirt with a blue-and-white striped bowtie.

"Okay, Elena and I are going in to pay a quick visit to the town's chief of police," said Grant to Maclean. "While I'm gone, why don't you walk to the nearest convenience store and get us a couple days' worth of bottled water and some bug spray. I think we're going to need both in this heat."

"Got it," replied his friend.

"What about me?" asked Hayes, looking around. "What do you want me to do?"

Grant pointed at the café next door. "You keep telling us you're the expert; pop inside and introduce yourself. Maybe someone saw the meteor coming down."

Hayes walked off mumbling something to himself.

"So, what do you normally do in these situations?" Grant asked Elena.

"Follow my lead," she replied, reaching for the station's front door.

Inside the air-conditioned building they were met by the station's receptionist, an elderly woman whose desk nameplate identified her as Sheryl. At the sight of them, Sheryl put her hardcover book down on her desk. "Good morning, and welcome to Robertson's Mine police station. Can I be of assistance?"

Elena smiled and held out her hand in greeting. "Good morning to you too. My name is Elena Leon, and my friend's name is David Grant. We're with the North American UFO Investigation Society and were wondering if the sheriff was in so we could pay him a courtesy call."

"Did you say UFO?" said Sheryl, looking over the top of her reading glasses.

"Yes," Elena replied, handing Sheryl a business card. "We're investigating the mysterious object that flew over your town late last night."

Sheryl skimmed the card. "This says you're from Colorado Springs. Boy, you sure got here in a hurry."

"You know what they say. The early bird gets the worm."

Sheryl got out of her chair and smiled. "Please wait here a minute while I fetch the sheriff."

Grant leaned over and whispered in Elena's ear, "I thought that woman was going to break out laughing when you said UFO."

"I'm used to it," she replied. "I'd be more concerned if they welcomed us with open arms."

Sheryl returned and ushered them to Robin Black's office.

"Please come in," said Black.

They walked in, and Grant liked what he saw. Robin Black exuded confidence and had a no-nonsense look about her. She looked like she was someone he could rely on to get things done.

After Elena had made the introductions, they sat down across from Black in old wooden chairs.

"Sheryl told me that you're here in town to investigate a

possible UFO sighting?" said Black as she read Elena's business card.

"That's correct," said Elena. "My people and I flew up here to gather information on your close encounter of the first kind."

"Our what?"

"Sorry. I'm so used to speaking as if everyone knows all there is to know about UFOs. There were reports of a power outage and a strange object flying over your town late last night, and we've come up here to interview anyone who may have seen something in the night sky they cannot explain."

Black raised an eyebrow. "Word sure travels fast."

"In our community, nothing stays a secret for very long. Everyone wants to be the first person on site, in case there is something to the story. You don't get a television special made about you by being the second or third person to investigate a possible UFO sighting."

"As far as I'm aware, the only person who claims to have seen anything so far is old Edgar Bedard. However, I wouldn't put too much faith in what he has to say."

"Why not?" asked Grant.

"Edgar tends to drink too much and spends a fair bit of his time in my cells, sobering up."

"Where might we find Mr. Bedard?" said Elena.

"He lives in the small trailer park on the outskirts of town. I'll give you his address," said Black, scribbling the information down on a piece of paper and handing it to Elena.

"Thanks. Trust me, we won't be a bother to the town's citizens while we're here. If people don't want to talk with us, that's fine. We're not known for being pushy."

"That's good because most folks who live in and around the town like their privacy. Are there more than just the two of you?"

"Yes, there are four of us altogether."

"Do you have somewhere to stay while you're here?"

"Yes. We called ahead and reserved rooms at a place called

Aunt Rebeca's Inn."

"It's far from being a five-star hotel, but it's the best you're going to find for hundreds of miles. As an added bonus they serve some really good food there. Try the steak and eggs for breakfast. It's one of my favorites."

"Thanks for the heads-up. I'm sure we'll try it. However, I doubt we'll be here very long."

"Sheriff, would it be possible to get two town maps from your office?" asked Grant.

Black nodded. "Sure, just ask Sheryl on your way out, and she'll provide you with them."

"Well, all I wanted to do was pop in and say hello," said Elena as she stood up. "We really should get going. The last thing we want to do is keep you from your duties."

Black got out of her chair. "Aside from the power outage and a couple of dogs being mauled to death last night, things here are as quiet as always."

Elena brought a hand to her mouth. "Oh my, how horrible. What happened?"

"We think there's a grizzly bear on the prowl. The dogs must have attacked it and were killed in the ensuing fight."

"Did this happen close to town?" asked Grant.

"No. It happened on Ellen Marshall's property. She lives about ten kilometers north of here. If you're thinking about going out there, be careful. This isn't the lower forty-eight. We've got bears up here that won't think twice about attacking and killing a man."

"Thanks for your advice, Sheriff. We'll be careful."

With that, Grant and Elena exited the station, stopping briefly to pick up some maps from Sheryl on their way out.

Robin Black watched the pair of newcomers head toward the café next door before freshening up her coffee and making her way to Sheryl's desk. "So, what do you make of our visitors?"

Sheryl shrugged. "They seem harmless enough. I'm not sure I buy into all this UFO hokum, but in this economy, if they want to spend some of their hard-earned cash here in town, who am I to complain?"

Black looked down at the card in her hand and shook her head. "If that man isn't in the military, he's definitely ex-military."

"What makes you say that?"

"His mannerisms gave him away. He sat far too straight in his chair and didn't look like any UFO investigator I've ever seen on television. As my late uncle used to say, you can take the boy out of the army, but you can't take the army out of the boy."

"If they're from the government, what are you going to do?"

"For now, nothing. As long as they don't break any laws, I'll let them be. Earlier, I was curious if the military had something to do with last night's blackout. Now, I'm almost sure they did. What I'd like to know is what they find so damn interesting about a meteorite."

Sheryl giggled. "Maybe a real UFO crashed in the woods, and they're here to find it?"

Black smiled, a knot forming in her belly. Her gut was telling her that something had gone wrong, and she wondered if she was being kept in the dark.

16

Grant and Elena linked up with their friends in the café next door to the police station. They all ordered some lunch, and as they waited for their food, they discussed options for their next course of action.

"I got us a ton of water and bug juice," reported Maclean. "The guy at the store also sold me some noise-makers and some bear repellent. He said they've been coming really close to town this year."

"The sheriff told us the same thing," said Grant. "In fact, a couple of dogs were mauled to death earlier in the day by a bear."

"Did you say a bear ate some dogs?" said Hayes.

"You're not in sunny old England anymore, Professor," said Maclean. "The store owner also told us to watch for moose near the lakes and ponds that surround the town. He said if we hit one with one of our cars, it could end up going through the windshield and killing whoever is in the front seat."

"On a far more pleasant note," said Hayes. "While you were all away, I ran into a fellow called Edgar Bedard."

Elena smiled. "What a stroke of luck. He's the man Sheriff Black told us to speak with about last night. What did he have to say?"

"When you get past the revolting smell of alcohol on his breath, he's not a bad eyewitness. He recalled when and where he saw the object in the night sky. From his description of an orange glowing ball passing over the top of the town, I've been able to roughly plot where it may have come down."

Grant was impressed. "How did you manage that?"

"By using geometry, that's how. He took me outside and showed me where he first saw it to where he lost sight of it behind the hills outside of town. Combine those together and I was able to determine its rate of descent."

"I hate math," said Maclean. "Thank God you've got a mind for it."

Grant placed a map on the table. "Do you think you can you plot the landing site on this?"

Hayes reached into a shirt pocket and withdrew a small black book. He re-read his notes from the interview and began to jot down the calculations on the map. A few seconds later, he grabbed a pen and marked an X on the map. "That should be the location, give or take a few hundred meters."

Grant turned the map around so he could read it. The spot Hayes selected was near a lake about twenty-five kilometers outside of town. There was only one home marked on the map near the lake. "Are you sure this is the spot?"

"As sure as I can be using eyewitness testimony."

"Did you call back to the ops center with this info?"

"I did, and they passed it onto NORAD, but they still can't see anything. Captain Jones says the image is still being distorted by something on the ground."

"This happened to me once before, during a UFO investigation in the Florida Everglades," said Elena.

"Let's not jump to any conclusions without any hard evidence. I know of several reasonable explanations for this disturbance," said Hayes.

"Well, whatever is going on, at least your calculations give us something to go on," said Maclean. "What happens if we do find something out there?"

"Then we call the colonel and let him decide what happens next," said Grant. "It's not like the four of us on our own could recover a downed craft. We're here to get information and nothing else."

"That's precisely what Colonel Andrews said our mission was," added Elena.

Their waitress returned with their meal. The two soldiers had ordered cheeseburgers and fries, while Elena ate a salad, and Hayes enjoyed a bowl of tomato soup.

"Before we head out there," said Grant, "I'd like to brainstorm about what we may find out there and how to deal with any possible hazards we may face."

"In my humble opinion, there are two realistic options to explain why NORAD is having a hard time focusing their satellites on this part of Alaska," said Hayes. "What crashed in the woods is either a highly radioactive meteorite or a satellite."

"Whose satellite could it be?" asked Maclean.

"Since it's most likely not one of ours, it leaves the Russians or the Chinese as the main culprits. Both nations have been known to power some of their surveillance satellites using tiny nuclear reactors."

"So, radiation is a possible danger no matter what we find?" said Grant.

"Yes. That's why I brought along several handheld Geiger counters with us."

"What about you, Doc, what do you think?" Maclean asked Elena.

"Well, you know what I think," she replied. "Radiation may have helped trigger the initial electrical blackout, but there's no way it could have caused the NORAD satellites in orbit above Alaska to malfunction. There has to be another explanation other than a meteor or a crashed satellite."

"If Professor Hayes' calculations are correct," said Grant, "an hour from now we may have our answer."

"What do you say?" said Maclean, "How about a little wager?"

"What kind of wager?" asked Elena.

"The first team to find whatever it is out there gets dinner bought for them by the losing team."

Grant chuckled. "Why not? I'm in."

"As am I," said Elena.

Maclean nudged Hayes. "Come on. You've got me on your team. You can't lose."

With an exasperated sigh, Hayes raised a hand. "All right, but I get to choose the restaurant. I'm not going to eat at some greasy fast food spot."

Maclean took a sip of his Coke and sat back in his chair. "I've got a good feeling about this. Today could turn out to be my lucky day."

The drive to the lake took them just over half an hour. After turning off the gravel road, they drove on a dirt trail that was barely wide enough for the vehicles. The sound of tree branches scraping down the sides of the car made Elena cringe. They came out in a mountain clearing overlooking an oval-shaped lake. Grant and Maclean parked their cars side by side and got out. Everyone met at the back of Maclean's vehicle.

Hayes opened the trunk and retrieved three black plastic cases. He opened them and stood back. Inside one case was a pair of Geiger counters. In the next was a small green and black drone with a control box. The last one held two handguns. Hayes picked up one of the Geiger counters and switched it on. He walked to the front of the vehicles and stood there, staring at the small screen on the top of the device.

"So, Doc, what's the story?" said Maclean. "Are you reading any abnormal levels of radiation?"

Hayes shook his head. "No. The level of radiation in the air is what I would expect us to find. We're safe."

"I take that as good news," said Grant.

Hayes turned off his Geiger counter, walked back, and put it back in its box. He pulled the container with the weapons toward him. Hayes looked over at Grant and Maclean. "Gents, I brought along two Heckler and Koch Mark 23 pistols. They fire .45 caliber ammunition and have a small rail built under the barrel, which allows the firer to add a detachable laser aiming device, a suppressor, or a small light, should he wish to. In the case, you will find six full magazines for each weapon."

Maclean picked one up and felt the weight in his hand. "Nice choice, Doc. This will do nicely."

"As Alaska allows people to openly carry firearms, there shouldn't be an issue with you having them on you from now on. There are permits for both weapons in your names in the case as well."

"What about the drone?" asked Grant. "What kind of range does it have?"

"It can travel up to twenty kilometers away from the controller and remain aloft for ninety minutes before needing to be recharged," explained Hayes. "There is a camera on it, which can send back live feed to my laptop."

"What are we waiting for?" said Maclean. "Let's get it airborne."

"Have you ever flown this type of drone before?" Grant asked Hayes.

The academic shook his head. "No, it's brand new. I was hoping one of you two had experience with it."

"My nephew has a toy kind of like this," said Maclean. "If I don't crash it on takeoff, we should be okay."

Hayes removed the drone from its case and placed it on the ground. It had four arms with a propeller on each. Suspended underneath was a miniature camera. Hayes switched the drone on before activating the handheld control device, which he quickly handed over to Maclean.

"Here goes nothing," said Maclean, pressing a red button, which applied power to the propellers. The drone slowly lifted off the ground and pitched over to the right for a second before righting itself. Maclean quickly got a feel for the controls and brought the drone to a stop right in front of him, hovering about three meters in the air. "See, I told you I could get it aloft."

"Wait a second," said Hayes as he checked the image on his laptop.

"How do things look?" asked Elena, peering over Hayes' shoulder.

"Perfect," replied Hayes. "Sergeant, the anomaly should have come down about a kilometer to the west of us. Please maneuver the craft over in that direction."

Maclean moved a small stick with his thumb. The drone rose up in the air and flew off in the direction of the alleged crash site.

Grant and Elena watched the image on the screen. The lakeshore was deserted. There weren't any animals to be seen, which struck Grant as odd. He lifted his head and looked around. It was the same. They were completely alone. Only the insects seemed to have stuck around. Goosebumps ran up Grant's arms.

"Wow, David, take a look at this," said Elena.

Grant turned his head, saw what was on the computer screen, and let out a low whistle. In a straight line leading to the edge of the lake, the tops of the trees looked like they had been neatly sawed off.

"Please hold the drone where it is," said Hayes.

"Will do, Doc," replied Maclean.

"How far back does this go?" asked Elena.

"There's only one way to find out," said Hayes. "Sergeant, please raise the drone up in the air until I tell you to stop."

Maclean gently applied power to the drone allowing it to ascend higher in the sky.

"That'll do," said Hayes. "Please hold it there."

The swath of destruction went back for almost a kilometer through the woods.

"My God, it must have been coming in at an incredibly fast

speed to do that much damage," said Elena.

"If you look at the width of the path, you can see that the object was probably about fifty meters across," explained Hayes as he pointed at the screen.

"Well, I think that rules out a satellite," said Maclean. "You're recording this, aren't you?"

"Of course," said Hayes. "This is an incredible find."

"That leaves only one other culprit," said Maclean. "From what I can see on the screen, it must have been one hell of a meteor."

"No way. A meteor didn't do that," said Elena firmly. "The Tunguska event of 1908 in Siberia was caused by a fifty-meter wide meteorite exploding high in the air. The resulting blast was equivalent to ten megatons of TNT going off. All the trees in a thirty-kilometer radius were flattened. As the lake and most of the countryside doesn't look like it was touched, I think we can safely rule out a meteor."

"Whatever it was, it must have carried on and gone down in the lake," said Grant. "I wonder how deep it is."

"It's hard to tell," said Elena. "I wonder if the sheriff would know."

"We'll give her a call when we're ready to leave. After that, we can ask the ops center to arrange for a navy ROV to be shipped to us."

"What's an ROV?" asked Elena.

"It stands for remotely operated underwater vehicle," explained Grant. "It's a kind of unmanned mini-sub. The navy use them all the time to look for things lost at sea."

Hayes lowered his head and leaned in toward the screen. "Excuse me, Sergeant—"

"For the love of God, Doc, we're supposed to be undercover. Please drop the rank," cried Maclean.

"Sorry, er…James, could you maneuver the drone back toward the lake, and then slightly to the right of the path cut through the trees?"

"Do you see something?" asked Grant.

"I'm not sure. What do you take that to be?" said Hayes, pointing at a shiny tube lying on the ground in a clearing.

"I don't know. But it doesn't look like a piece of meteor or any other naturally made object to me," said Grant.

"How far away is it?" asked Elena.

"About eight hundred meters," said Hayes.

"What are you thinking?" Grant asked Elena.

"We have to take a look at whatever it is lying out there in the woods. It's not that far, and the sun won't be going down until around eight o'clock tonight."

Grant looked over at Hayes. "Doc?"

"While I'd rather not go traipsing blindly through the woods, I'm forced to agree with Elena," said Hayes. "Our job is to investigate, and this could be an escape pod from some highly advanced Russian plane we have yet to learn about."

"Okay, I guess that settles it," said Grant. "Jim, bring the drone back home, and let's all grab what we need for a walk through the woods."

17

Robin Black placed her black Stetson on her head and checked her uniform over in a mirror on the wall before leaving. She always insisted on looking professional, which was something she also expected from her officers. A breeze outside helped cool down the unseasonably warm mid-September temperatures. She walked to her Suburban and was about to open the door when she spotted a truck parked farther down the street. It wasn't the vehicle so much as the people standing outside of it that caught her eye. There were five men, all dressed as if they were going camping. There was something about the way they acted that made her uneasy. Black decided to check them out and walked toward them.

As she got closer, she could see that all but one of them looked to be in their early thirties and appeared to be in peak physical condition. The odd man out was in his late forties, with blond hair and a neatly trimmed goatee.

"Good afternoon, gentlemen, going camping?" Black asked congenially.

The blond-haired man smiled at Black. "Yes, we are, Sheriff." The man's accent betrayed a hint of German. "We just stopped in town to grab a few supplies before driving a few klicks out of town to set up our camp for the evening."

Civvies don't say klicks, thought Black. *More goddamned government agents poking their noses around in my town.* "Do you gentlemen plan on doing any fishing?"

"We sure do."

"Do you have fishing licenses?"

"No. That's another reason why we stopped here. We're going to pick some up at the hardware store before leaving town. Say, you must know where the best lakes to fish at are around here."

"Jonas Lake, about ten minutes' drive out of town, is a good spot, as is Bear Lake."

"Thanks for the tip, Sheriff."

"Whatever you do, be careful out there, as we've got a grizzly bear roaming the woods north of the town, and it's already killed a couple of dogs today."

The man opened the back of his truck. On the floor were several hunting rifles. "We came prepared to protect ourselves."

"I can see that," replied Black, looking over the weapons. "Take care of yourselves, and have a nice day."

"We will," replied the man.

Black walked back to her vehicle, got in, and dug out her cell phone. She decided to call her old military friend at Elmendorf.

"Hello." A woman's voice came across the line.

"Anne, it's me, Robin. Sorry to bother you, but I need you to do me a favor."

"It's never a bother hearing from you," said Anne. "How can I help?"

"I don't need to know the particulars, but could you confirm for me if the military has people in my neck of the woods right now?"

"Hold on," said Anne before setting her phone down. A minute later she picked it back up. "We don't have anything on the books, Robin. Why? Are there some drunken soldiers in town on leave causing you a spot of trouble?"

"No, nothing like that."

"If you like, I can ask higher up if they have something on the go."

"I'd appreciate that."

"This may take some time."

"That's all right. I can wait for your answer. Nothing important is going on here right now."

"Talk to you later," said Anne before hanging up.

Black sat in her seat and watched the five men as they got back in their truck and drove off. She drummed her fingers on the steering wheel for a few seconds before starting her Suburban and placing it in reverse. Black waited for a car to pass her, then pulled out of her parking spot and onto the road. Ellen Marshall had called her a few minutes ago and had been crying over the loss of her dogs. Black decided she would pay her a visit before popping in to say hello to some of the other people in the area where the grizzly's tracks had been spotted. She figured the trip would eat up what was left of the afternoon. With two possible teams of government agents nosing around in her jurisdiction, Black doubted she would get much rest until they were gone and life returned to normal in Robertson's Mine.

18

Grant took hold of a tree branch blocking the trail and pushed it aside, while Elena, Hayes, and Maclean walked past him. The path through the forest was tight, but well-worn. Grant suspected if they stayed on it long enough that it would eventually come out at the lone cabin marked on the map.

"The object should be about forty meters that way," said Maclean, pointing off to the right. In his hand was a GPS with the coordinates of the pod inputted into it.

"Any sign of radiation?" Grant asked.

"None," replied Hayes, checking his Geiger counter.

"At least we have that going in our favor," said Elena as she swatted a mosquito on her neck. "This place is unbelievable. I've never seen so many bloodsucking insects in all my life."

Maclean tossed her some bug spray. "Put some more on. It's the only way to keep the little bloodsuckers away. I remember this one time in East Timor, one of my mates got bitten by something which swelled up his leg so bad he had to be flown home. Poor bugger almost lost his leg. Ever since then, I smother myself with bug spray wherever I go."

Elena nodded and hurriedly sprayed the exposed parts of her face and hands.

Minutes later, they emerged out of the wood and into the clearing. Grant and Maclean drew their sidearms.

Grant looked at his colleagues. "Okay, you two stay here until James and I have checked out the pod and determined that it is safe for you two to come and inspect it," he said firmly.

Elena placed a hand on Grant's arm. "Be careful."

"We will," said Maclean.

With their weapons held out at the ready, the two soldiers walked toward the pod. They stopped a few meters short and looked over the device. It was about four meters long and one and a half meters wide. The metal was smooth and didn't appear to have any rivets or welds on it. A door lay on the ground next to the pod.

"Do you know what I don't see lying anywhere around here?" said Maclean.

"What?" replied Grant.

"A parachute. If this were a Russian ejection pod, where's the parachute?"

"I hadn't thought of that. Perhaps it never deployed."

"Then where's the pilot?"

"Another good question."

Maclean stepped away from the pod and stopped next to the door. On the ground was a pair of boot prints, which dwarfed his own size-twelve feet. "Hey, Dave, come over here and check this out."

Grant's eyes widened when he saw the tracks. "The Russians must be breeding them big and heavy these days. Those boots must be at least size twenty, and the pilot had to weigh a couple of hundred kilos to leave an imprint that deep in the ground."

"The tracks lead off to the east," said Maclean, pointing to the far woodline.

"Did you find something?" called out Elena.

"Yes, footprints," responded Grant. Before he could say another word, the two scientists were on the move.

"Nobody said it was safe to come over here," said Grant.

"I know, but I couldn't wait a single second longer," replied Elena as she got down on one knee to look inside the pod. She started snapping pictures with her camera.

Grant joined her. He had expected to see a seat or at least some harnesses to keep the pilot securely in place after ejection, but there was nothing. The inside of the device was completely bare. He placed his hand on the outer casing. Although the sun was directly overhead, the metal was cool to the touch. Grant pushed down gently on the casing, and to his surprise, he saw his hand leave an imprint on it. A second later, the metal rose up and erased the print.

Elena looked up at Hayes with a bright twinkle in her eyes.

Maclean patted Hayes on the shoulder. "Okay, Doc, there's no way in hell you can tell me that's Russian."

"We won't know that for sure until we've had a better chance to study the metallurgy," replied the scientist.

Elena stepped back and brought up her camera. "David, would you please stand beside the pod, so I can use you for scale?"

Grant nodded and stood ramrod straight next to the ejection pod.

Elena took a half-dozen photos before lowering her camera. "Now, where are these tracks that you found?"

"They're over here," said Maclean.

Elena and Hayes walked to the soldier's side and looked down at the imprints in the ground. Elena placed her foot next to a track and snapped off a couple more pictures.

"My God, those boot prints are enormous," remarked Elena.

"That they are," said Maclean. "Now, can either of you two fine doctors tell me what is odd about those boot tracks?"

"I have no idea," said Hayes with a shrug.

"Neither do I," added Elena.

"I'm not a fashion expert, as my boots come free of charge from the army. But I find it quite odd that there no ridges on the soles of his boots. They are as flat as an ironing board. Not the best footwear to have on one's feet when one is slogging through the woods of Alaska."

"I would never have thought of that," said Elena.

"So, folks, what do you want to do?" said Grant. "It's nearly three in the afternoon. Do you want to head back to town and inform Colonel Andrews about what we've found so far, or would you like to follow these tracks for a few hours before calling it a day?"

"We can't go back now," said Elena. "I have to see where these tracks lead."

"I disagree," said Hayes. "The pilot is clearly still alive and could see us as his enemy. I'm in no mood to get shot by a scared Russian test pilot. It's time to bring in more people to help with the investigation."

"Jim, your thoughts?" asked Grant.

"I'm with Elena," he replied, winking at her. "We've got plenty of time before the sun goes down. As long as we're cautious, we should be okay."

Grant grinned. He knew his comrade would want to push on. "I agree with James and Elena. We'll follow the tracks for another hour or two before heading back to town."

Hayes let out a moan and shook his head. "Captain, please, I'm an analyst, not a field operative."

"Quit yer griping, Doc," said Maclean. "Live a little. You can't sit behind a desk all your life. Consider this a crash course in fieldwork."

"Let's go," said Grant. "Jim, you've got the lead."

With that, Maclean began to walk slowly, following the tracks in the mud. Less than ten minutes had passed before they emerged out of the woods and into another open space. In the middle of the clearing were the remains of a destroyed log cabin. Although there were no visible signs of a fire, the roof and most of the front of the building was gone. Shattered wooden timbers covered the ground.

Grant placed a hand firmly on Elena's shoulder. "I want you to listen to me this time. You two have to stay here while Jim and I check this place out."

Elena nodded solemnly and reached for her phone to take more pictures.

Both men drew their pistols and walked toward the cabin.

"Hello, is there anyone in there?" called out Grant.

Silence greeted his call.

"This happened only hours ago," said Maclean.

"How can you be so sure?"

"Because the pilot's footprints lead right up to where the front door would have been on this cabin."

Grant edged up to an opening on the side of the cabin and peered inside. Everything was a mess. The interior looked as if a tornado had gone through the home. All the furniture had been flipped over and thrown about inside the tiny cabin.

"I'll check around back," said Maclean.

Grant walked to the front of the cabin and stepped over an old iron stove lying on its side. He threaded his way through the debris until he was near the back of the small home. There was no sign of the pilot or the person who had lived in the cabin. However, Grant was surprised by the number of destroyed bird cages littering the floor.

"Dave, out here," cried out James.

Grant pushed his way past the kitchen table blocking the back door and ran outside. "What's up?"

"I think I've found the homeowner," said Maclean who was on his knees, cradling an old man in his arms. The man was wearing a dirty red-and-white checkered shirt underneath his denim overalls. His face was wrinkled and in need of a shave. He had long, scraggly, white hair.

"Is he alive?" asked Grant.

"Yeah. He's breathing. I think he was knocked out cold by whoever, or whatever, did that to his place."

Grant looked around. The pilot's boot prints were nowhere to be seen. A chill ran down his spine. He cupped a hand to his mouth and shouted, "Elena, Jeremy, come here please."

"Oh my. Is he all right?" said Elena when she saw the old man.

"He seems okay. I think he was knocked out by the blast,"

explained Maclean.

"That man clearly needs to see a doctor," said Hayes. "We should stop what we're doing and take him into town without delay."

"I think you're right," said Grant. "We've done all we can today."

Maclean scooped up the man in his arms and struggled to stand. He raised his eyebrows and let out a deep grunt. "Whoa, this old bugger is a might bit heavier than he looks."

Grant pointed toward a trail in the woods. "I think that will lead us back to our cars."

"I'll take the lead and anytime you need a break, Jim, holler out, and I'll take a turn carrying the old man," said Grant.

Maclean gritted his teeth. "I'll be fine. Lead on, boss."

After thirty minutes of bashing through the woods, Grant helped Maclean lay the sleeping man down on the backseat of his Ford Mustang before stepping back so he could stretch out his back.

"My feet feel as if they've marched one hundred kilometers today," complained Hayes as he deposited his tired body onto a seat in the front of the vehicle.

The old man suddenly sat straight up and opened his eyes. "My birds! Where are my birds?"

Elena ran over and took one of the man's gnarled and callused hands in hers. "Sir, you're okay. You're with friends. My name is Elena, what's yours?"

"Joe. Joe Sparks."

The old man looked from person to person. "I don't know any of you. Have you seen my birds?"

Maclean handed the man a bottle of water. "Here, Joe, drink some of this."

Sparks eyed the bottle suspiciously before taking a sip. "Where are we?"

"We're just over a mile from your cabin," said Grant, suspecting the old-timer wouldn't have a good grasp of the metric system. "We found you lying on the ground outside your home. Joe, what's the last thing you remember?"

Sparks took a long drink of water. He scrunched up his weathered face. "I thought I heard someone moving around outside, so I went to grab my shotgun. A split second later, there was a flash of light. No noise, just a light as bright as the sun. After that, I don't recall a thing until I woke up here with you people. Can you take me back to my cabin? I also got some cats to look after. They and my birds are going to need to be fed."

"Sir, your home was blown to pieces," said Grant. "I'm sorry, but we didn't see any of your pets when we looked through your cabin. They were either killed in the explosion or ran off."

Sparks' shoulders drooped. His eyes filled with tears. "They were all I had to keep me company after my wife died."

"Sir, we're sorry for your loss, but you need to see a doctor," said Elena. "I think you may have suffered a concussion when your cabin exploded."

"I guess there's no point going back now. There's a clinic in town that I go to a couple times a year. You can take me there."

"Okay, that settles it," said Grant. "We'll take you to the clinic, and then let the police know what happened. I'm sure they'll want to investigate the explosion."

"Dear God," said Hayes, his voice was tight with fear.

"What is it Doc?" Grant asked.

"The lake..." Hayes mumbled, pointing a shaking finger at the water.

Everyone turned their heads and stared in disbelief as a cloud of steam began to rise from the middle of the lake. Within seconds, the entire lake became a bubbling, frothing mass. An unusual orange glow appeared at the far end of the lake and grew so bright that it was near impossible to look at.

"Time to leave," called out Grant. He ran to his vehicle and started it up. Elena opened her door and jumped in next to him.

The two cars had barely pulled back ten meters when a tall plume of water shot out of the lake and rocketed up into the sky. A couple seconds later, the water began to rain down to earth, covering the vehicles. Grant hurried to turn on his windshield wipers so he could see what was going on. With a loud crunch, a fish landed on the windshield, cracking it.

Elena jumped back in her seat. "What the hell was that?"

"A trout...I think," replied Grant, trying to sound calm. Inside, his heart was pounding away.

"Stop backing up," said Elena, peering out through the cracked windshield.

Grant placed the vehicle in park. "Why, what's wrong?"

"The lake...I think it's gone."

Grant opened his door and stepped outside.

"Be careful out there," said Elena.

"Not to worry," he replied, placing his hand on his holster. A thick, humid mist hung in the air. It felt like Grant was standing inside a sauna. The ground was soaked. Dozens of dead fish lay scattered all around the vehicle. Grant watched for a few moments as the fog began to dissipate. He looked over at the lake and shook his head. Elena was right; the lake was gone. There wasn't a drop of water left in it. Grant stared at the muddy lake bottom, bewildered. His mind was unable to process what his eyes were seeing.

"Now that was something," said Maclean, joining his comrade.

Grant blinked a couple of times as if he were in a dream. "Jim, where's the lake?"

"Dave, that's not the problem."

"Really?" Grant's eyebrows shot up to his hairline. "What would you say the problem is, then?"

"The UFO. Where's the friggin' craft that Elena thinks may have crashed into the lake? I don't see it, do you?"

Both men stood there staring at the empty crater, which less than thirty seconds ago had been full of water.

Grant looked over his shoulder at Elena and Hayes. "A crashed experimental Russian airplane my ass. I think it's high time the two good doctors learned to trust us and opened up a little bit more about what's really going on."

"Gents, we've got to go," said Hayes, waving a handheld Geiger counter in the air. "The ground at our feet is highly radioactive. We'll need to wash both cars before entering the town, if we can. Also, we're going to need to change all of our clothes and shower the instant we get back to our hotel."

Neither soldier had to hear another word. They ran back to their cars. Before long, they were speeding down the dirt trail back toward town, desperate to find a working car wash.

19

Robin Black parked her Suburban and got out. She could see Ellen Marshall sitting on her front steps. In one hand was a glass, in the other was a half empty bottle of bourbon.

"I'm sorry to hear about your dogs, Ellen," said Black.

"I'd raised them ever since they were pups," bemoaned Ellen. "They were good dogs. Why did the Good Lord have to take them away from me?"

Black took a seat next to Marshall. "There's no rhyme or reason as to why these things happen. They just do. I called the State Wildlife Troopers, and they're going to send a few officers to look for the bear that got your dogs."

"Thanks," said Ellen as she poured herself another stiff drink.

"Ellen, do you have any family or friends nearby who you could stay with for a couple of days while the troopers hunt down this bear?"

Ellen nodded. "Gladys Wright is on her way here to pick me up and take me into town for a few days."

Black smiled. Gladys was the wife of the town's church minister, and a kind-hearted soul. Marshall would be in good hands until the dust settled. As if on cue, Gladys' car came into sight.

"You'd best hide the bottle," whispered Black to Ellen. "Pastor Wright isn't fond of people who overindulge."

Ellen shrugged. "This is nothing. I can finish a bottle by myself without even batting an eye."

"That may be so, but you'd best behave yourself while you're living under their roof."

"I guess I should go and pack a few things to take with me." Ellen stood and shuffled back inside her home.

Black got to her feet and walked toward Gladys' car. "Afternoon, Gladys," she said in greeting.

"Afternoon to you, too, Robin," replied Gladys, as cheerful as ever.

"It's awfully good of you to take in Ellen on such short notice."

"Nonsense. Ellen may not come to church as much as she used to, but she's a person in need, and it's our job to help people like her."

"Well, I, for one, will sleep better knowing she's not out here by herself for the next few days."

"Do you think we've got a rogue grizzly on our hands?"

"I don't know. I'll leave it the wildlife troopers to sort it out."

Ellen Marshall walked out of her home carrying a small bag jammed with clothes, locked the front door, and got in Gladys' car.

"I'll come by and see you in a day or so," said Black to Marshall. With that, Gladys turned her car around and drove off. Black stood still, studying the woods which surrounded Ellen's home. The hair on her arms stood on end. The same as it did when she got the feeling she was being watched. Black was used to being in the woods and didn't fear any animal which lived there. Her father had taken her hunting as soon as she was old enough to carry a rifle. Something felt off. She shook her head and put it all down to nerves. Black got back into her SUV and pressed the button to start her engine. She had intended to go back to the station, but instead decided to pay a quick visit to Ronald Deering, as his home was only a couple of kilometers down the road.

The moment she saw the front door standing wide open at Deering's house, Black knew something was wrong. The man was almost a recluse. He liked his privacy and rarely dealt with anyone in town unless he needed something. She had never seen his door open in all the years she had been with the police force.

Black parked her vehicle and got out. She stopped at the front of her SUV and called out, "Ron, it's me, Sheriff Black. Are you home? Are you in need of assistance?"

Silence.

Black reached down and pushed the thumb break on her holster forward, allowing her instant access to the firearm should she need it. Her heart began to race when she spotted several discharged shotgun shells lying on the ground.

She edged toward the door. "Ron, are you okay? Do you need help?"

Black stopped by the open door and drew her pistol. She took a deep breath to calm herself and stepped inside. "Ron, it's me, Robin. If you're here, please call out." She walked through the tiny, well-kept bungalow until she came to the back door, which was also wide open.

Black holstered her pistol, shook her head, and mumbled to herself, "What the hell happened here, Ron?"

Black walked out back and looked down. There were more fired shotgun shells. She noticed a set of footprints leading away from the house. Black brought a hand to her mouth and yelled, "Ron, it's me, Sheriff Black. Are you out in the woods?"

Aside from a couple of birds chirping in a tree next to the house, the woods were silent.

Black followed the tracks until they stopped at an old brick well, from which Deering still got his water. On the ground lay a double-barreled shotgun. Black picked it up and popped it open. There were two more fired shells inside the barrels. She looked around but couldn't see what Deering had been trying to hit. Black turned to leave, when out of the corner of her eye she spotted peculiar-looking tracks in the wet ground. She bent down to examine the imprints in the ground. There were several large three-toed tracks that looked as if they came out of the woods to the well and then went back again. Black struggled to identify the tracks. They looked more like a giant bird's footprint than any other animal she had ever seen. There wasn't a sign of a struggle, nor was there blood on the ground. It was as if Deering had simply vanished. Black checked the time. It would be getting dark in a couple of hours. If she were going to organize a search party, she would have to get back to town right away.

Black jogged back to her Suburban and reached for her radio. "Sheryl, this is Sheriff Black, do you read me, over?"

"I read you, loud and clear, over," responded Sheryl.

"Sheryl, I'm up at Ronald Deering's place, and it looks like he's gone missing. I think he may have been taken by a wild animal. Have Kyle and Tracey report in early for work, and let the wildlife troopers know what's happened. I'm heading back to you to organize a search party to look for Ronald, over."

"Wilco, over."

"Roger, Black, out." She started her vehicle and drove away from Deering's home. Black felt a shiver go down her spine. She glanced more than once in her rearview mirror and couldn't shake the feeling that things were about to get a lot worse.

20

"How's Mr. Sparks doing?" asked Elena the instant Grant walked into his room back at the hotel. The rest of the group sat around a small oval table in the corner of the suite. Like Grant, everyone had showered and changed.

"He's doing fine," he replied, closing the door behind him. "He's still pretty distraught about his pets, but aside from that, I think he'll be okay. I told the nurse I'd swing by after supper to see how he's doing."

"Maybe I'll come with you," said Elena.

"Did he say anything to the staff at the clinic about his house, or what happened at the lake?" asked Hayes.

Grant shook his head. "I'm not sure if he was conscious or not when the lake disappeared. As for his house, Joe still can't recall a thing."

"I think the poor old bugger passed out before the lake went poof," said Maclean, making an explosion gesture with his hands. "I know for sure that he wasn't exposed to any of the contaminated lake water, as he was lying down in the back of my vehicle safe and sound."

"Speaking of that," said Grant. "We were damned lucky to find a gas station with a do-it-yourself car wash on the outskirts of town. I'd hate to think what we would have had to do if we hadn't been able to wash our cars."

"I would have suggested that we drive them to the nearest river and wash them by hand," said Hayes. "We wouldn't have won any awards from the people at the EPA, but we couldn't risk bringing any contaminated dirt or water into the town."

Maclean leaned forward in his chair. "Doc, please don't try to tell me that was a naturally occurring phenomenon we witnessed today."

"I've been thinking about it, and there is a plausible explanation for what happened," replied Hayes.

Grant pulled a chair out at the table and took a seat. "This, I have to hear."

"We all witnessed a bright orange glow before the lake evaporated," said Hayes. "I believe volcanic activity may have caused the lake to disappear. There are dozens of active and inactive volcanoes spread throughout Alaska. I think we may have stumbled upon a yet-to-be identified volcano."

Grant rolled his eyes. "Come on, Jeremy, do you take me for an idiot? We get that part of your job is to spread disinformation to protect secret government programs, but don't try that crap with Jim and me. Something's going on around here, and we deserve to know the truth from both of you."

Hayes sat back in his chair, avoiding eye contact for a few seconds.

"What would you like to know, Captain?" said Elena.

"Elena! Colonel Andrews hasn't given us permission to divulge any national security secrets to them," argued Hayes.

"For God's sake, Jeremy, they, more than anyone we have ever worked with in the past, deserve to know the truth and not just snippets of it."

"I don't agree."

Elena glared at Hayes. "And right now, I don't care what you think. David's right. This isn't some simple disinformation operation. Something neither of us has ever encountered before is happening right here, right now, and I don't mind telling you that I'm more than a little scared." She looked at the two soldiers. "Gents, what is it you'd like to know?"

"For starters, I'm beginning to suspect there's more to this UFO business than either of you have let on," said Grant.

"And you would be correct," replied Hayes reluctantly. "You

have to understand. People like you two come and go from Project Gauntlet. They get used for a specific task and then sent on their way, without ever really learning what we do. The fewer people who know, the better, as far as Colonel Andrews is concerned. Also, I suspect you've already determined that the constant verbal sparring between Elena and me is just an act to confuse people and make them believe that UFOs are entirely man-made and not from outer space."

"So, were you lying about the Nazi flying discs and what happened at Roswell?" asked Maclean.

"No, everything I said back at the base is true. The vast majority of sightings are misidentification of natural phenomena, or secret military drones and planes. It's the one or two percent that can't easily be explained away on which we focus almost all of our attention."

"Okay, without betraying any state secrets, what can you tell us?" said Grant.

"I'm going to Leavenworth for the rest of my life," mumbled Hayes. He composed himself and sat up in his chair. "The retrieval of downed UAV and airplanes, both foreign and domestic, is our stated primary role. In reality, it is the Directorate for Science and Technology of the Defense Intelligence Agency who do all the real legwork. Our people work very hard, but we lack the tools required to search for downed craft outside of the United States. However, the DIA has satellites spread all around the globe, as well as deep-cover operatives in almost every country around the world. It was their black-ops retrieval team which was wiped out in the ambush at the airport."

"I've been meaning to ask who they were, but thought you would have told me by now," said Grant.

"It drives the colonel around the bend that we have absolutely no control over the DIA's people," said Hayes. "As you saw, the moment they decided to launch their people to take the plane, there was no stopping them."

"What is Colonel Andrews' part in this grand deception?" asked Maclean.

"He asked to be assigned to Project Gauntlet, thinking he was going to be leading missions around the world to recover crashed craft," replied Hayes. "I wasn't there at the time, but I was told he was crushed when he found out that he lacked the manpower and had to rely on others to do his job. However, on a positive note, over the past few years, he has given Elena and me a great deal of autonomy to conduct our studies into extraterrestrial encounters."

"I don't get it," said Maclean. "Why didn't the colonel just speak with his superiors and ask for his budget to be increased so he could run Gauntlet the way it should be?"

"He did and was told that the budget he had was more than sufficient."

"I suspect that funds allocated for us have been siphoned off to the DIA since 2000," said Elena. "It's no secret that the annual six hundred-billion-dollar defense budget is one massive shell game."

Maclean shook his head. "This is unbelievable."

Grant looked Hayes in the eyes. "Enough of this budget and command relationship nonsense. Professor, do you believe in UFOs?"

Hayes nodded. "Yes. Just not in the same fervent way Elena does, but yes, I do. My job, as you already know, is to be able to counter any and all UFO sightings with realistic and plausible scientific explanations."

"And what's your job?" said Grant to Elena.

"No change," she replied. "I advise Colonel Andrews on all matters pertaining to UFOs."

"My head's beginning to spin," said Maclean. "I'm a simple soldier. In simple terms, I want to know precisely what Gauntlet does."

"On paper, Gauntlet works directly for General McLeod, the C-in-C of NORAD, who to the best of my knowledge, is aware of our symbiotic relationship with the DIA," explained Hayes. "We do three things: Firstly, we cooperate with the DIA to retrieve crashed UAVs and planes anywhere in the world. Secondly, we covertly spread disinformation on any possible UFO sighting. And lastly, we gather what information we can on any unexplainable UFO encounter."

"Now why didn't you say that way back in Colorado?" asked Maclean.

"Because I didn't know if I could trust you," said Hayes. "Please understand, trust is hard to come by in our line of work."

"Well, we're not the enemy, so you had best learn to trust us," said Grant.

"I'll try." Hayes placed his hands on the table. "Gentleman, all of the U.S. government studies into the UFO phenomenon have always come up with the same conclusion. Namely, the objects being reported by the public were not of extraterrestrial origin, and that none of the sightings represented a threat to the security of the United States. However, not everyone in the military agreed with the findings. That's why Gauntlet was established. For decades, its efforts were mainly focused on debunking UFO sightings. But at the beginning of the twenty-first century, things had changed. There seemed to be an unusual spike in UFO activity, especially around military installations in the U.S. and elsewhere."

"You're worried they're probing us and looking for our weaknesses, aren't you?" said Maclean.

Hayes nodded. "I am. We only need to look at our own history to give us a lesson in the negative consequences of an advanced civilization contacting a less-advanced one. Every time this has occurred, the less-advanced people have suffered grievously. There is no hard evidence that the extraterrestrials visiting Earth are hostile, but we know so little about them and their intentions. As they say, to be forewarned is to be forearmed."

"Back in Colorado, you said that you two had investigated thirteen sightings," said Grant to Elena. "Were any of them similar to this one?"

"None of them have even been remotely like this case," she replied. "The closest we've ever come to finding evidence of extraterrestrial visitation was two years ago in northern Maine, when we found imprints in the ground from an alleged UFO landing site."

"There were also traces of radiation in the soil that couldn't easily be explained away," added Hayes.

"So how did you hide your discovery?" asked Maclean.

"We didn't. This was one of the rare occasions where we decided to let people believe that they had been visited."

"Why would you do that?" said Grant.

"Two reasons. First off, it helped distract the other UFO investigators from looking elsewhere, and secondly, the Air Force was testing a new stealth drone along the U.S.- Canadian border, so any sightings of the craft would naturally have been reported as another UFO and not a military UAV."

"Ingenious," said Maclean. "But what about that ship in Iraq, which cost my mates their lives? Was it a Russian drone or a UFO?"

Elena cleared her throat. "Professor Hayes and I believe that it was a possible downed UFO. I'm truly sorry your friends were murdered. Regrettably, the DIA didn't see fit to bring us in on their investigation until after the attack on your camp."

Grant nearly fell out of his chair. "Someone back home in the States knew something was there? Why the hell didn't they warn us, or do something about it before it was too late?"

"The DIA's satellites detected the crashed disc the day after that massive sandstorm passed through your part of Iraq. Unfortunately, at the time, the DIA was focused on gathering intelligence on the Chinese naval build-up off the coast of Taiwan. No one above us thought time was of the essence."

"Bloody hell," muttered Maclean. "Bureaucratic inertia knows no bounds."

"As Jeremy said earlier, we just don't have the resources to do these kinds of missions by ourselves. By the time the DIA decided to bring Colonel Andrews into the planning process, the disc was already gone, and your friends were dead."

"Also, until two weeks ago, we were unaware of a non-state organization that was as interested in UFOs as we are," said Hayes. "A new and deadly variable has been added to an already volatile situation."

Grant let out a deep sigh. "At least you're both finally being honest with us, and for that, I thank you."

"Now that we've cleared the air, what do you two doctors think is going on around here?" asked Maclean.

"Well, let's begin by looking at what we do know," said Hayes. "Less than twenty-four hours ago an unknown object flew over Robertson's Mine, causing an electrical blackout, which lasted several hours. Even though the power has returned, NORAD satellites in orbit above the town still cannot see the ground."

"Wait a second, Doc," said Grant. "Before we go any further, could you please call back to the ops center and see if the jamming is still in place? I'm willing to bet the satellites can see the town quite clearly now. Also, have them look in the woods near the lake for the ejection pod."

Hayes made the call. When he hung up, he looked at Grant and said, "I'll be damned. You're right. NORAD has no problem seeing the town and the surrounding area now."

"Whatever was causing the interference was in the lake, and when it exploded, if that's what happened, it ceased to jam the satellites," explained Grant.

"What about the escape pod?" asked Elena. "Is it still there?"

Hayes shook his head. "It's gone as well."

"Damn. So much for our only piece of hard evidence of extraterrestrial visitation."

"What about the pictures you took?" asked Grant.

"They're not there," replied Elena, holding up her camera. "I don't know how, but the memory has been wiped clean."

"Figures."

"Folks, you're forgetting the biggest puzzle of them all," said Maclean.

"And what would that be?" said Hayes.

"What I'd like to know is, where's the big bastard who walked away from the crash site and seemed to vanish into thin air at Joe Sparks' front door?"

21

Black parked in front of the police station and got out of her vehicle. For the first time since being elected sheriff, she could feel the full weight of her responsibilities pushing down on her shoulders. Inside, police officers Scott and McCartney were sitting at a desk chatting with Sheryl. The two other members of the town's police force, Kyle Harrison and Tracey Tibeluk, were standing by the coffee machine.

Sheryl saw Black and stood. "Sheriff, I called Liam Jones, and he said he'd meet you at Deering's place with his dogs."

"Thanks," said Black. Jones' bloodhounds were among the best in Robertson's Mine and the surrounding area. They'd been used twice already during the summer to look for campers lost in the backwoods north of the town.

"Evening, Sheriff," said Tibeluk. Like Black, she was an Alaskan native.

"Evening, Tracey," replied Black. "Sorry to call you and Kyle in a couple of hours before your shift starts."

"No one ever said it was going to be only shift work when I signed up."

Black poured herself a cup of coffee and sat down on the edge of a table. "I take it the word has already gone out to the state troopers that Mr. Deering has gone missing?"

Sheryl nodded. "I called them right after I got off the phone with you. I also did a quick call around town to see who is available to help with the search."

"And?"

"I've got a dozen people on standby should you need them. But we can't count on much help from the state troopers on account of that massive forest fire burning out of control to the northwest of Valdez."

Black smiled all too briefly. Sheryl was worth her weight in gold. "Well, for now we'll have to do the best we can with our own people. Call everyone in and have them meet us at Deering's home, and we'll do a quick search tonight. If we strike out, we'll enlarge the search at first light, and ask the state troopers to send us what they can. Even if all they can spare are a couple more officers, I'll take them."

Sheryl picked up her phone and started dialing.

"What do you think happened to Mr. Deering?" asked Scott.

"I don't know," replied Black. "He fired off a half-dozen shots at something before his tracks seemed to vanish at the edge of his property."

"I wonder if the bear that killed Ellen Marshall's dogs is to blame?" said McCartney.

"I didn't see any bear tracks," said Black. "There were some tracks there, but I didn't recognize them. Perhaps Liam can tell us what they are. He's spent more time in the backwoods than the lot of us put together." Black placed her half-finished cup of coffee down. "Okay, people, let's get to work. I'm just going to call my son, and then I'll meet you all outside."

Black quickly spoke with her son to let him know she wouldn't be home until late, if not sometime in the morning. As she went to leave, Sheryl's phone rang. Black was almost past her desk and out the door when Sheryl raised a hand to stop her.

"What's up?" asked Black.

There was a troubled look in Sheryl's eyes. "Mrs. Moore was just on the phone. She said her husband and son haven't come home."

Black glanced up at the clock on the wall. "It's still early. If I know those two, they probably went fishing and lost track of time. They'll probably stroll in the front door any time now, with something to cook for supper."

"That's what I told her, but their dogs came home an hour ago without them. There was blood on one of them. She sounds really worried."

Black bit her lip. One person missing was easy to rationalize, but three was almost unheard of. "Damn. Tell her that I'll send two of my officers up there right away to look for them."

Sheryl nodded and picked up the phone.

Black stepped outside. Too many things were happening for all of it just to be a series of random occurrences. She looked over at Harrison and Tibeluk and dispatched them to Mrs. Moore's home.

"Sheriff, something ain't right with all these disappearances," said Scott as he opened the truck of his vehicle and pulled out a shotgun.

Black nodded. "I know. Let's hope the state troopers get here before we lose any more people."

It took less than an hour for the volunteers to arrive at Deering's home. Black was relieved when Liam Jones' beat-up truck came spluttering up the dirt road. The old hunter parked his vehicle and opened his door. Three bloodhounds jumped out, pulling Jones along with them.

"Evening, Liam," said Black. "Sorry to call you out like this, but Ronald Deering's gone missing."

Jones spat a mouthful of tobacco juice on the ground. "Ain't no trouble whatsoever, Sheriff. You know me, I'm always ready to help the police."

Black called out, "Okay, folks, everyone move in on me."

The gaggle of volunteers and police officers formed a semi-circle in front of Black. They were all armed and had flashlights in their hands. "As you're all aware, Ronald Deering went missing some time this afternoon. The last place I saw his tracks were behind his house near his well. We'll let Liam lead off with his dogs and follow them wherever they take us. Before we begin, does anyone have any questions?"

"Sheriff, I heard talk of a rogue grizzly stalking the woods," said a man with a thick black beard. "Is that true?"

"Yes, it is. So, keep your wits about you." Black looked over at Jones. "After you, Liam."

Jones let his dogs sniff a hat belonging to Ronald Deering. In seconds, the dogs were running to the back of the house. When they got to the well, the unexpected happened. The dogs stopped in their tracks and began to whine.

"Go on, yah damn cowards," said Jones to his dogs.

With a howl of fear, the dogs bolted for the safety of the truck. Jones had to let go of their leashes or he would have been pulled off his feet.

"What the hell spooked them?" asked Black.

"I don't know, Sheriff. I've never seen them act like this. They usually ain't afraid of anything."

Black patted Jones on the shoulder. "You had best see to your dogs. We'll carry on without them as far as the river before calling it a night."

Jones nodded and ambled off back to his truck, cursing his dogs to high heaven.

"Okay, folks, I guess we're on our own. Let's spread out in a line and look for clues," said Black to the rest of the group.

"Jesus, will you take a look at this," cried out one of the volunteers. Lit up by a couple of flashlights were the three-toed tracks Black had seen earlier.

"I think those belong to whatever Deering was shooting at," said Black.

"Whatever it is, it's big," said Scott.

Black could see fear in the eyes of some of the men. "Come on, let's push on as far as the river before we call it a night. It's the least we can do for Ronald."

Black took a step forward and pushed some branches aside. With no great sense of urgency, the search party followed her, one by one, into the dark woods.

22

"What's the word?" Maclean asked Grant in between bites of his club sandwich.

"The ops center back home has nothing new to report," replied Grant as he put his phone away. "As far as NORAD Headquarters is concerned, everything is back to normal. With their satellites no longer being jammed, they're back to focusing on their primary job of defending North America. The North Koreans are once again threatening to fire an ICBM over Japan. Naturally, the Japanese aren't too thrilled with the decision and have threatened to shoot it down. NORAD is keeping a close eye on that situation in case it turns into a shooting match."

"One day, the people in North Korea are going to wake up and depose the lunatic running the country," said Maclean.

"We can only hope so. My brother's somewhere out there in the Pacific Ocean; no doubt keeping a close eye on the North Korean fleet."

Elena's phone buzzed. She set down her fork and read a text message. "Colonel Andrews says the hearings in Washington are probably going to last a couple more days. He says there's been a lot of partisan bickering among the committee members, which is dragging the whole thing out. In the morning, Colonel Andrews wants us to take another look around Mr. Sparks' home to see if we can learn what happened to the pilot of the downed craft."

"I thought he'd say that," said Grant.

"I wish there were more of us," said Hayes. "My feet are killing me from all the walking we did today."

"Buck up, Doc," said Maclean. "That was nothing. When I was training to be in the SAS, we had to march farther than that, and with heavy packs on our backs. Today was a mere stroll through the woods."

Hayes shook his head. "If you say so."

"David, what would you like to do after supper?" asked Elena.

"Jim and I will pay a visit to the clinic to see how Joe is doing. I'm hoping that he's over his shock and is able to shed some light on what happened to his home. I know we should have done this earlier, but I'd like you and Jeremy to pay another courtesy call to the police and let them know that we found Sparks' home destroyed and we brought him into town for medical attention."

"Sounds good. Do you want me to tell them about the lake?"

"You might as well. Someone's bound to go up there in the next day or two and find it drained. Jeremy can use his unknown volcano story on them to explain what occurred."

"It's a plausible enough explanation," said Hayes. "You'd be amazed how easily you can convince people to accept a theory if you give them your credentials first."

"We didn't buy your story," said Maclean.

"That's because you two are a pair of cynics, and thanks to my big mouth, you now know far more than the average person on the street about what is going on."

After finishing their supper meal, they parted and went their separate ways. At the clinic, Grant and Maclean were met by the receptionist, who asked them to take a seat while she called the night shift nurse. Less than a minute later, a woman in her mid-forties came from behind the counter to greet the men. She smiled when she recognized Grant.

"Mr. Grant, I didn't expect to see you until later tonight," said the nurse.

"Sorry, Mrs. Norton, I hope we haven't come at an inconvenient time," replied Grant.

Norton shook her head. "No, not at all. Mr. Sparks doesn't have any living relatives, so I don't see any harm in you paying him a quick visit."

"How's he been since we brought him in?"

"He seems to be unhurt, but he's been very cranky. He keeps telling me he wants to leave and go home. But I told him that he had to stay overnight, in case he'd suffered a concussion."

"Where is he now?" asked Maclean.

"In his room," replied Norton.

"Sorry, where are my manners?" said Grant. "James Maclean, please meet Mrs. Jane Norton, the senior nurse here at the clinic."

"My pleasure," said Maclean, offering his hand in greeting.

Mrs. Norton shook Maclean's hand. "This way, gentlemen." She led them past the receptionist and down a short corridor; they came to a closed door at the end of the hall. She knocked on the door. "Mr. Sparks, are you awake? I have a couple of men who'd like to see you."

There was no response.

Mrs. Norton turned the doorknob and slowly pushed the door open. The room was dark. The nurse reached over and flipped on a light.

Grant swore the instant he saw the bed was empty and a window on the far wall open.

"It looks like our friend has flown the coop," said Maclean.

Mrs. Norton opened the small clothes closet in the room and shook her head. "His clothes are gone. The crazy old coot should have stayed in bed. If he's suffered a concussion, he's only going to make it worse."

"I guess you had best call your boss and let her know what's happened," said Grant. "In the meantime, Jim and I will take a look around town and see if we can find Mr. Sparks and try to convince him to come back to the clinic."

"Thanks," said Mrs. Norton as she hurried back to the front desk to make the call.

"So, what do you think is up with Mr. Sparks?" said Maclean.

Grant shrugged. "Beats me. But then again, who knows what happened at his home. He could be mentally deranged for all we know."

The telephone was ringing off the hook as Elena and Hayes opened the front door to the police station. A frazzled Sheryl waved them in as she answered the calls.

"Looks like bedlam has taken hold," whispered Hayes.

"Having a bad night?" Elena asked.

Sheryl leaned back in her chair and let out an exasperated sigh. "I've never seen it this busy, and I've been working here for close to fifty years."

"What's wrong?"

"What isn't?"

Elena took a seat across from Sheryl. "I'm sorry; I don't understand."

"First, Mrs. Marshall's dogs went missing, and were later found dead. Then Mr. Deering disappears from his home. Add to that, Mrs. Moore's husband and son have also been reported missing. And that's only the half of it. In the last half hour alone, I've received half a dozen calls from people telling me that their dogs, chickens, horses—you name it—have been killed or taken by some kind of predator."

The hair on the back of Elena's neck stood straight up. "Did any of them see this predator?"

"No. Almost everyone reported the same thing. They said they heard their animals making a ruckus outside, and by the time they got out there, their animals were either dead or missing."

"You look like you could use some help. Why don't I plot all of these reports on the map hanging on the wall for you?"

"Thanks, that would be great," said Sheryl, handing Elena a handful of hastily scribbled reports.

The phone at Sheryl's desk rang again, sending her scrambling to answer the call.

"Okay, I'll read out the address and you mark it on the map with a yellow sticky," said Elena to Hayes.

"If she has the time when the person called in, I'll write that down on the note as well," said Hayes.

Being unfamiliar with the town and the many homes spread around it, Elena and Hayes struggled to find some of the places on the reports. Ten minutes later, they stepped back from the map.

"Good God," said Hayes under his breath. "They're all south of Mr. Sparks' home."

"Yeah, and it looks like they're moving toward the town."

23

"What's the Geiger counter reading?" Max asked one of his men, a red-haired mercenary with a thick goatee and arms like tree trunks.

"It's way above the red line," replied the man. "We need to limit our exposure to the radiation."

"How long do we have?"

"Five minutes, and no more."

"Okay, Dan, you and the rest of the team get back in the trucks, and honk the horn when my five minutes are up."

The barrel-chested mercenary didn't have to be told twice. He and the rest of Max's men sprinted away from the empty lake bed.

After several hours of driving through the woods, they had stumbled upon what had at first appeared to be a crater in the ground. Upon closer inspection, it turned out to be a recently drained lake. In the back of his mind, Max knew it had to be connected to the UFO sighting. With his flashlight in his hand, Max walked to the edge of the empty lake and shone his light all around. The foul stench of dead fish assaulted his nostrils. Some of the lake water had drained back into the hole, creating dozens of small ponds, which glimmered in the moonlight. Max turned off his flashlight and put a set of NVGs over his eyes. He switched them on and smiled. In the middle of the empty lake was a bright white blob of heat where something had once been. Max doubted, by the scale of the destruction, that there was anything left of the craft. He pulled his NVGs off and turned to walk back to his truck, when, out of the corner of his eye, he thought he saw something moving through the shadows. Instinctively, he drew his pistol, flipped off the safety, and dropped to one knee. Max could only hear the sound of his own breathing. He was about to replace his pistol in its holster when he heard footsteps creeping toward him from behind. His body broke out in a cold sweat. Max gripped his pistol tight in his hand. With his left hand, he brought up his flashlight, spun around, and turned it on.

Max's heart skipped a beat when he saw a three-meter-tall bird with a massive beak and long, clawed legs, frozen in the light less than an arm's length away from him. As fast as he could, Max pulled the trigger. He fired his weapon at point-blank range into the bird's chest. With a loud, terrifying squawk, the bird pulled its head back and took a step forward as if ready to strike.

A sharp crack rang out from behind Max.

The animal's head flew to one side as a portion of its skull was blasted away. The animal wobbled on its feet for a couple of seconds before tumbling over onto its side.

Max's heart was racing. He ejected his empty magazine and quickly inserted a fresh one. He looked down at the bird and saw it was severely wounded, but still alive. The animal opened its beak and tried lifting its blood-splattered head. Max took a breath to steady his shaking hand, aimed his pistol at its head, and fired off three rounds, killing it.

"Jesus, Mr. Roth, are you okay?" asked Dan as he ran to his boss' side.

"Yeah, I'm all right," replied Max. He was lying. Max had never been so horrified in his entire life. His guts felt like jelly, and he thought he was going to be sick at any moment.

"What the hell is that thing?" asked Dan.

"How the hell would I know?" snapped Roth. "I've never seen anything like this before."

"That's a prehistoric terror bird," said a short gunman with a shaved head, shining his flashlight on the bloody carcass.

"Like you'd know what a prehistoric bird would look like,"

chided Dan.

"My sister's kid is nuts about dinosaurs," replied the bald man. "I've taken him to the Smithsonian a couple of times this year, and I'm telling you this thing shouldn't exist."

"Carter, you're out of your mind. This can't be a dinosaur. They died out millions of years ago."

"I didn't say it was a dinosaur. It's from the time after the dinosaurs died out. You know, when woolly mammoths and saber-toothed cats roamed the Earth."

"Are you buying any of this, Mr. Roth?" asked Dan.

Roth holstered his pistol. "Carter's explanation is as good as any right now. Let's get the hell out of here in case there are any more of them nearby."

In the safety of their truck, Dan looked over at Max. "Boss, what do you want to do now?"

"Let's head back to our campsite. I need to make a few calls before I decide on our next move."

Dan nodded, started his vehicle, and drove back down the rocky trail toward the main road.

Three darkened shapes crept out of the forest and stopped at the body lying in the dirt. One of the animals bent down and nudged the carcass with its beak. When the animal didn't move or make a sound, the three other birds instinctively knew it was dead. The closest animal let out a loud squawk before plunging its razor-sharp beak into the belly of the dead bird, ripping it open. The two other animals could smell the warm blood, which sent them diving in and tearing large pieces of flesh from the lifeless carcass. Within minutes, all that remained were some bloody feathers and fragments of bone. For now, the terror birds' hunger had been sated. But before the sun came up, they would be hungry again, and the hunt would begin anew for something else to eat.

24

Robin Black removed her hat and wiped the sweat from her brow, letting the cool night air brush against her face. It was late, and Black was growing tired and frustrated. The search for Ronald Deering had turned up nothing but more odd-looking tracks. She waited by her vehicle until the last volunteer drove home to get some sleep before the search resumed in the morning. Black removed her hat, got into her Suburban, and picked up the radio handset to call back to the police station.

"Sheryl, this is Sheriff Black, how do you read me, over?"

"Five by five," replied Sheryl. She sounded relieved to hear from Black.

"The search for Ronald Deering was a bust. Have you heard from Kyle or Tracey, over?"

"No, I haven't, Sheriff. Are you on your way back, because it's been unbelievably busy back here, over?"

Black didn't like the news that two of her officers hadn't been heard from in a couple of hours. Protocol dictated that they should have called back to the station when they arrived at Mrs. Moore's home. She bit her lip. Black waited a second before keying her mic. "Sheryl, I'm going to swing by Mrs. Moore's place and see what's going on before coming back to the station. Bill and Sean are already on their way back to help you, over."

"Acknowledged. Thanks."

"How are things going at your end, over?"

Sheryl's tired sigh echoed across the CB radio. "More animals have been reported missing, Sheriff, a lot of them."

Black frowned. What the hell was going on? "Okay, fill Bill and Sean in when they get there, and I'll contact you when I get to the Moore's place, over."

"Thanks, Sheriff. Something really odd is happening out there tonight, be careful out there."

"I will, out."

Black started up her SUV and drove down the pitch-black trail leading away from Deering's home. She turned her high beams on and sat back in her seat. Her mind was racing; Black doubted she would get any sleep over the next few days. As she pulled out onto the highway, she looked up and saw a bright orange light shoot across the star-filled sky. Black pulled over onto the shoulder and stopped her vehicle to get a better look at the light. Oddly, the glowing orange light seemed to come to a complete stop over the peak of a tall hill a couple of kilometers away before spinning around in the air and flying straight down the road toward Black. As it got closer, she could see that the mysterious light was disc-shaped. There were a series of colored lights on the underside of the craft, which lit up the road beneath it. Her vehicle's engine inexplicably switched off. Black tried to start it again, but the attempt was in vain.

The disc slowed down and came to a stop directly above the Suburban. The light from the disc was blinding. Black raised a hand to block the glow in an attempt to get a better look at the object silently hovering above her. Instead of feeling scared, Black was surprised to find she was quite calm. Seconds later, curiosity got the better of her. She opened her door and stepped out onto the road. Black squinted, trying to see the craft floating in the night sky.

In the blink of an eye, the disc went dark. Then a single, bluish-white light shone down onto Black. An uneasy feeling washed over her the longer the light was on her. She felt it was intrusive and unwelcome. A second later, the light vanished, leaving Black on the darkened road staring up at the belly of the craft. Without making a sound, the disc raced off at treetop level into the night.

The SUV's lights and engine came on, startling Black. She looked back at her vehicle and saw the power was back on. Black hurried to get back into her Suburban and reached for her radio handset but stopped before she could pick it up. Black wasn't sure what had just happened to her. She had no idea what she would report. With so many strange things happening, she decided to wait until she got back into town, and then track down the team of UFO investigators. Perhaps they could help her understand what she had just witnessed. But first, she had to check on her people. Black had to know if they were all right.

25

"Well, that was the last house on this side of the street," said Maclean to Grant, "and I didn't see hide nor hair of Joe in the alleyway, either."

"I wonder if he flagged down a passing car and got a lift back to his place?" pondered Grant.

"Not sure why he'd go back. His place is a wreck, and he's hardly in any shape to repair the place by himself."

"He's distraught over the loss of his pets and isn't thinking straight."

"Yeah, I guess you're right. I think this is going to turn out to be a dead end. Why don't we go and see how the other half is doing with the police?"

Grant nodded and turned to leave when a brilliant orange light flew right over the town without making a sound.

"My God, did you see that?" said Maclean, wide-eyed.

"I sure as hell did. It looked like it was heading toward the lake."

"We've got to tell Elena and Jeremy what we just saw."

At a gas station across the street, a dog started barking loudly as if trying to frighten someone off.

"Somebody sure sounds pissed," said Maclean.

"There's probably a raccoon rummaging through the garbage." Grant paid the animal no heed as he continued on his way to the police station. All of a sudden, the dog yelped in pain and then went silent.

Maclean spun on his heel and took off running. Grant drew his pistol from behind his back and ran after him. At the gas station, they found the front door slightly ajar. Grant dug out his Maglite and turned it on, as did Maclean, after drawing his own weapon. Both men shone their lights all around the inside of the darkened store.

"There," said Maclean, shining his light on a pool of blood on the linoleum floor.

Grant's pulse quickened. "You go left, and I'll go right."

Maclean nodded and slid inside.

As quietly as he could, Grant stepped inside, keeping his hands out in front of him. The sound of several cans of food hitting the ground surprised Grant. He swung his light over to the left and took up the slack on his pistol's trigger.

"Don't shoot," cried out Sparks, standing there with his hands in the air.

"For the love of God, Mr. Sparks, what are you doing in here?" asked Grant, lowering his weapon.

"I heard a dog cry out and ran to see if I could help," replied Sparks.

Grant and Maclean walked to the old man's side. At his feet was a dead pit bull. Its throat looked like it had been ripped from its muscular neck. The floor was slick with blood.

"Did you see what did this?" Maclean asked Sparks.

Sparks shook his head. "Sorry, no. It was too dark in here to see anything until you two arrived."

Grant placed his pistol back in its holster. "Mr. Sparks, would you please tell me why you left the clinic?"

Sparks furrowed his brow. "What are you talking about? I wasn't at any clinic."

"Yes, you were. We left you at one late this afternoon."

"I don't recall being dropped off at a clinic. Are you fellas sure it was me?"

Grant looked into the old man's eyes and saw confusion. "Sir, if you'll come with us, we'll take you back to the clinic to get you checked out by one of the nurses working there. I think you may have bumped your head earlier in the day and are suffering from post-concussion amnesia."

"Yeah, let us take you back," added Maclean, draping a tarp on top of the dead dog.

"If you insist," said Sparks.

Outside, Grant looked at Maclean. "Why don't you head to the police station and let them know that the gas station was broken into and that the guard dog has been killed, while I take Mr. Sparks back to the clinic."

"All right, boss, I'll meet you there." Maclean took off jogging toward the station.

"It's a good thing everything is so close in this town," said Grant to Sparks, guiding him by the arm.

"It sure is," replied the old man.

"Sir, do you remember anything before you heard the dog yelping?"

Sparks didn't say a word; his gaze was fixed on the night sky.

Grant stopped walking and looked down at the old man. "Sir, can you recall what you were doing before the dog was killed?"

Sparks said nothing. He just stood there, staring up at the stars.

Grant decided to try a different line of questioning. "Joe, did you see that orange light fly over the town a couple of minutes ago?"

"Why, yes, I did," replied Sparks, smiling from ear to ear.

Grant tried to push his luck. "Think hard, Joe. Did you see something similar last night over the lake by your home?"

"You know about the other light?"

"Yes." Before Grant could say another word, Sparks balled up his fist, and with lightning-fast speed, smashed it straight into the side of Grant's jaw. The soldier dropped to the ground like a sack of potatoes.

Sparks looked down at Grant and saw the man was unconscious. He quickly looked around to make sure no one had seen what had happened as he reached down, grabbed Grant by his shirt collar, and dragged him between two buildings, dropping the body on the ground. He bent down and studied the face of the man he had subdued. Sparks couldn't decide if he should kill the man or not. His death wouldn't mean a thing to him, just another in a long line of dead adversaries. He stood up and left Grant lying in a heap. Although unfamiliar, the man had shown him kindness. Sparks decided, for now, to let him live. If, however, the man came after him, then he would be forced to kill him. He walked out of the dark and onto the street. Sparks looked back up at the star-filled sky and smiled. He couldn't believe his luck. Another ship had arrived. Yesterday, he would have given himself less than a five percent chance of completing his experiment and getting away alive. Now, his odds were nearly fifty-fifty. Sparks began to run. He had to get back before the new arrival found out what he was up to and tried to put an end to his life's work.

26

A light fog blanketed the road.

A flash of light caught Sheriff Black's eye. She turned off her high beams and slowed down. She came to a halt on the shoulder and parked her car. Black bit her lip when she realized she was looking at the back of a vehicle belonging to the state troopers. It sat askew off the edge of the highway. She opened her door and got out. The air was damp and cold. She removed the flashlight from her belt and switched it on. The light barely penetrated the mist. Black slowly moved her light around and discovered that the front end of the cruiser was submerged in the black water of a marsh. She walked to the open driver's side door and looked inside.

The car was empty. The front seats were covered in fetid water, and the front windshield was shattered inward. It looked to Black as if the state troopers had unexpectedly hit something, causing them to swerve off the road and into the swamp. Her blood turned to ice when her flashlight picked up blood smeared on the leather seats.

Something had gone horribly wrong. Black clenched her jaw and shone her light all around. "Hello, this is Sheriff Black, is anyone out there?"

The only reply came from the frogs croaking in the water next to the road.

Black walked around the cruiser looking for footprints. In the soft ground by the driver's-side door were a set of human footprints leading away from the vehicle. Black placed her hand on her pistol and followed the trail. The tracks abruptly stopped at the edge of the swamp.

"God, no. Not again," muttered Black to herself when she found several expended 9mm casings lying on the ground. She moved her light all over the ground and found a strange-looking track. It looked like a cat's paw print, only much larger. Black had tracked mountain lions before, but she had never seen a track as large as the ones by her feet. She had seen enough. Black drew her sidearm and removed the safety with her thumb. With her hand tight around her weapon's pistol grip, Black followed the trail. A couple of seconds later, she stopped in her tracks. A shiver ran down her spine when she saw obvious signs of a struggle, and blood on the damp grass. Fear for her people gripped her heart. Kyle Harrison and Tracey Tibeluk's faces flashed before her eyes. Black spun around and sprinted for her SUV. She yanked open the door and jumped inside. She reached for her radio handset.

"Officer Harrison, Officer Tibeluk, this is Sheriff Black, do you read me, over?"

There was only silence.

Black repeated her message. Again, there was no response. She fought the growing feeling of desperation taking hold in her chest.

"Any call sign, this is Sheriff Black, do you read me, over?"

When no one answered, Black let out a scream and threw the handset against the dash of her SUV. She started her Suburban, threw the vehicle in drive, and jammed her foot down hard on the accelerator. Rocks and dirt flew up in the air behind her vehicle as it sped off into the night.

Less than five minutes had passed before she saw the road leading to Mrs. Moore's home. Without bothering to slow down, Black spun the steering wheel and shot up the narrow dirt track leading through the woods. In her headlights, she saw the other officers' police vehicle. Black drove as fast as she could to the Suburban before jamming her foot down on the brake pedal. Her vehicle fishtailed from side to side as it came to a sliding halt next to the other SUV. Black pushed open her door and ran to the side of the vehicle and looked inside.

Just like the other vehicle, it was empty.

"No," croaked Black. "Please, Lord, not my people."

A light shone out of the dark, blinding her.

"Sheriff Black, is that you?" said a familiar voice.

Robin Black could have leaped for joy when she recognized Tracey's voice. She turned and walked toward the person holding the flashlight. "Officer Tibeluk, why didn't you call back to the station when you got here?" Black's tone was firm.

"We did, Sheriff," said Tibeluk. "Ask Mrs. Moore, she can tell you that we tried at least a couple of dozen times before giving up."

Black looked around. "Where's Kyle?"

"He's resting inside. The damned fool broke his right leg when he stepped in a rabbit hole in the dark."

"At least he's alive." Black patted the younger officer on the shoulder as she walked past her and into Mrs. Moore's home. Harrison was propped up on an old blue couch with his foot resting on a pile of pillows.

"Sorry, Sheriff," said Harrison. "Some days I think if I didn't have bad luck, I'd have no luck at all."

Black smiled. She bent down and checked out the injury. His ankle was dark purplish-blue and swollen. "I don't think you broke your leg. It does, however, look like you may have broken your ankle."

"Evening, Sheriff," said Mrs. Moore, sounding very tired.

"Evening to you, too, Wendy," replied Black. "I take it you haven't heard from your husband or your son?"

Tears filled Moore's eyes. "No, I haven't, Sheriff. This isn't like them. I know in my heart something has gone wrong."

Black didn't doubt that for one second. "Since my officers' radio doesn't seem to be working, could I please use your phone to call back to town?"

"It's not working, either," said Tibeluk. "We tried using it after our radio crapped out."

Black chewed her lip for a second. "Well, we can't stay out here all night. Kyle needs to see a doctor, and I don't think it would be wise if Wendy were to stay out here by herself."

"What if Raymond and Bob come back?" asked Mrs. Moore.

"Write them a note and tell them to stay put until first light. I'll drop you and Kyle off at the clinic. They can find you there."

"Okay, Sheriff," said Mrs. Moore as she looked around for a pen and paper.

"What do you want us to do?" asked Tibeluk.

"You and I will help Kyle into the backseat of your vehicle," said Black. "Mrs. Moore can ride with me."

"What about my foot?" asked Harrison.

Black smiled. "Tracey, fetch me a fairly thick magazine, and ask Wendy for a tensor bandage. I'll show you how to make an expedient splint."

"Is it going to hurt?" queried Harrison.

"Sure, but it won't bother me in the slightest."

When everyone was safe and secure in the two police vehicles, Black waved for Tibeluk to follow them back to town. With the radios and phones unable to transmit, Black was more convinced than ever that the military was somehow behind what was going on, and she intended to find out what it was.

27

Grant sat straight up. His jaw hurt like hell. It took him a few seconds to realize he was sitting on the ground between two buildings. Grant hadn't been coldcocked since he was a freshman at West Point, when he had foolishly tried to break up a fight between a couple of his drunken classmates at a bar. He rubbed the side of his face and stood up. Grant walked out onto the road and looked around. Sparks was nowhere in sight. For an old man, Sparks had been able to land one hell of a blow. Why he had hit Grant was a mystery to him. He shook his head. If Sparks didn't want their help, with everything else that was going on, then he could go to hell as far as Grant was concerned.

He walked to the police station. Inside, he found his friends sitting at a table, drinking coffee.

"Hey, you look like crap," said Maclean. "What happened to you?"

"Sparks sucker-punched me and then ran off," replied Grant.

"What? Are you telling me that sweet old man was able to knock you down?" said Elena.

"Yes. And in my books, he isn't so sweet and lovable anymore."

"Where is he now?" asked Hayes.

"Beats me," said Grant. "I suspect he took off back home."

"What, in the dark?"

"I guess so," said Grant, pulling out a chair to sit down on. Maclean poured him a cup of coffee and handed it to him.

"I hope Mr. Sparks knows what he's doing," said Elena.

Grant looked at Maclean. "Did you tell the receptionist that the gas station has been broken into, and the guard dog is dead?"

"Yeah, she tried calling the owner," replied Maclean. "But the phone lines aren't working."

"Come again?"

"The phone, the internet, the police radios, cell service…you name it. Every form of communication in town all went dead at the same time," said Hayes.

Grant reached for his phone and saw there were no bars on the screen. "Is the disturbance localized to just the town?"

"Right now, it's impossible to determine how far this goes."

"What's all this?" asked Grant, pointing at the map covered in yellow sticky notes.

"It would appear that there has been a rash of disappearances to the north of town," said Elena.

Grant leaned forward in his chair. "What kind of disappearances?"

"A fair number of animals and people have gone missing since the UFO flew over the town last night."

Grant's pulse quickened. "How many people are we talking about?"

"Right now, three that we're aware of. The phones were ringing off the hook up until about five minutes ago, when the lines went dead."

"What do you want to bet that NORAD's satellites can't see the town again?"

"I wouldn't take that bet," said Maclean. "Ever since that orange orb flew over the town, we have been cut off from the outside world."

"What orange orb?" asked Elena, leaping out of her seat.

Maclean hit his forehead with his palm. "Sorry, I got so sidetracked reporting the break-in to Sheryl that I forgot to tell you we saw a bright orange light streak across the sky."

"When?" asked Hayes.

"I dunno, about ten, maybe fifteen minutes ago."

"Did you see where it went?"

"Yeah, to the north."

Elena began to pace back and forth. "David, we've got to leave here immediately and check it out."

"Are you sure that's a wise move?" said Grant. "It's dark outside, and all of those yellow notes plastered on that map don't fill me with too much confidence."

"David, we have to investigate," pleaded Elena.

"What do you think, Doc?" Grant asked Hayes.

"While I'd rather not drive around in the dark, something very peculiar is going on around here," said Hayes. "As a military scientist, I'm duty-bound to investigate."

"Okay, saddle up. We'll take both vehicles. I'll lead. Elena, please let Sheryl know that we're going to take a drive to the north of the town; you know, just in case we don't come back."

"Will do," she replied.

"Jeremy, do you have any more toys in the back of your vehicle?" Grant asked.

"As a matter of fact, I do."

On the street, Grant and Maclean waited while Hayes opened one of his black plastic storage boxes.

"For added firepower, I brought along two Heckler and Koch MP7 submachine guns," explained Hayes as he handed over the weapons. "They fire 4.6 x 30mm ammunition, which is more than capable of penetrating military-grade body armor and Kevlar helmets. There are both twenty- and forty-round magazines for the MP7. You can use the weapons' iron sights, or a detachable laser sight if you wish."

Grant studied the weapon in his hands. It was small with a collapsible butt. There was also a folding handgrip forward of the magazine housing, allowing the weapon to be fired as either a pistol or a submachine gun.

"Another good choice, Doc," said Maclean, holding the lightweight weapon out in front of him. "What about you two?"

"We aren't trained in the use of firearms," replied Hayes. "I did, however, bring along a couple of powerful police Tasers for Ms. Leon and me to use in self-defense."

"Consider them needed," said Grant. "Did you think to bring any body armor?"

"Of course I did," responded Hayes, flipping open another box.

Grant picked up the slender vest and held it in his hands. "This is really light. What's this made of?"

"Liquid body armor. I brought along four sets, just in case we needed them."

"How's it work?" asked Maclean.

"The tissues inside the vest have been coated with a shear-thickening fluid, which will instantly harden when struck. It's lighter to wear and far superior to normal body armor."

"I'll take your word for it," said Grant, slipping one on under his shirt. He was pleased to see it was comfortable and didn't restrict his movements.

"Are they heavy?" asked Elena, watching Hayes adjust his.

"No," replied Grant. "Remember, safety first."

"Say, you're right," she replied, slipping hers on. "It's not bad at all."

"If we're all good to go, I say we get moving before anything else goes wrong around here."

28

"Look out!" yelled Mrs. Moore, recoiling back in her seat as she frantically pointed at the windshield.

Sheriff Black's eyes widened as she swerved to miss a person standing in the middle of the fog-covered road. Black slammed her foot down on the brake pedal and brought her vehicle to a screeching halt.

Behind her, Tracey Tibeluk reacted likewise.

"Stay here," said Black to Mrs. Moore as she opened her door. The smell of burnt rubber hung in the air. Black walked to the person standing on the road.

Tibeluk's vehicle's headlights lit up the mist.

As she got closer, Black could see it was a girl in her late teens. She was wearing blue jeans and a yellow fleece top. The girl's dark hair was matted to her pale face. "Are you all right?" Black asked.

The girl stood there, staring straight ahead, shivering.

Black looked at the girl. She didn't appear to be hurt.

Tibeluk joined them. "Hon, can you tell me your name?"

The girl remained silent.

"Do you recognize her?" Black asked Tibeluk.

"No. She's not from around here," replied the officer. "Perhaps her family was camping in the woods nearby?"

Black gently placed her hands on the girl's shoulders and turned her so she could look into her brown eyes. She made sure her voice was as soothing as possible. "Is that it? Is your family somewhere nearby?"

The girl was still unresponsive.

"What do you want to do, Sheriff?" asked Tibeluk.

"I'll take her in my vehicle. We can drop her off at the clinic with Kyle and Mrs. Moore. After that, we'll head to the station. Bill and Sean can come back up here and look around for her parents."

"Come on, hon," said Tibeluk, guiding the girl to Black's Suburban.

Black removed the flashlight from her belt, switched it on, and walked to the trees lining the road. She shone her light on the forest, trying to see if there was anyone else out there in need of help. All she saw were dark, crooked shadows among the trees, and more fog. Black shook her head and turned on her heel to leave, when out of the corner of her eye she spied a large boot print in the dirt. Black bent down to examine it. The imprint looked fresh, but it wasn't from the girl. Black estimated the track was at least three times the size of the girl's foot.

"Hello, is anyone out there?" called out Black.

Only the incessant buzzing of insects and the croaking of frogs answered her call.

Black stood up and stepped back onto the road. She pursed her lips. Something bizarre was happening around her town, and she was having trouble trying to make sense of what it was. She walked back to her vehicle and got in. The girl was sitting in the backseat with a blanket draped over her shoulders. Mrs. Moore had moved back there with her and held her tight in her arms.

"Is everyone good to go?" asked Black.

"I can't say for my young friend, but I sure as heck am," answered Mrs. Moore.

"Okay, then let's head back to town and get ourselves some coffee and a bite to eat." Black placed her SUV in drive, and with a gentle push on the accelerator, she drove off into the swirling mist.

29

"Nothing, absolutely nothing works!" screamed Max, slamming his satellite phone's handset down.

"Have you tried your secure laptop?" asked Dan.

"Yes, of course, I tried the damned thing. It, along with my cell phone, can't send or receive a bloody thing."

"Why would anyone want to jam all of our comms equipment?" asked Carter.

Max shrugged. "The U.S. military, maybe? It would be prudent to assume that they've got people up here looking for the downed craft."

"What about that silent orange disc we saw fly over the hills?" asked a stocky, black-bearded mercenary. "It could be behind all of this."

"Yeah, there's that possibility too, Raoul."

"Sir, what do our mission protocols say in the event of a total comms failure?" asked Dan.

"We carry on with the original mission until ordered to cease our operation," replied Max.

"The only problem is that, in my opinion, the mission has changed," said Raoul. "The craft we were looking for is no longer here. We all agree that it was most likely vaporized when the water evaporated. Aside from some dangerously strong radiation readings on the Geiger counter at the edge of the lake, we have found nothing of the UFO."

Max tapped his right foot on the ground while he thought.

"You're right, Raoul. Let's pack up our gear and drive to the last spot we saw the new disc before it disappeared. Maybe we'll get lucky and stumble across this other craft before someone else does."

A couple of minutes later, they were on the road, heading back into the hills. The men in Max's truck sat in silence. The thought of running into another terror bird weighed heavily on their minds.

Just before the turnoff to the lake, the lead vehicle began to decelerate.

"Why are we slowing down?" asked Max.

"Sir, there's a man on the road," replied Dan.

Max leaned forward in his seat. Sure enough, there was an old man jogging on the side of the road as if he didn't have a care in the world. Max shook his head and said, "Go around him."

"Sure thing." Dan turned the steering wheel in his hands and gave the man a wide berth, as did the car behind them.

The man paid the vehicles no heed as they drove around him. He just kept on running. The odd thing about the old man—other than the fact that he was out for a leisurely jog in the middle of the night—was that he wasn't wearing any running attire. He was jogging along in his normal clothes, with a pair of old leather boots on his feet.

"This is one awfully strange place," said Max under his breath.

"Sir, rather than go back to the lake, why don't we take the side road and come out on the hill overlooking it?" asked Dan. "I'm sure we'll be able to get a better view from up there."

Max could hear the hesitancy in his colleague's voice. He didn't blame him; he was nervous too. "Sure, why not. We can launch the drone from up there and survey the entire valley."

After they had parked and assembled their drone, it took off into the night sky. A cold breeze came from the north, accompanied by the faint sound of thunder. Max could see a long line of dark clouds approaching as it blocked out the stars. Max stood, resting his back on the warm front grill of his truck, hoping the clouds didn't bring rain. He dug out his cigarettes and lit one. He had tried to stop smoking several times in the past to no avail. Max's life and his job were far too stressful to let him quit.

"What are we looking for?" asked Carter at the controls of the drone.

"Heat signatures…the bigger, the better," replied Max.

"Won't whatever we're looking for be shielded or invisible to the naked eye?"

"That's why you're looking for heat. I doubt they can mask the heat from an engine or the ground the disc may be sitting on."

The air was tense. While Carter and Max waited for the drone to find something, the other three men stood guard.

"Boss, I've got something you may want to see," Carter announced suddenly.

"What is it?" asked Max, tossing aside his cigarette.

"There are two cars parked at the bottom of the hill, and I can see people moving around the vehicles."

"How many of them are there?"

"Four," said Carter, turning the screen so his boss could see.

"Can you get in close without them hearing the drone?"

"Sure. This baby's engine is barely audible to the human ear. I could bring it within a meter, and you'd think there was a mosquito flying around your ear. It's that quiet."

Max watched as the UAV descended from the sky toward the unsuspecting group of people. When it was less than fifty meters above them, Carter focused the drone's camera on a tall man with short hair and a tough-looking face. Max studied the image for a moment before pointing it at another man standing next to one of the cars with a weapon in his hands. The state-of-the-art camera swung over and zeroed in. Max clenched his jaw when he thought he recognized the man as someone he had seen running from the airplane hangar in Batumi, Georgia.

"Do you recognize him, boss?" asked Carter.

"Perhaps. I think that man was in Georgia a few weeks back.

Show me the faces of the other people."

Carter moved his thumb on the control pad until the last two people in the group appeared on the screen.

Max swore. "Elena Leon and Jeremy Hayes. I should have known those fools from Gauntlet would come sniffing around here."

"Are they trouble?" asked Carter.

"Hayes and Leon are a pair of government scientists and, as such, they are no physical threat to us. The other two, I don't know." Max waved Raoul to his side. "Take Clive with you and eliminate those four people. Place their dead bodies in their vehicles and then drive them deep into the woods."

Raoul nodded and left with his comrade to kill the interlopers.

Max patted Carter on the arm. "It'll take them about five minutes to get down the hill. Until then, let's do what we came here to do and continue looking for that craft."

30

"Do you hear something?" asked Elena, looking up at the night sky.

Grant shook his head. "No. What did you hear?"

"It sounds like a strange buzzing sound coming from right above us."

Grant looked up and saw nothing. "It could be a dragonfly hunting mosquitos. They can make a fair bit of racket with their wings."

"Yeah, that's probably it."

Grant walked over to the back of Maclean's vehicle and patted his colleague on the shoulder. "How long until you can get our drone airborne?"

"Not long at all. Give me thirty seconds more and we'll be good to go."

Grant joined Hayes, who was hunched over, checking the ground for radiation. "What's the word, Doc?"

"There's no sign of radiation in the soil," replied Hayes. "Luckily, the water from the lake didn't get this far."

Moments later, their drone shot skyward.

"Circle the lake and look for any large hot spots on the ground," said Elena to Maclean.

"Will do," replied the Australian, sending the UAV flying toward the drained lake.

"Uh…Captain Grant, you need to come and see this," said Hayes. His voice quivered with fear.

Grant flipped on his flashlight and spotted Hayes looking at something on the ground. "What have you found?"

"I'm not a paleontologist, but I don't think these tracks should be here," Hayes said, shining his light on several sets of large three-toed tracks.

Grant got down on one knee to study the tracks up close. "What do you think could have made those?"

"If I'm right, and I think I am, they belong to a large, predatory, flightless bird. The problem is that they died out tens of millions of years ago, and to date, their fossils have never been found this far north."

Grant moved his light around on the ground and found dozens of tracks. His mouth turned dry with fear when he realized the tracks led in and out of the woods right next to where they were parked. He flipped the safety off his MP7 SMG and shone his light at the forest where the tracks had come from and was reassured when he saw that they were alone.

"Back to the car, Doc," said Grant as he walked backward with his weapon aimed at the woods.

"What's wrong, David?" asked Elena as Hayes ran past her, jumped inside his vehicle, and locked the door.

"I'll explain when we're on the road. Please get in the vehicle right away."

"Okay," replied Elena, reaching for the passenger-side door.

"Jim, where's the drone?" Grant asked.

"On the far side of the lake. Why?"

"There's not enough time to bring it back. I want you to crash it into the lake. We still have a second one in the back of your vehicle, should we need to use it."

Maclean looked over at Grant. "Are you sure you want to do this?"

"Yes! Do it and get behind the wheel of your vehicle, ASAP. We're leaving."

Maclean didn't question his friend's orders. With a flick of his thumb, he sent the drone flying into the muddy bottom of the crater. He threw the controller into the back of his Mustang, slammed the trunk closed, and ran to get inside his vehicle.

In the rearview mirror, Grant saw Maclean wave at him. He started his car, put it in drive, and jammed his foot on the gas pedal. He spun the wheel around in his hands until his Mustang was facing the dirt trail leading back toward town. Grant never let up on the accelerator. His vehicle's tires clawed at the wet ground for traction. Dirt and sand shot into the air as his tires spun on the ground. A second later, they gripped some large rocks, and the vehicle shot forward like a racehorse hearing the starter's pistol.

"You're frightening me, David," said Elena. "What did you and Jeremy find?"

"We found tracks belonging to a large carnivorous bird that has no place being here in Alaska," responded Grant, steering around a deep pothole on the narrow path.

"My God, I would have loved to have seen it."

"No, you wouldn't. There were dozens of tracks, which means there are a whole lot of them out there in the woods."

"David, look out!" screamed Elena as two men emerged from the woods and stepped out onto the path holding M4 carbines.

For a moment, Grant thought about running the men over, but when one of them brought his weapon up to his shoulder and fired off a burst into the grill of his car, he thrust his foot onto the brake pedal. His vehicle came to a sliding halt a meter away from the men.

"Turn off your vehicle, and get out nice and slowly," ordered a short man with a thick, black beard.

"What are we going to do?" whispered Elena.

"We do what he says, and play for time," replied Grant. He switched off the engine, opened his door, and raised his hands to show he was unarmed. Grant got out of his vehicle and stood motionless with his hands in the air.

"Walk to the front of your car, and then get down on your

knees," said the man.

Grant and Elena moved to the front of their vehicle and knelt on the gravel.

"Get the people in the other vehicle," said the bearded man to his partner.

The man nodded and walked to the other Mustang with his M4 at the ready. He returned a minute later with Hayes, who was shaking like a leaf caught in a storm.

"Where's the other person?" asked the bearded man. "There's supposed to be four of them."

The man's accomplice shrugged and turned to look back.

As silent as a thief in the night, a darkened shape walked out of the woods and jammed a pistol into the side of the bearded man's head. "I'm right here…surprise!" said Maclean. He reached over and quickly disarmed the man.

Grant smiled. Maclean had made for the woods the instant his vehicle had come to a stop and snuck his way around.

The second thug looked at his comrade and hesitated.

"Don't be an idiot. Drop your weapon, or I swear to God I'll kill this man," warned Maclean.

"Do it," said the bearded man.

The second mercenary glared at Grant as he tossed his M4 to the ground.

Grant jumped up and grabbed the dropped weapon. He thrust the carbine's barrel into the hired gun's ribs, causing him to wince in pain. "Walk!"

Elena and Hayes stood.

"Get back in the vehicles and flip the lights on," said Grant.

They two scientists almost tripped over one another to get away from the mercenaries.

"Now it's your turn," said Maclean to the two men. "Place your hands on your heads and get down on your knees,"

"Cover me," said Grant to Maclean while he quickly searched through the men's pockets, taking their wallets and anything else of value he found. He dug out the men's driver's licenses and read their names. "Raoul Morales and Clive Barnes. I doubt these are real. So, who are you, and why did you stop us?"

"You're right, they're fake," moaned Raoul. "Only our first names are correct."

"I'll ask you again, who are you, and why did you stop us?"

"Who we are is none of your business, and why we stopped you is because we were told to deal with you."

"Wrong answer," said Maclean, cuffing Raoul on the side of his head with his pistol.

Raoul grimaced. Blood trickled down the side of his head. He looked up and smiled at Maclean. "If you think either of us will break, you're going to be sadly mistaken. We swore an oath years ago to a higher power. Our word is more important to us than our lives. Torture us all you want, neither of us will tell you what you want to know."

"Who do you think you are, the bloody Nazi SS?"

Raoul turned his head away.

"What do you want to do with them?" Maclean asked Grant.

"We're not coldblooded murderers, so we can't shoot them in the back of the head and leave their bodies for the animals to eat," said Grant. "Let's tie them up and hand them over to the sheriff for questioning."

"I think I've got some rope in the back of my vehicle."

"Fetch it."

"You're making a big mistake," said Raoul. "Think of your families. Do you want them to die because of your stupidity?"

Grant's blood began to boil. "Don't you even think about touching anyone in my family. Got it?"

"You have no idea what you've gotten yourself involved with," said Clive. "Let us go, and we'll see about only killing you and not your family."

Grant couldn't believe his ears. Even with a gun at their heads, they were threatening him. "For God's sake, hurry up, Jim," he said coolly. "I'm really getting tired of listening to this crap."

A chilly breeze stirred the trees.

The hair on the back of Grant's neck went up. His brain reminded him of a time when he was a teen and had gone hunting with his father. The musky smell was unmistakable. There was a bear nearby.

"Found it," announced Maclean, holding the rope in his hands.

The sound of heavy breathing and twigs cracking just off to the right made Grant turn and bring up his weapon.

The attack was sudden and brutal. A gigantic bear charged out of the woods and clamped its massive jaws around Clive's neck, snapping it like a twig. Blood shot out like a fountain from the doomed man's severed neck.

Grant jumped back to one side and fired off a burst into the side of the bear's head. He might as well have fired his bullets into the air. The animal's flesh and skull were far too thick for the bullets to penetrate.

"Run!" yelled Maclean, shooting at the bear as it shook Clive's body from side to side in its bloody jaws before dragging him back into the woods.

Grant sprinted back to his vehicle and jumped in. Elena had already started the ignition. He shifted into drive and thrust his foot down so hard on the accelerator that it hurt. His car slowly picked up speed and whipped past the bear as it tore chunks of flesh from the dead man's body.

"Where's the other man?" asked Elena, looking out her window

"I don't know, and right now I don't care," responded Grant, willing his vehicle to go even faster. He spun the steering wheel around in his hands and sped off toward town.

Max watched the whole affair on the screen of his laptop computer. He ground his teeth and clenched his fists in anger. If their comms weren't jammed, he could have warned his men that a predator was stalking them. Instead, he had to watch impotently as the monstrously large bear killed and devoured one of his men.

"Sir, it looks like one of our men got away," said Carter.

"Where is he?" asked Max. His black mood lifted slightly.

"On the road. There's a man running back our way. I think it's Raoul."

Max snapped his fingers. "Dan, take one of the trucks and help him."

The mercenary nodded, jumped into the nearest vehicle, started it up, and drove off.

Max took a deep breath through his nostrils and forced himself to relax. He had a job to do, and he wasn't going to leave Alaska empty-handed. He looked at Carter. "There's no point in wasting any more time. Let's carry on with our aerial search. This time, I want you to head to the south of the lake and let's see if we can spot anything out of the ordinary."

"But what about the animals, sir?"

"What about them?"

"They're not normal. What if one or more of them is nearby?"

"Worry about me, not the animals. My brother and I don't take failure lightly."

Carter gulped. "Yes, sir. I'm moving the drone to the south of the lake as you asked."

31

Black walked into the police station, raised a hand to stave off Sheryl's imminent questions, and made her way to her office. She removed her hat and let out a weary sigh. Black was tired and confused. Nothing she had ever done in the past could have prepared her for what was going on around her town. After dropping off Officer Kyle Harrison, Mrs. Moore, and the mysterious girl at the clinic, she was ready for some time off her feet, but by the sound of raised voices in the main office, she wasn't going to get much rest. Black, reluctantly, left her office and went in search of some coffee. She poured herself a full mug and took a seat next to Sheryl.

"Sheriff, forgive me for saying so, but you look like you could use a week off," said Sheryl.

Black patted her friend on the hand. "Only a week? Okay, Sheryl, please tell me what's been going on since I was last here."

"Well, as you are aware, all of our communications have failed. The phones, the internet, you name it, they seemed to go offline all at once."

"When did that happen?"

Sheryl glanced at her watch. "It all went dead about an hour, maybe an hour and a half ago. I can't be sure. It was somewhat crazy until then; the phones wouldn't stop ringing."

"What's all this?" Black asked, looking over at the map with the yellow notes on it.

"Two of the UFO investigators were kind enough to help me

plot all of the calls that were coming in on that map."

Black stood up and checked out the map. All the calls were clustered to the north of the town. "Did anyone report seeing what was taking their livestock and pets?"

Sheryl shook her head. "Strange, isn't it?"

"Strange doesn't begin to cover what's going on around here." Black drummed her fingers on Sheryl's tabletop for a few seconds before standing back up. She glanced around at her remaining officers. "Okay, folks, this is what we're going to do. Since we can't talk to anyone, Tracey, I want you to take your car and drive to Valdez and let the state troopers there know that we badly need their help."

Tibeluk picked up her hat. "What should I tell them, Sheriff?"

"After you tell them about our comms problems, let them know we've got a couple of wild animals terrorizing the town, and that we need their help to locate the people who have gone missing and to track down and kill these rogue animals." Black scribbled down the license plate of the abandoned state trooper's vehicle she had come across. "Let them know they have a couple of missing troopers as well."

Tibeluk stood. "Got it. I should be back in about twelve hours. Hopefully with a couple of dozen troopers to help us out."

"What would you like us to do?" asked Bill Scott.

"Take your vehicle and patrol the streets," said Black. "I don't want a single one of these animals getting into the downtown core. If you come across anyone, tell them to head home right away and to stay there until they hear otherwise."

"You got it, Sheriff," said Scott as he got his feet, his partner, Sean, right behind him.

Black flashed a weary smile at Sheryl. "With the radios and phone lines down, you might as well head home and get a few hours of sleep."

"I don't sleep much these days, Sheriff," said Sheryl. "I think I'll stay here, just in case everything comes back online."

"Thanks." Black drank a mouthful of coffee and rubbed her aching neck.

"Is your son going to be okay by himself?"

Black had been so busy she hadn't even had time to think about Sam. "He'll be fine. He knows to lock all the doors at night, and he knows how to use a gun. In fact, he's a better shot than I am."

"Hopefully, he won't need to shoot at anything."

"Did those UFO people say where they were going when they left here?"

"No. But I did hear one of them say something about heading in the direction of the lake by Joe Sparks' place."

Black glanced back over at the map and the line of disappearances just below the lake. "Bloody fools!"

Grant brought his vehicle to a halt outside their hotel and switched the engine off. He got out and waited for everyone else to join him on the street. Grant looked at Elena and Hayes. "Those two men were trained killers. They undoubtedly intended to torture us for information and then kill us. Men like that never work alone. If it were just Sergeant Maclean and me here, we'd go hunting for these men and put an end to them. However, it's not, so I'm willing to entertain any suggestions you two might have."

"The problem is, we can't call anyone for help," said Hayes. "Nor can we afford to sit idle. There is something decidedly odd going on around here, and we need to find a way to stop it before any more civilians are hurt or killed."

"Jeremy's right," said Elena, rubbing her tired eyes. "Right now, those thugs are the least of our problems. I've never read anything remotely similar to what is happening in the woods north of the town."

"Four people don't make an army," pointed out Maclean. "If we're going to do something, whatever that may be, we're going to need the help of the sheriff's department."

"Jim's got a point there," said Grant. "We can't keep all of this information to ourselves. I think we should inform the sheriff who we are, but not necessarily what we're really doing up here. While we do that, let's hope the comms come back online soon, so we can call Colonel Andrews and have him convince his superiors to dispatch some troops here to help defend the town."

"I don't see any other alternative open to us," said Hayes.

"Okay, that settles it," said Grant. "Let's walk over to the police station and see if the good sheriff will buy what we're selling."

Sheryl met them at the door and smiled as she waved them inside. She looked relieved to see them. Sheryl led them to Sheriff Black's office and knocked on the open door. "Sheriff, look who's back."

Black stood and motioned for them to step inside her office. Maclean grabbed more chairs so everyone could sit down.

"Sheriff, before we begin, could I have your word that what we're about to discuss stays between us?" said Grant, showing her his military ID.

Black nodded.

"Thanks. I guess I'll cut right to the chase then. We're not civilian UFO investigators."

"I had a feeling you weren't. So, what are you, then?"

"We're a team of civilian and military investigators who work for the U.S. Air Force."

"I gathered that the minute I set eyes on you," said Black. "You don't act or look like those people on TV."

"I guess we'll have to work on that. Sheriff, we believe something unexplainable is happening to the wildlife to the north of the town."

"Why would you say that?"

"Less than an hour ago, we came across what we believe to be the tracks from a giant, flightless bird which has been extinct for millions of years. Barely five minutes later, we were stopped by some hired guns who are also looking into the same UFO sighting as we are. During this standoff, one of the men was attacked and killed by a giant bear."

"If the internet was still up, I'm willing to bet I could prove that the bear and the predator birds come from the same time period," said Hayes.

"Perhaps we still can prove your theory," said Black. "In the storeroom is an old set of encyclopedias. They were here when I took over. I just didn't have the heart to throw them away."

Hayes stood. "May I?"

Black nodded. "Of course. Turn right outside of my office and go down the hall. Second door on the left. There's a bookshelf in the back of the room."

"Thank you," Hayes said as he walked out of the room.

"While he's gone, I'll let you in on what I know. So far, we've got two missing state troopers and three missing civilians. I've also seen tracks I can't explain, so I'm willing to give your theory, as crazy as it sounds, some credence. Also, when I was on my way to Mrs. Moore's home, I had an encounter with a bright orange disc in the sky, which has left me troubled."

"How so, Sheriff?" said Elena.

"This craft didn't make any noise and was able to move through the air in ways I can't begin to explain. When it closed in on me, my vehicle lost power. At first, I didn't feel threatened. In fact, I was quite calm. When I stepped outside to get a better look at the disc, a blinding light was shone down on me, and I had the distinct feeling I was being scanned. The second it flew off into the night, my vehicle came back to life."

"Loss of power and reports of being scanned by UFOs are quite commonplace. Did you experience any loss of time?"

Black shook her head. "It all happened in under five minutes."

"I envy you. I've never had a close encounter of the first kind."

"I don't know, I feel violated."

Hayes walked back into Black's office holding an encyclopedia in his hands. He took a seat and opened the book on the sheriff's desk so everyone could see. "The tracks we found belongs to a *Phorusrhacidae*, also known as a terror bird. It was an apex predator in South America but died off about 1.8 million years ago. Some of them stood well over three meters tall and could run up to fifty kilometers an hour. It killed its prey using its razor-sharp beak and clawed toes."

"But you never actually saw any of these terror birds, did you?" said Black.

"That's correct. We only saw their tracks," said Grant.

"But we did see this," Hayes said, flipping to another page. "This is a short-faced bear, which went extinct about 11,000 years ago. The one we saw was enormous. It must have been as tall as a man in the shoulders and was at least five meters long."

"Are you positive? Sometimes people mistake things, especially when they're scared or in the dark."

"I won't lie, Sheriff, I was terrified. But I'm a trained observer, and I know what I…what we saw."

"It sure as hell looked like that bear to me," said Maclean, tapping his finger on the picture of the animal.

"Let me see if I'm following you people," said Black. "You claim there are people trying to kill you because of your interest in an alleged UFO sighting. You also claim animals that went extinct eons ago are now somehow back alive and are killing people?"

"Yes," replied Grant. "That is exactly what we're saying."

"If I hadn't seen the tracks at Ronald Deering's home, which look awfully similar to the ones in the encyclopedia, I'd say you were all crazy and kick you out of my town. Not to mention that encounter with the glowing orange disc I had a few hours ago. While we're all laying our cards on the table, you should know that I saw some other strange-looking tracks near an abandoned state trooper's car."

"What did they look like, Sheriff?" asked Hayes.

"A mountain lion's paw print, only much larger."

"How much larger?"

"Two to three times larger than any track I've ever seen."

Hayes picked up the encyclopedia and thumbed through it until he found what he was looking for. He placed the book down in front of Black. "*Smilodon*, more colloquially know as a saber-toothed tiger. Another apex predator that vanished around the same time as the short-faced bear. This animal was quite common to North America. It would be safe to assume that the tracks you found were left by this animal."

Black shook her head. "I don't get it. How did all of these animals get here?"

"Right now, we have no idea," said Elena. "They weren't here before the first UFO flew over your town, so I think it's safe to say they're somehow related to its arrival."

"Sheriff, can you please come here?" called out Sheryl.

Black stood and walked out of her office. Grant and Maclean followed her.

Mrs. Norton from the town's clinic was standing next to Sheryl's desk.

"Is something wrong, Jane?" asked Black.

"Yes. That girl you dropped off an hour ago has gone missing," replied Mrs. Norton.

"What girl?" said Grant.

"I found a teenage girl on the road outside of town," explained Black. "She was alone and looked to be in shock, so I took her to the clinic."

"After you left, the girl seemed to come to life," said Mrs. Norton. "I never got her name, but she seemed real interested in the room Joe Sparks had stayed in."

"How did she know about Joe?" asked Grant. "Did you tell her he had been there in the afternoon?"

"That's the strange thing. I never once mentioned his name, but she knew he had been a patient and insisted on looking at the room he had stayed in. I told her she would have to wait until I had looked at Officer Harrison's broken ankle. The girl couldn't be reasoned with. She walked right past me to Sparks' old room. When I finally went to see what the girl was doing, she wasn't there. She had gone out through an open window just like Mr. Sparks had."

"Déjà friggin' vu," said Maclean under his breath.

"I know where she's gone," said Grant.

"Where?" asked Black.

"The gas station."

"Why would she go there?"

"Because that's where Sparks went. Sheriff, you seem strapped for staff right now. If you don't mind, Sergeant Maclean and I will go and see if we can find this girl and bring her back here before she disappears into the night."

"I'd rather send my own people, but I have no way to get in touch with them, so I can't say no to your help right now."

"Hopefully, we'll be back in a couple of minutes with this girl. I have a feeling in my gut that this girl knows more than any of us about what is going on around here."

32

"So, what are you thinking?" Maclean asked as they jogged toward the gas station.

"If she's there, we'll try and talk her into coming back to the police station with us," replied Grant.

"And if she doesn't want to?"

"Then there isn't much we can do. She hasn't committed any crimes that I'm aware of that we could hold her on."

They split apart as they got closer to the station. The lights were off, but the front door was once again wide open. Both men drew their pistols.

Grant poked his head inside and saw a dark figure standing next to the tarp covering the dead pit bull's body. By the size and shape of the figure, Grant could tell they had found the missing girl. In the darkness, it was hard to tell, but it looked like she had something in her hand and was pointing it around the room. Grant called out, "Hello in there. My name is David Grant, and I mean you no harm. Why don't you come outside, and we can talk?"

The girl didn't respond. Instead, she got down on one knee to examine the dog's remains.

"Cover me," whispered Grant to his colleague as he slipped inside the gas station. He walked slowly toward the girl, so as not to frighten her. When he was a couple of steps away from her, the girl stood up and looked at Grant. In the darkened room it was nearly impossible to see her face, but Grant felt certain she was studying him.

In the far corner of the store, a narrow blue light appeared and moved across the room as if it were searching for something. Before Grant could say a word, the girl dove at him and tackled him to the floor.

For a small person, she packs quite the wallop, thought Grant as he lay there looking up at the roof. He felt a hand on his mouth, warning him to be quiet. Grant turned his head and saw the girl reaching into a pocket on her jeans.

The light stopped right above them and moved from side to side as it tried to find them.

"Are you okay in there?" called out Maclean.

In the blink of an eye, the light swung over and lit up the doorway. Maclean leaped back as the front door began to glow brightly before disappearing altogether a split second later.

Like a gymnast, the girl leaped up onto one knee and aimed something that looked like a miniature pistol at the light and activated it. An orange burst of light shot from the device, noiselessly creating a red glowing hole in the wall several meters wide where the blue light had once been.

Grant lay there, wide-eyed. He couldn't believe what he had just witnessed. There weren't any weapons on Earth that could have done that. He got up and looked down at the girl. "Thanks. I don't want to sound ungrateful, but I'd like to know who you are and what just happened."

The girl looked back at him.

Grant gently placed a hand on the girl's arm and tried to move her. She didn't budge a millimeter. It was like trying to move a statue. "You can trust me when I say I mean you no harm. Please step outside so we can talk."

With a slight nod, the girl walked out onto the street.

"What the frig was that light, and how the hell did it melt that door?" Maclean asked the girl.

"It was a trap left for me," said the girl as she lashed out and kicked a rock, sending it flying across the street. Her accent sounded somewhat Russian.

"What do you mean, it was a trap?" said Grant.

"It's a long story, and one I don't think either of you will believe."

Grant motioned for her to take a seat on an old wooden bench. "Before we go any farther, I'd like to know your name."

"You can call me Nadia," replied the girl as she took a seat. "It's not my real name, but for now, it will do."

"Okay, Nadia, my name is Dave, and my friend is called Jim. I think you'll find that we're not as closed-minded as you may think."

"That's good to hear."

"If you're not from these parts," said Maclean, "how can you speak English so well?"

"I can't. You're just hearing me in your minds."

Maclean looked over at Grant and shook his head. "I'm not buying that explanation. I can see her lips moving when she speaks. I bet she's nothing more than a Russian agent in possession of some very high-tech weaponry."

"I thought I was supposed to be the pragmatic one in our partnership," said Grant.

Nadia stood. "I'm not Russian, nor am I an agent. I just like the accent. And think about it for a few seconds; you both know that there are no weapons anywhere on your planet that could equal the destructive power I possess."

"Okay, we can discuss all of that later," said Grant. "Nadia, can you please tell us what is going on around here?"

She smiled. "Why not? It's not as if anyone is going to believe a single word about what I'm going to tell you. To be succinct, gentlemen, I have been dispatched here to kill or capture a renegade general who has no authority to be on your planet."

"Who sent you?" asked Maclean.

"That, you don't need to know," replied Nadia bluntly. "What you need to know is that you and all the people living around here are in great danger."

"Is this general of yours behind the sightings of strange animals roaming the woods to the north of the town?"

"Yes. He had been secretly working on a bio-weapon that would regress an animal's DNA to a point in the past where it was far larger and more aggressive than it is today."

"If I'm following you, you're saying that if I were to use this weapon on a cat, it could conceivably regress into something like a saber-toothed tiger?"

"I'm not wholly familiar with those animals, but in theory, yes, it would alter the animal's DNA."

"Jesus," muttered Maclean. "How fast does this weapon take to change a furry little kitten into a killer?"

"Not very long at all. From the time the subject is sprayed with the vapor, it takes less than ten minutes for the animal to change. These regressed animals must eat constantly, or they will die. It's a kind of built-in safety feature designed to prevent the animals from thinking about breeding."

"You seem to know a lot about this weapon," said Grant.

"I had to. It was my job to keep an eye on the general and report his findings to my superiors. I worked in his lab as a research assistant for close to a year before he discovered who I was and tried to kill me. I went after him, but he got away, and now I am here trying to stop this unauthorized incursion."

"Girlie, you don't look old enough to have ever worked in a military laboratory," said Maclean.

Nadia smiled. "Trust me; looks can be deceiving."

"I have no doubt about that," said Grant. "So, what were you doing on the road when the sheriff drove by?"

"I had just arrived and was disoriented from my long journey. Luckily, your sheriff came by and dropped me off at the medical clinic. That's when my tracking device picked up the general's scent. I foolishly followed his trail to the store behind us, where he left a motion sensor behind to kill me or any of my kind that showed up to try and stop him. He didn't get to be where he is by being nice to his contemporaries. I won't be that naïve ever again."

"Wait a second, are you telling me little old Joe Sparks is your general?"

Nadia's brown eyes lit up. "Who is this man, and where can I find him?"

"The birds and cats that Sparks was going on about when we first met him," recalled Maclean. "He...or whoever it was...must have used this weapon on Sparks' pets. That's where these bloody terror birds and saber-toothed tigers are coming from."

Nadia nodded. "Yes, that all makes sense. You have to take me to this man before he gets away."

"I'm sorry, Nadia, but you're going to have to meet some associates of mine before we go anywhere," said Grant.

"You don't understand. Time is critical here. If he can prove that his weapon works, there are people in our military who would forgive him for coming here without authority. I fear he may secretly be given carte blanche to mass-produce this weapon on an industrial scale. My culture has almost wiped itself out several times in the past. It seems we never learn from our mistakes. The last thing we need are new and more exotic weapons of mass destruction."

"Nadia, how can this general get back to where he came from if his ship was destroyed when the lake it crashed in evaporated?"

"He'll look for my ship, and if he's half as smart as I believe him to be, it won't take him more than a few hours to find it."

Grant looked over at his friend. "What do you make of all of this?"

Maclean chuckled grimly. "A month ago, if someone had approached me with a story about UFOs, aliens, and a DNA super weapon which can change household pets into killers, I would have laughed in their face. But right now, it's the only thing that makes even the remotest bit of sense. If this young lady, or whatever she is, thinks Sparks is a threat, then we have to help her stop him."

"Please, we're wasting time," pleaded Nadia.

"Okay, we'll help, but we first have to warn the town's sheriff of the threat that's coming her way," said Grant.

Nadia pressed her lips tightly together and gave a curt nod.

As they walked toward the police station, Grant looked at Nadia. "I'm glad you trusted us enough to tell us what you're doing here."

Nadia stopped and fixed Grant with a cool stare. "Dave, I need your help to locate and stop the general, and I don't ever recall saying that I trust you or your friend. Understand this. I have a mission to accomplish, and you're a means to an end…nothing more."

Overhead, jagged bolts of silver lightning lit up the night sky. Seconds later, the first drops of rain fell from the heavens. The storm had arrived.

33

Tracey Tibeluk tapped her hands on the steering wheel of her Suburban while singing an old Johnny Cash tune to herself. She had rolled her window down to let the cool night air wash over her face, helping to keep her awake and alert. Tibeluk drove along with her high beams on. The last thing she wanted to do was smash headlong into a moose. She glanced down at the odometer and saw that she had driven almost sixty kilometers when, without warning, her vehicle's engine shut off. Tibeluk was plunged into complete darkness. Fear gripped her heart. She brought her vehicle to a rolling halt on the gravel road.

"What the hell?" she said to herself, trying to restart the Suburban. After five tries, she sat back and shook her head.

Tibeluk grabbed her flashlight and tried turning it on. Like the vehicle, it wouldn't work. She opened her door, stepped out onto the road and looked around. The world all around her was pitch-black. A feeling of dread seeped into her chest. First, they had lost their communications, and now this. Tibeluk began to wonder if someone didn't want anyone getting in or out of the area.

An idea crossed her mind. She walked back about twenty meters from her vehicle and tried turning on her flashlight. Nothing. Tibeluk continued walking back until she was fifty meters away and pressed the button again. She could have jumped for joy when it lit up. Tibeluk left the light on the road as a marker, walked back to her Suburban, and shifted the vehicle in neutral, before grabbing hold of the door frame with her hands. She dug her boot tips into the ground, and with a grunt, tried pushing her vehicle backward. At first, it didn't move. Then, ever so slowly, the SUV began to creep backward.

"At least it isn't raining," Tibeluk said in an attempt to cheer herself up. As if on cue there was a brilliant flash of lightning right above her, followed a split second later by a thunderous boom. Rain began to fall. It didn't take long for her to become soaked to the bone. She dropped her shoulders, sighed, and cursed up a streak that would have made her mother blush.

Tibeluk looked up and smiled when she saw her flashlight growing closer. The nearer she got to the light, the safer she felt. The thought of being trapped on the side of the road all alone in a dead vehicle in the dark didn't thrill her at all.

With a loud click, the Suburban's lights switched back on, startling her. Tibeluk pumped her fist in the air, jumped into her vehicle, said a quick prayer, and turned over the ignition. With a loud roar, the engine came to life. Without bothering to pick up her flashlight, Tibeluk slammed her door closed and spun the wheel around in her hands. As soon as she was facing back toward Robertson's Mine, she floored the gas pedal and shot off down the road.

Before long, she had the SUV bouncing up and down as she sped over the bumpy dirt road. Whatever was going on, Tibeluk knew there would be safety in numbers. The sooner she got back to the police station and her friends, the better, as far as she was concerned.

34

Grant escorted Nadia inside the police station and had her take a seat next to Elena, who smiled warmly at the teenager.

"You look a whole lot better than when I found you on the road," said Black, coming to stand by the girl.

"I'm feeling better, thank you," Nadia replied.

"I hope some coffee is fine with you?" Grant said, walking over to Nadia with two cups in his hands.

Nadia sniffed it before taking a small taste. She shrugged and took another sip. "I don't think it will kill me."

"David, is this the young lady you were looking for?" said Elena to Grant.

"Yes, sorry. Everyone, this is Nadia." Grant went around the room, quickly introducing everyone to the young woman.

"Can you recall where your parents are, my dear?" asked Black.

"I'm alone," replied Nadia. "I'm sorry for the deception, but I wasn't fully in charge of my faculties when you found me."

Black canted her head slightly. "I'm sorry, I don't understand. What does that mean?"

"I cannot say," responded Nadia. Her sharp tone made it clear she wasn't going to divulge any more information.

"Okay. Can you at least tell us why you left the clinic?"

Grant raised a hand. "If I may? It's kind of complicated. I think it'll be easier if I take it from here. To be blunt, Nadia isn't from around here. In fact, she's not even from this planet. She's on a mission and is looking for someone she calls the general. This man is a military scientist who came here without any authority to test a new form of weapon."

"What kind of weapon?" asked Hayes, sitting up straight in his chair.

"It radically changes an animal's DNA, allowing it to revert back hundreds of thousands, if not millions, of years in a matter of minutes."

"My God," blurted out Elena. "This can't be true."

"I'm afraid it is," said Grant.

"So, is this why we're suddenly having these disappearances?" asked Black.

Grant nodded. "The problem is that these abominations have a one-track mind. They have to eat constantly in order to survive, and they're moving south toward the town, consuming whatever they can find."

Maclean looked over at the town map on the wall. "If we take a brisk walking pace of five to six kilometers an hour, the animals should be on the outskirts of town by first light."

"Do we know how many animals we're dealing with?" Black asked.

Nadia shook her head. "He took enough weaponized vapor to change hundreds, perhaps thousands, of animals. The problem is getting close to the animals without them running away or attacking the person administering the spray. The domesticated ones in Mr. Sparks' home would have been a blessing to the general."

"We found at least a couple of dozen wrecked birdcages at Joe's home," said Grant. "So, we have to assume that all of these birds have been changed, along with an undetermined number of cats."

Black stood and glared at Nadia. "Why the hell did this general of yours have to come here to test his accursed weapon? What have we done to deserve this?"

"Because your planet is remarkably similar to ours—"

Black interrupted. "What do you mean, our planet is similar to yours?"

"Sheriff," Grant said quickly, intent on keeping the conversation moving. "I know we've all had a long and stressful night. We can talk about what Nadia means later. Right now, we have more important things to worry about."

Black pursed her lips and frowned at Grant. "As a soldier, you of all people should understand my growing anger and frustration. I've got five missing people who are most likely dead because of this general." She turned to stare at Nadia. "How many more of my people will have to die before this madness is brought to an end?"

"I'm sorry," Nadia replied. "I wish I had killed the general when I had the chance, but I failed, and now I'm here to try and right that mistake. As for how many more people will die, that's up to you. Their lives are in your hands, not mine."

Grant saw Black's eye twitch and raced to stand between the two women before they came to blows. "Assigning guilt can come later. Right now, Sheriff, we have to warn everyone in town to stay where they are and barricade themselves in their homes until help arrives."

"How are we going to do that if none of the radios or telephones are working?" asked Elena.

"I know how," said Sheryl, raising a hand. "We can use the town's old civil defense alarms. They haven't been used since the big fire of 1998, but they get tested every year on the Fourth of July, so we know they still work. All we need to do is go to city hall and access the speaker system and broadcast our message from there."

Grant winked at Sheryl. "Genius…pure genius."

"What about the people living by themselves, or who are too far away to hear the alarm?" asked Maclean.

"The next time I see my officers, I'll get them to drive down the side roads and use the speaker system on the top of their vehicle to pass the message," said Black.

"Sheriff, what would you say is the sturdiest building in town?" asked Grant.

"Without a doubt, it's the school. It was built in the 1950s and is made of brick. Why do you ask?"

"Not everyone is going to want to stay in their homes. Those who are scared will naturally head to where they feel the safest, and that's here in town. You need to get those people into the school and make it as defensible as possible. I'd suggest moving anyone still in the clinic into the school as well."

"Officer Harrison may be injured, but he can take charge at the school until I get there," said Black.

"Sheriff, what about the people living on the Munroe farm?" said Sheryl.

"Crap, I forgot about them."

"Is there a problem?" asked Maclean.

"The Munroes are several generations of the same family living together on a farm about twenty kilometers outside of town," explained the sheriff. "They're devout pacifists who don't believe in owning guns, even for hunting."

"How many of them are there?"

Black bit her lip. "I'm not sure."

"I think there are about thirty of them," offered Sheryl. "I think they have a truck or two up there, but not enough to haul everyone away in one haul."

"Well, we can't leave them out there to die," said Maclean. "I'll take a vehicle and bring them all back here to the school."

"The keys for the community school bus will be hanging in the administration office at the school," said Black. "Sheryl has the spare keys to the front doors of the school in her desk."

Sheryl opened the top drawer and began to search for the keys.

"Okay, while Jim does that, Nadia and I are going to try and track down this general and put a stop to whatever he's up to," said Grant.

Elena reached over and placed a hand on Grant's arm. "I want to come with you. I've waited my entire life for an opportunity like this. Please don't turn me away."

"Elena, please think about what you're saying. This isn't some benign UFO investigation where you drive around taking statements from alleged eyewitnesses. People are dying out there."

"And if I stay here, who's to say I won't die in town if these monsters find a way inside this building or the school?"

Grant couldn't fault her logic. "What do you think?" he asked Nadia.

"I don't care," she replied. "Do as you want. The woman is not my responsibility."

"Please, David, I have to come with you," implored Elena. "I promise I won't get in the way of whatever you have to do."

Grant gnashed his teeth for a couple of seconds before relenting. "Okay, this is against my better judgment. You can come, but keep behind me at all times."

"I found your keys," announced Sheryl, holding them up in the air.

"Well, I'm out of here, then," said Maclean. He stood and eyed Hayes. "Care to come for a ride with me, Doc? You can read the map while I drive."

Hayes' face blanched. "You can't be serious. You want me to go back out there with all of those creatures running around on the loose in the dark?"

"I'll put it another way. Do you want the deaths of thirty people, including women and children, on your conscience because I took the wrong turn in the pouring rain and arrived too late to help those people?"

"No."

"Good, now grab a spare map, have Sheryl mark the Munroe farm on it, and follow me to the school."

Hayes shook his head and mumbled to himself as he got out of his seat.

"I take it that leaves me to head to city hall to bring the civil defense system online," said Black.

Grant stood. He held out his hand. "Good luck, Sheriff, hopefully, we'll all meet back here in a couple of hours."

"Good luck to you too, soldier boy," replied Black. "Hopefully, Tracey will be back here before too long with the state troopers and the National Guard in tow."

35

Max Roth sat in his truck, chewing on the end of a pen he had found. The sudden downpour had put an end to their search of the countryside with their drone. He reviewed the recorded feed on his laptop but couldn't find a single heat signature he could attribute to a craft sitting on the ground.

The driver's-side door opened, Dan climbed in and took a seat. His clothes were soaked and stuck to his skin.

"How's Raoul doing?" asked Max.

"He's still pretty shaken up," replied the mercenary. "I gave him a shot of brandy, and that seemed to help calm him down."

"Good thinking."

"Did you find anything, boss?"

Max let out a deep sigh. "Not yet."

"Sir, I've been thinking about that man we passed on the road. Didn't it strike you as a little bit odd how he was dressed?"

"Sure. What's your point?"

"Earlier, I was reviewing the feed taken by the UAV of the land south of the lake and saw a heat signature making its way through the forest to what looked like a cabin."

"So?"

Dan held out his hands. "It's better if I show you."

Max slid the laptop over and reached for his cigarettes. He opened his window slightly and lit one of his smokes.

"Here it is," said Dan, turning the screen. The image on the screen was frozen. On it was the bright white silhouette of a man running through the woods. "I didn't pay much attention to this when I first saw it, as we were looking for a large thermal target and not a lone person."

Max rubbed the back of his neck with his hand. "Dan, it's late and I'm starting to lose my patience. What is so important about this man?"

Dan pressed the button to resume the playback. Right away, the figure began to move. Instead of plodding along like an old man, the shape was sprinting down the narrow trail to the cabin. "Sir, according to the information received from the camera, that person is moving more than thirty kilometers an hour in the dark and the rain. I doubt that's our old man. Someone or something else is down there."

"For the love of God, Dan, why did you wait so long to tell me?"

"I was about to tell you a while ago, but you yanked the laptop from my hands and kicked me out of the vehicle. You told me to check on Raoul and not to come back for at least thirty minutes. Carter also saw the image when he was operating the UAV, but he thought you were too worked up and angry to listen to him."

Max closed his eyes and clenched his fists together. He took a long, slow breath in through his nostrils. His volcanic temper was barely being held in check. "I'm sorry, Dan, I've been a little too short with you and rest of the team this time out. I apologize. Please let Carter and Raoul know that we're going to check out this person right away."

Dan opened his door and stepped back out into the rain. He turned back and looked at Max. "Sir, what about Clive? I've never once left a fallen comrade behind in the field. Aren't we going to retrieve his remains?"

"Do you honestly think there will be much left of him to bury?"

"It doesn't matter, sir. He was a loyal soldier and deserves better than to be left for the scavengers to eat."

Max nodded. "You're right. Before we leave here, I promise

you that we'll recover what we can and return it home for a proper burial."

"Thanks, sir," said Dan, closing the door.

Max had to give it to his people; they might not always be the brightest, but they were loyal to each other and, more importantly, to the cause. He looked down at the screen and fixed his eyes on the person running at great speed through the woods. Max's lips began to curl into a sadistic grin. "I've got you...you son of a bitch. Now give me what I want."

36

Grant dropped Maclean and Hayes off at the school before taking a dirt road out of town. Elena sat up front with him, while Nadia sat silently in the back.

Grant glanced up at the rearview mirror and saw that Nadia was fidgeting with the device she had used to vaporize the motion sensor trap. It looked like a very small pistol. "What is that thing?" he asked.

Nadia held up the weapon so Grant could see it in the mirror. "It's what we call a phase pistol."

"How accurate is it?"

"It's good to about fifty meters. After that, forget it."

Elena turned in her seat. "May I take a look at it?"

"No, you may not," replied Nadia, sliding the weapon back into a pocket on her pants.

"I'm sorry, I didn't mean to offend you."

"You didn't. You're not a soldier like Dave, so you don't need to see it."

"I never told you I was a soldier," said Grant.

"You don't have to," responded Nadia. "I can read your mind."

"What else can you do?" asked Elena.

"I'm not a performing animal. I'm highly educated and have traveled thousands of light-years to get here. So please treat me with some respect."

Elena turned about and looked over at Grant with a puzzled look on her face. He smiled and shook his head. It was obvious to Grant that Nadia didn't like having another woman around.

"Nadia, if you can read our minds, why do you need me to take you to Sparks' home?" said Grant. "Surely, you've already read my thoughts and know precisely where he lives?"

"You may be a lesser species, but I was taught to use what you could around you to achieve your mission," replied Nadia. "You're a skilled warrior, so it would have been foolish of me not to have brought you along."

"I guess I'll take that as a compliment. So, what's your plan when we catch up with the general?"

"I'm hoping to take him peacefully. But if he resists, I won't hesitate to kill him."

"How will we recognize this general?" asked Elena.

"Sorry, I mustn't have been clear back at the police station," said Grant. "Sweet old Joe Sparks is the man we're after."

"Him? I don't believe you."

"It's not him," said Nadia. "It only looks like him. The real man is most likely dead."

Elena's mouth hung open for a few seconds. Finally, she said, "My God, you're a Reptilian…aren't you?"

"Who and what I am are unimportant. I have a job to do, and that's all you need to know."

"Don't take it too personally," said Grant to Elena. "I tried playing twenty questions with Nadia when we first met. Suffice it to say, Nadia's not too forthcoming on details."

"Can't this thing go any faster?" asked Nadia.

"No. Not unless you want to end up in a ditch on the side of the road. I'm already driving too fast for the road conditions. Just sit back and we'll get there soon enough."

Nadia let out a deep huff and sat back in her seat. She reached into her pocket, pulled out her pistol, and once again began to absentmindedly play with it.

"Are you sure this is the right road?" Maclean asked Hayes as he turned off the road onto a dirt track leading through the woods.

"It's the only one on the map," replied Hayes, thrusting his map in front of Maclean's face.

Maclean brushed the map aside. "I can't drive and read the map at the same time—that's why you're here."

"Then please do me the courtesy of not questioning my map-reading skills every time I tell you to take a new road."

"Sorry, it's just so damned dark out, and this friggin' rain isn't making it any easier to see."

"It's all right. My nerves are on edge as well. I never thought I'd be doing this when I agreed to come over from England to help with Project Gauntlet."

"When I joined the army, I did it so I could fight the Taliban in Afghanistan. I don't remember the recruiting officer saying anything about UFOs and having to dodge prehistoric killer animals running around the backwoods of Alaska."

"Do you always have to make a joke out of everything?"

Maclean chuckled. "It's a defensive mechanism. I'm not as confident as I look. Right now it helps mask how bloody scared I am inside."

"I'm glad you can admit that you're scared, as I'm just about ready to pee my pants."

"Let's not be doing that now, Doc. How much farther would you say it is to the Munroes' farm?"

Hayes checked the map. "No more than another ten kilometers."

"Okay, at this speed, we should get there in less than fifteen minutes."

"Good. Let's hope these people aren't unreasonable and will willingly come back to town with us."

"After you tell them that a rabid, oversized grizzly bear is headed their way, I bet they'll be more than willing to come with us."

"Why do I have to tell them?"

"Because you look like you know what you're talking about, and your Oxford-educated, English accent is easier to understand than my Australian one."

"Whatever works."

"That's right, Doc, whatever works."

Robin Black sat down behind a wooden desk and pulled the old metal microphone toward her. She closed her eyes and composed her thoughts. When she was ready, Black activated the town's sirens and let them blare a warning tone for a minute before switching it off.

Black pressed the talk button. "People of Robertson's Mine, this is Sheriff Black speaking. This is not a drill. I say again, this is not a drill. A couple of wild animals have been spotted heading for the town. They are believed to be sick and are extremely dangerous. They will kill you if they catch you outside your homes. I am asking all of you to remain indoors until further notice. Lock your doors and windows and keep as quiet as possible. If, however, you don't feel safe in your home, please make your way to Eisenhower School, where Officer Harrison will be there to meet you. If Officers Scott and McCartney can hear this message, I want you to report back to the station immediately."

Black sat back in her chair and waited a few seconds before repeating the message to ensure as many people as possible heard it. When she felt she was done, Black switched off the power to the microphone and stood. Before she did anything else, she knew she had to drive home and bring her son to the school. Like her, Sam was an accomplished hunter. Black wanted him to be near her until the danger had passed. She was going to use him as a lookout on the school roof. If any of the animals got into the town, his job would be to bring them down before anyone else got hurt.

37

Max Roth got out of his truck and looked around. With the rain coming down, he couldn't see more than a few meters into the pitch-black woods. He reached back into his vehicle, grabbed hold of a set of NVGs, and switched them on before placing them over his eyes. Right away, the world turned into myriad shades of green. He adjusted the lenses until everything around him was in focus. Max scanned the countryside and saw they were alone. He flipped up his NVGs and looked over at the three men still with him.

"Okay, we stopped about five hundred meters shy of the path leading to the old man's house," explained Max. "I didn't see any point in potentially alerting him that someone is coming his way. Carter will take point, followed by myself, then Raoul, and lastly, Dan. Our aim here is to capture the old man alive and force him to help us. Under no circumstances are you to fire at him without my authority. Got it?"

No one said a word. They were all ex-soldiers who knew precisely what was expected of them.

"All right then, lead on, Carter," said Max, stepping to one side to let the mercenary lead them to the old man's cabin in the woods. He brought his NVGs back down over his eyes and clenched his M4 carbine tight in his hands.

Max, unlike his older brother, had served in the armed forces and had once been a captain in Argentina's elite Special Operations Forces Group before leaving the military to work for his family. Over the past few years, Max had killed dozens of men, mostly in cold blood. Anyone who got too close to his brother and any other member of the Aurora Group was fair game as far as he was concerned.

It didn't take long in the pouring rain for Max's clothes to become drenched. Through his NVGs, he could see Carter's breath hanging like a mist in the cold night air. A hardened assassin, Max ignored the minor discomfort, knowing his family's future was in his hands.

"Damn, I hope we're not too late," said Elena, pointing at the two trucks parked just off the narrow road.

Grant immediately turned off his car's headlights, slowed down, and parked his vehicle. "Wait here," he said to his passengers as he picked up his MP7 submachine gun, flipped off the safety, and opened his door. With his weapon at the ready, Grant crept toward the two vehicles. In the rain, he doubted he would hear anyone moving around in the dark until he was standing right next to them. Grant took a quick look inside each truck and saw they were empty. His gut told him the vehicles belonged to the opposition, so he dug out a knife from his jacket and dashed from truck to truck, slashing the front tires. With a loud hiss, the tires rapidly deflated until the metal rims were almost on the ground.

Grant placed his knife away and walked back to his car. He gently tapped on the window and waved for Elena and Nadia to join him.

"What did you do?" Elena asked, looking over at the trucks.

"I made sure that our friends, should they decide to come back suddenly, won't be going anywhere fast," replied Grant.

"Which way is it to the man's house?" asked Nadia.

"It's just up the road a ways, and then a couple of hundred meters through the woods."

Nadia started to walk down the road.

"Whoa, hold on just a minute," said Grant, grabbing her

shoulder.

She stopped and faced Grant.

"Nadia, we can't just go walking blindly into an ambush. There are men like me out here, undoubtedly trying to get their hands on your craft or the general. We need to work together. I don't care how advanced your pistol is, the men we are going up against are cold-blooded killers. They won't hesitate to kill all of us to get what they want."

"I'm highly trained in all forms of combat," replied Nadia. "I can handle myself, should they open fire on us."

"That's nice. You can fool yourself all you want about being well-trained and ready for a fight, but all that misplaced bravado goes out the window the instant you realize someone's trying to kill you. If you think you're good enough to proceed on your own, please don't let me stop you. Elena and I will hold back a few paces and use your body as a shield against the hail of incoming bullets."

"Please don't run off and get yourself killed," said Elena.

Nadia shook her head. "Okay, soldier, what are you proposing?"

Grant smiled at Elena. "Did you remember to bring your Taser with you?"

"Yes," she replied, showing the handheld device to Grant.

"Surprise is one of the principles of war, so here's what we're going to do."

Carter's hand went straight up beside his head.

Everyone behind him saw the signal, stopped, and silently dropped to one knee.

"What is it?" whispered Max into his colleague's ear.

"About thirty meters ahead, there's someone digging in the ground outside a run-down cabin," explained Carter.

Max moved around his comrade and peered down the trail. Through his goggles, he could see a light green shape furiously tearing at the ground with his bare hands. With his back to them, the man wouldn't see them until it was too late to do anything about it.

"Follow me, and remember…no shooting!" stressed Max to his team. With his weapon tight against his shoulder, Max walked straight toward his unsuspecting prey. He couldn't believe his stroke of good luck. For once, everything was falling into place. When he was less than ten meters away, he stopped. His men fanned out around him with their weapons aimed at the old man's back.

"Hey, you!" cried out Max. "Stop what you're doing, stand up with your hands in the air, and then turn around nice and slowly."

Sparks' shoulders drooped. He shook his head, rolled over, and turned to face Max. The old man wiped his mud-caked hands on his coveralls and sat there on the ground, mumbling to himself.

"Hey, Grandpa, I told you to stand up," said Max, lifting his NVGs up.

"Give me a minute," said Sparks. "I'm old and need a minute to catch my breath."

"Get him on his feet," said Max to Raoul.

The mercenary stepped forward and grabbed Sparks with his left hand. When he went to pull him to his feet, his hand slid off Sparks' arm. It was as if the man weighed several hundred kilos. Raoul slung his carbine over his back, grabbed hold of Sparks' arm with both of his hands, and pulled as hard as he could. He leaned back and let out a deep grunt. Sparks remained sitting there with a blank look on his face.

"Step aside, Raoul," ordered Max. "Okay, mister, I don't know who or what you are, but the order still stands. On your feet, now!"

Sparks smiled at Max and did what he was told. "Would you mind if I had a bite of my plug tobacco? I keep some in my pocket."

"Yes, I bloody well do mind. Keep your hands where I can see them."

Sparks shrugged and wiped the rain from his wrinkled face with the sleeve of his shirt. "So, what do you boys want with me?"

"Let's drop the façade, shall we, mister? I know you're from another planet. I also know your ship must have been damaged when it crashed, that's why it eventually self-destructed and took most of the water in the lake with it. What I want you to do is show me where that second craft is located."

Sparks smiled and let out a mirthful chuckle. "My what? Have you boys been drinking too much of the local hooch?"

"Don't screw with me, old man. You know precisely what I'm talking about. A few hours ago, my men and I saw another ship fly in this direction. Start talking, or I'll have my associates convince you to tell me what I want to know."

"You can try. But that would be an awfully dumb move on your behalf."

Max snapped his fingers. "Dan, teach this old fool some manners."

"With pleasure," replied the mercenary. He slung his weapon and drew a long knife from a sheath hidden behind his back. The blade shimmered in the flashes of lightning tearing across the night sky.

"I'd think long and hard before trying to stick me with your knife, son," said Sparks to Dan.

At that moment, Elena staggered out of the woods and stopped next to Max. She placed a hand on his shoulder as she fought to catch her breath.

Max turned and looked at her. "Ms. Leon, what a surprise to see you. What on earth are you doing out here at this hour?"

"This," she replied, jamming her Taser into his ribs and turning it on. In the blink of an eye, 1200 volts of electricity shot through Max's body. He let out a pained moan and dropped to his knees, writhing in agony.

"Don't anybody move!" warned Grant as he burst from his hiding spot in the woods and jammed the barrel of his MP7 into the side of Dan's skull.

Both Carter and Raoul stood their ground and swung their weapons toward Grant. Like a creature coming out of the pits of hell, Nadia stood up between the two killers. She was covered from head to toe in mud. With lightning-fast reflexes, she lashed out at both men, sending them flying back onto the muddy ground.

"Drop the knife, or I'll blast your brains all over the ground," growled Grant.

Dan knew when he was beaten and tossed the blade away.

"Good boy," said Grant as he grabbed the mercenary by the collar and thrust him over to where Max was kneeling on the ground, trying to catch his breath.

Elena ran from man to man and picked up their dropped carbines. When she had them all, she walked to the edge of the woods and tossed them as far away as she could.

"Thanks for coming to my aid," said Sparks. "These boys have to be on drugs or something. They said they were gonna carve me up."

Grant spun around and aimed his submachine gun at the old man. "Last time we were alone together, you knocked me out cold. No more games, Sparks. Step aside. I want to know why you were digging in the mud."

Before Sparks could move, Nadia screamed at the top of her lungs and charged at the old man. Her eyes were aglow, her face distorted with hate and anger.

Sparks saw her coming and jumped into a fighting stance. In the instant before they collided, both combatants changed their shapes and became who they truly were. Their human camouflage vanished and their lizard-like bodies were revealed. Both aliens were at least a head taller than Grant and had scaly faces with golden-colored eyes. Their bodies were covered from their feet to their necks in formfitting, segmented body armor.

Grant jumped aside as Nadia plowed straight into the general, sending them both tumbling to the ground. He staggered back. His mind couldn't comprehend what he was seeing.

Nadia and the general hissed and bit at each other's faces. She may have had youth and anger on her side, but the older alien was more experienced and a far better fighter than she could ever hope to be. He brought up his right leg and thrust it into Nadia's stomach, flipping her off him.

Grant saw Nadia hit the ground and brought his weapon up to fire. He was fast, but not as fast as his opponent. The general reached out, grabbed Grant's MP7 by the barrel, and yanked it out of his arms.

"Look out!" screamed Elena.

Grant never saw the clenched fist coming out of the dark. The next thing he knew, his head shot over to the left. The coppery taste of blood filled his mouth as his legs buckled underneath his body. Grant fell on his back in the muddy field. Out of the corner of his eye, Grant watched as the general drew his pistol and fired it. A bright orange flash filled his eyes. When the light faded, one of the mercenaries was gone, and the alien was nowhere in sight. A split second later, the three surviving killers jumped to their feet and ran for their lives.

Elena ran to Grant and placed her hands on either side of his pounding head. "David, are you all right?"

He slowly sat up, leaned to one side, and spat out a mouthful of blood. "What happened?"

"The male alien killed the man who had the knife and then ran off," explained Elena.

Grant moved his aching head around. "Where's Nadia?"

A darkened shape sat up, wobbled, and waved. "You're right, I guess I'm not as good a fighter as I thought I was."

With his teeth clenched, Grant struggled to stand. Even in the dark, he could see Nadia's alien facial features. She had a small snout on her face with two small slits for her nostrils on the top of it.

"So, is this the real you?"

"Yes," she replied.

Grant blinked. "How did you do that? I didn't see your lips move."

"I told you, I can read your mind. I'm using telepathy to talk with you."

Elena clapped her hands together and let out a small whoop of joy. She had forgotten the horrors of a few seconds ago and was happily lost in the moment. Her life's work had come to fruition. Smiling from ear to ear, Elena reached up and wiped the tears from her eyes. "I'm sorry," she said. "I'm just a little overwhelmed right now."

"Why didn't the general kill us all when he had the chance?" asked Grant. "You and I were both down, and the mercenaries were unarmed."

"He's in a lot of pain," she replied.

"He didn't look hurt to me."

"He's strong; I'll give him that. However, before he escaped to come here, there was a firefight in the laboratory. I thought I had wounded him, but it wasn't until I saw the scar on the left side of his face that I was sure. Also, he could have suffered internal injuries when he ejected from his doomed ship."

"Perhaps we can use this information to our advantage when the time comes."

"I can assure you the only thing on General Nagan's mind right now is escape."

"Your ship, where is it?"

"My ship isn't very large. I was able to land it inside an old abandoned mine."

Grant ran a hand across his throbbing jaw. "Is it invisible to the naked eye?"

She nodded. "Yes, it's shielded from view."

"Do you think the general will be able to find it?"

"Given time…yes."

"Guys, what's this?" said Elena, pointing at the hole the general had dug in the ground.

Grant dug out his flashlight, turned it on, and shone the light around inside the hole. A small metal box with no lid sat nestled in the dirt. Inside were several slender, colored vials.

"It looks like he took a handful of DNA weapons with him when he left," said Nadia.

"Okay, that's not good," said Grant. "We've got to go after him. But before we do, Nadia, I want you to destroy what's left in that box."

"Gladly," she replied as she brought up her phase pistol and pulled the trigger. The box glowed brightly for a second before disappearing completely.

"Let's head back to the car and make our way to the mine before the general or any of those fanatical mercenaries get there."

With that, Grant took Elena by the hand. With Nadia in the lead, they ran as fast as their legs could carry them through the darkened woods. The race was on, and it was one Grant did not intend to lose.

38

"There…over there, that looks like a cabin to me," said Hayes, gesturing with his hand at a darkened building just off the dirt road.

"That it does," replied Maclean as he applied the brakes. With a loud squeal, the vehicle came to a halt. Maclean picked up his MP7, opened the door, and stepped outside. In the dark, he could just make out a handful of dwellings and a couple of large barns. Maclean switched on his flashlight and shone it all around to make sure the area was safe.

The rain was now only a gentle drizzle.

"Come on, Doc, we've got work to do," said Maclean.

Hayes did up his jacket and joined his colleague on the muddy field. He whispered, "Do you think the creatures will have gotten this far south by now?"

"Probably. Also, there's no point in whispering. If they were here, they'd have been on us before we got ten paces from the bus."

"Which house should we knock on?"

Maclean shone his light on a large cabin in the middle of the farm. "Ten-to-one, that's where we'll find Mr. Munroe."

Maclean balled up his fist and smashed it against the wooden door a couple of times before calling out, "Mr. Munroe, are you in there?"

No one answered.

"Perhaps no one's home?" said Hayes.

"Nah, the old bugger's probably just fast asleep," said Maclean, again banging his fist hard on the door.

A light switched on inside the cabin. "Whoever you are, you can stop doing that," bellowed an angry-sounding man.

The door swung open and light flooded out onto the porch. A man with long, unkempt white hair and a full beard stood there in his plaid pajama bottoms with a faded and stretched blue T-shirt. His bloodshot eyes fixed on the two unwelcome guests. "Who the hell are you, and why are you banging on my door at this ungodly hour of the morning?"

"Very sorry to disturb you, sir. My name is Sergeant James Maclean, and this is Doctor Jeremy Hayes," said the Aussie. "Sheriff Black sent us here to evacuate you and your family back into town."

Munroe belched and scratched his backside. "I don't understand. Why would we leave our homes in the middle of the night and head into town?"

"Sir, let me explain," said Hayes. "There's an usually large grizzly bear on the prowl. The beast has already killed several farm animals and is reported to be infected with rabies. It was last seen heading in the direction of your farm."

Munroe looked from Maclean to Hayes, and then back to Maclean. "You didn't have to drive all the way out here to tell me that. Why didn't you just call me on the telephone?"

"Sir, I know this may all look a little bit odd, but I can assure you that we're on the level. If you were to try your phone, you would find that it does not work. In fact, absolutely no forms of communication are working right now. That's why Sheriff Black insisted that we drive up here and evacuate your family before anything horrible happens."

"We've got a school bus waiting to drive you all to safety," said Maclean, pointing over his shoulder at the yellow vehicle. "All you have to do is wake your family up and get them on board. Please do as we ask. I've seen this bear. It's huge, and it's not going to stop until the state troopers get here and bring it down."

"What's all the fuss about, Harold?" said an older woman dressed in a pink housecoat with short, silvery hair.

"Trudy, these men want us to pack up the family and head into town," replied Mr. Munroe.

Mrs. Munroe looked up at the two strangers. "Why, is something wrong?"

Mere seconds after Hayes described the threat, the old couple helped Maclean and Hayes and ran from cabin to cabin, banging on doors and yelling for everyone to get up. People rushed to grab what they could before running to the idling bus. At the last home, they ran into trouble.

A woman in her forties grabbed Trudy by the hand and started crying.

"What's the matter?" asked Maclean.

"It's her two boys," replied Trudy. "They went camping down by the river a day ago and aren't due back until sometime after noon today."

"Damn," muttered Maclean under his breath. "Tell her to get on the bus. I'll get her kids and bring them into town."

"Sergeant, we have a quad you can use," said Trudy.

"Bless you. Where is it?"

"It's in the big storage barn, right behind the main house."

Maclean nodded. "And what are the kids' names?"

"Jacob and Patrick."

Maclean repeated their names to himself a couple of times to memorize them.

Behind them, the lights from an approaching vehicle lit up the farm. Maclean watched, suddenly tense, as the Suburban stopped next to the school bus and a single occupant got out.

"Morning Trudy," said the woman. She was wearing a police uniform. Maclean relaxed and exhaled quietly.

"Morning, Officer Tibeluk," replied Mrs. Munroe.

"I was on my way back into town when I saw the lights on your farm on and thought it most peculiar, considering how early it is. So, I decided to stop in and see what's going on."

Trudy looked at Maclean. "Sergeant Maclean told us that Sheriff Black wants us to pack up and move into town. He said a rabid bear was spotted in this neck of the woods."

Maclean held out his hand in greeting. "I don't think we've had the chance to meet yet. I'm Sergeant James Maclean. Sheriff Black kind of deputized me and my colleague to round up the Munroes, but we've hit a bit of a snag."

"I'm Officer Tracey Tibeluk. What kind of snag are you talking about?"

"Two kids aren't here. They're off camping in the woods."

"Where?"

"They're down by the Atna River," replied Trudy.

"I was just about to head out there and get the kids when you showed up," said Maclean.

"Do you know where Atna River is, Sergeant?" asked Tibeluk.

"No."

"I do, so I'm going with you. We can bring them back here, and then use my Suburban to drive them into town."

Maclean liked the confident tone and mannerisms displayed by Tibeluk. He smiled briefly and said, "Sounds like a plan to me. Now to break the news to Professor Hayes."

Aside from a couple of young children crying in their parents' arms, everyone on the bus was silent and pensive.

Hayes sat behind the wheel of the bus, shaking his head. "I've never driven anything this big before," he protested.

"You'll do fine, Doc," said Maclean. "Just remember this is a stick shift and not an automatic, and you'll be okay."

"If you say so."

Maclean patted the perturbed doctor on the shoulder and turned to face the two elder Munroes. "Jeremy will drive you all to the school, where you'll be able to stay until this all blows over."

"What about our animals? Who's going to look after them?"

asked Harold Munroe.

Maclean forced what he hoped would be a soothing smile on his face. "Don't worry, they'll be safe where they are. You'll probably be back in less than a day's time. Your animals should be okay until you get back." He cursed himself for his outright lies, but he knew that was what the Munroes wanted to hear.

"Please bring our grandchildren back to us," said Mrs. Munroe. Fear filled her voice.

Maclean winked and held up his MP7. "Don't you worry, ma'am, I'll have them to you safe and sound by breakfast." He climbed down out of the bus and waved as Hayes placed the vehicle in gear and slowly drove away. He walked behind the house to the storage shed and saw that Tibeluk had brought two quads out. Their engines rumbled quietly.

"Are you ready?" asked Tibeluk, sitting on a red quad.

"I should be. I drove something like this in Afghanistan. Say, what time is sunrise around here?"

Tibeluk checked her wristwatch. "In about two hours."

Maclean slipped on a helmet and sat down on the black, four-wheeled vehicle. He looked over at Tibeluk. "Ladies first."

Tibeluk applied power to the engine, turned her handlebar over, and drove toward a trail behind one of the Munroes' barns.

With a feeling of foreboding in his heart, Maclean sped after Tibeluk. He brought his submachine gun down and rested it on his lap. If something were to happen on the narrow trail, it would be quick and deadly, and Maclean didn't want to fall victim to the animals stalking the night.

39

"Son of a bitch," cried Grant.

"What's wrong?" asked Nadia.

"Those merc bastards stole our car!"

"What about their vehicles?" said Elena. "All we have to do is replace the flat tires, hotwire one, and we're back in business."

Grant closed his eyes and shook his head. "Have you ever hotwired a car before?"

"No. But you're a soldier, you should know how to do it…right?"

"Sorry, it's not a skill they taught at West Point," he replied as he walked to the nearest abandoned truck. He swore when he saw the spare tires for both vehicles were gone.

"Now what's the matter?" Elena asked.

"They took the bloody spares with them." Grant flipped up the vehicle's hood and looked inside. "And before you say anything else, it looks like they also took the engine alternators with them as well. From here on out, I guess we're on foot."

"It shouldn't be too bad; it's only about five and a half kilometers from here to my craft," said Nadia.

"Don't take this the wrong way," said Grant staring at Nadia's leathery face. "But are you going to remain as you are?"

"Yes. Why?"

"I don't know. I guess I'm just not used to seeing someone like you. The teenage girl's face looked far less threatening."

"It takes a lot out of me to be something other than myself. I'm going to need all my strength to see this through to the end. I think it's easier if I just stay as I am."

"You're the expert. I want you to take the lead, but keep your pace measured. We don't have legs as long as you do."

Nadia brought out her tracking device, got a fix on her craft, and began to walk.

A thought crossed Grant's mind. He cursed himself for not thinking of it earlier. He ran over and tapped her on the shoulder. "Nadia, all the comms systems in the local area went dead when you arrived. You're responsible for this communications blackout, aren't you?"

"Correct."

"Why don't you lift it, so we can call for help?"

Nadia stopped in her tracks. "I'm not going to lift the comms blackout, nor am I going to remove the electromagnetic shield which encompasses the town and the local countryside."

"The what?" said Elena.

"I have a shield in place, which prevents anything that relies on electricity to enter or leave this battlespace until I have completed my mission."

Nadia began to walk again.

"I don't get it. You say you want our help but won't allow us to call for assistance," said Grant.

"My mission orders are quite specific. Neither I nor the general can ever be taken alive by your armed forces. Similarly, all our technology must be destroyed if it looks like it's in danger of falling into your hands. You're a relatively primitive and immature species, but you're on the cusp of great advances in scientific technology. If any of our equipment were to be examined by your scientists, it wouldn't take them more than a decade or two to figure out how to reproduce whatever they got their hands on. And my people aren't about to let that happen."

"Please, you have to at least let us help the people in the town," pleaded Elena.

"Like I told the sheriff, they're on their own. I'm sorry, but I have strict noninterference orders."

"Aren't you breaking those orders by allowing Elena and me to help stop your rogue general?" posed Grant.

"Dave, if all you do is distract the general for a second or two before he kills you, then you will have aided me greatly. I give you at best a five percent chance of surviving the night. As for the woman, she has less than a one percent chance of living. The people back in the town, they're most likely all going to die. The creatures General Nagan created aren't just throwbacks to an earlier time. They're designed to be highly intelligent and will work together to bring down their prey. By moving everyone to one spot, all you've done is make it easier for them to find their next meal."

Anger surged through Grant's body. "Goddammit, Nadia, you could have told us this before we came up with our plan."

"I told you once before. You're a means to an end, and nothing more. You're the one who volunteered to help me. The people in the town will assist me by keeping the animals busy while I accomplish my mission." With that, Nadia spun on her heel and carried on walking.

Elena leaned in close and whispered, "My God, that woman's a real bitch."

Grant shrugged. "I don't know. I think she's just being honest. Besides, I don't think she expects to come out of this alive, either."

40

The night began to give way to the gray light of dawn.

Maclean saw Tibeluk apply the brakes to her ATV and did likewise. A couple of seconds later, they drove out of the woods and stopped in a small clearing. In front of them was the wide, and fast-flowing Atna River.

Maclean switched off his quad's engine, removed his helmet, and climbed off. The two boys were nowhere to be seen. He looked over at Tibeluk. "Do you have any idea where the boys could have set up their tents?"

"This river runs for hundreds of kilometers," replied Tibeluk. "They could be anywhere, but I suspect they're no more than five minutes from here."

"Why would you say that?"

"Because there's a great fishing spot just down the trail where my brothers and I used to go when we were kids. I bet we'll find them there."

Maclean placed his helmet back on his head and got onto his ATV. "Okay, then, let's get moving."

Tibeluk had called it correctly. They drove out of the woods and came to a halt right next to the shredded remains of a tent. Maclean jumped from his quad, slung his MP7, and ran to the pile of nylon, grabbing handfuls of it and lifting it into the air. The tent was empty. The boys' sleeping bags were ripped to pieces. Crumbs of food were scattered everywhere. Maclean stood up and studied the ground with his flashlight. There were at least three different sets of three-toed animal tracks around the tent.

"Are they...?" Tibeluk asked hesitantly.

"No, they're not in there. Nor is there any blood. I think the boys may have seen what was coming and made a run for it."

"We're up here," said a voice barely louder than a whisper.

Maclean and Tibeluk looked up into the trees and saw a teenage boy waving at them. A second dirt-covered face popped out from behind some branches.

Relief at seeing the boys alive replaced the fear in Maclean's heart. "Come on down, lads."

The boys scrambled down like monkeys from the tree.

"So, which one of you is Jacob, and which one of you is Patrick?" said Maclean.

"I'm Jacob," said the shorter of the two boys.

"And I'm Patrick," said the other boy, his face covered with freckles.

"Okay, I'm Sergeant Maclean, and I'm sure you already know Officer Tibeluk. Did you see what attacked your camp?"

"Yeah, but I'd never seen anything like them before in my life," said Patrick.

"What did you see?" asked Tibeluk.

"Officer, I'm not making this up; they were gigantic birds with massive beaks," replied Patrick.

"As crazy as your story sounds, trust me, after what's happened to me in the past few hours, I believe you."

"We were about to get some sleep, when I spotted one of them watching us from the woods. We knew we were in trouble, so we ran and climbed that tree."

"They couldn't climb up after us," said Jacob, "so they got really angry and tore our tent apart looking for food before heading back into the forest."

"You did the right thing, boys," said Maclean. "Now, Officer Tibeluk and I are going to take you to your parents, who are waiting for you in town," explained Maclean.

"What are they doing there?" asked Jacob.

"There's no time to explain right now," said Tibeluk. "Jacob, you get on my quad, Patrick can ride with Sergeant Maclean."

The boys nodded and ran to jump onto the ATVs.

"Sergeant, I'll lead us back to the farm," said Tibeluk to Maclean.

He smiled. "Not a problem, Officer. I like a woman who likes to take charge."

Tibeluk shook her head. *No matter where they come from, all men still think alike*, she thought.

When they came to the end of the trail, Tibeluk slowed her quad and brought it to a stop.

Maclean drove up next to her and looked over at the Munroes' farm. An early-morning mist covered the open ground. Tibeluk's police vehicle was parked on the road less than five hundred meters away. When he went to ask Tibeluk why they stopped, he saw her eyes were fixed on one of the farm's houses. "Do you see something?" he asked.

"I don't know. It may be nothing, but my gut's telling me to be careful," replied Tibeluk.

Maclean brought up his submachine gun and looked through its sights. He surveyed the farm but couldn't see anything.

"I guess I'm just imagining things," said Tibeluk.

Maclean lowered his weapon. "No. We're going to trust your gut instincts. It's worked for me in the past, and I'd rather err on the side of caution than end up dead. Let's go with the assumption that there is something out there waiting for us."

"What do you want to do?"

"We'll head straight for your vehicle. If something comes after us, I want you to keep going and let me deal with it."

"I have a gun too, and I'm one hell of a good shot."

"Tracey, I don't doubt you're handy with a gun, but you need to get Jacob to safety, and then worry about Patrick, and lastly, me."

Tibeluk nodded.

"What do you want me to do, sir?" Patrick asked.

"Can you drive this quad?"

Patrick's eyes lit up. "I sure can."

"Good, let's switch places. No matter what happens to me, I want you to follow Officer Tibeluk to her car. Got it?"

Patrick nodded and climbed in front of Maclean.

"Okay, let's do this," said Maclean.

Tibeluk revved her engine before releasing the brake and speeding out onto the open field. With Patrick right behind her, she raced for Suburban.

When they were halfway to the vehicle, three terror birds sprinted out from behind a barn and ran to catch their prey.

Out of the corner of his eye, Maclean saw them coming. He bought up his MP7 and aimed it at the closest bird. When it was less than ten meters away, he pulled the trigger, firing a sustained burst into the creature's chest. Blood and feathers flew as the bullets tore through its flesh. With a loud squawk the monster fell face-first to the ground.

The two other animals ran past the dying beast and closed in on Maclean's ATV. He switched his aim and sprayed what was left in his weapon's magazine at the birds. One of the creatures, hit in the leg, slowed down, but kept limping after the escaping vehicles.

With less than fifty meters to go, Tibeluk swerved around a stump partially hidden in the fog. Patrick saw the move but reacted a second too late. The tires on the right side of his quad hit the stump, knocking Patrick and Maclean from the vehicle. They landed on the soft ground and rolled end over end.

With adrenaline pumping through his veins, Maclean barely registered the fall from the quad and jumped to his feet. His submachine gun was gone. He ran to Patrick and helped the youngster to his feet. The last bird let out a loud shriek and charged at the two men trapped out in the open. Maclean pushed Patrick in the direction of the Suburban, reached behind his back, and drew his pistol. The bird was so close that he didn't bother to aim. As fast as he could pull the trigger, Maclean fired round after round into the monster. The bird's eyes rolled up in its head. A second later, it tripped over its own feet and tumbled to the ground right next to Maclean. He ejected the spent magazine from his pistol and jammed home a new one before loading a round into the chamber. His chest was heaving as if he had just run a marathon.

A shot rang out, surprising Maclean. He turned his head. Tibeluk was standing next to her vehicle with a smoking shotgun in her hands. In the field, the remaining wounded bird stopped walking and staggered from side to side like a drunk before dropping to the ground.

Maclean jogged to Tibeluk's side. "Thanks."

"I told you I was a good shot," she replied.

"I never doubted you for a second. Now, let's get the hell out of here."

Tibeluk got behind the wheel, started her Suburban, and placed it in drive. She glanced over at Maclean and said, "Care to tell me what we're up against, Sergeant?"

"I'm not sure what to tell you, other than there's a lot more of those things out there."

"Is this some sort of messed-up military experiment?"

Maclean chuckled. "Yeah, but your military isn't behind it."

"Then whose is?"

"You won't believe me."

"Try me."

Maclean sat back in his seat and let out a sigh of exhaustion. "Tracey, do you believe in UFOs?"

"For the love of God, you're not going to try and tell me something from outer space made those creatures, are you?"

"Well, kind of."

Tibeluk shook her head. "Save it. I'll get the sheriff to tell me what's going on. She's never lied to me."

"Your call," said Maclean. "But be prepared for the same story I was about to tell you." He looked out the window as they sped toward town, wondering how his friends were doing, and if they were still alive.

41

If Grant was having a hard time keeping up with Nadia, he knew Elena was having it ten times worse. The route Nadia had chosen through the woods had them traversing the side of a heavily wooded hill. The ground was slick and treacherous. Every few steps, Elena would trip on something and fall to the ground. After twenty minutes, she was covered from head to toe in mud and leaves.

"Slow down a little," said Grant to Nadia as he helped Elena back onto her feet.

"Dawn is coming," replied Nadia, pointing at the light on the horizon. "We should be picking up the pace, not slowing down."

"How much farther is it?" asked Elena between gasps of air.

Nadia checked her scanner. "Not far. Another two kilometers."

"Might as well be another twenty." She reached out and placed a hand on Grant's face. "Go on without me. I'll be okay."

"Like hell," replied Grant. "No one is going to be left behind. I'll carry you if I have to."

"Come on," urged Nadia. "We have to keep moving."

Grant took his friend by the arm and walked beside her, keeping her on her feet. When they got to the base of the hill, their luck changed from bad to worse. A wide, fast-flowing river blocked their way.

"For the love of God," mumbled Elena. "I can't seem to catch a break."

"We have to find a way across," said Nadia. "The mine isn't

that far from here."

"Which way is the mine?" asked Grant.

"That way," said Nadia, pointing downriver.

"Okay, then that's the way we'll go until we find a bridge or a log lying across the river that will support our weight."

They walked along in silence for nearly ten minutes until they stepped out onto a dirt road.

"Are you kidding me?" blurted out Elena. "Why the hell didn't we use this road instead of bashing our way through the woods?"

"I didn't know it was here," replied Nadia. "Or I would have taken it to speed things along."

"Aren't there any maps in your GPS of our planet?" quipped Grant.

"Pardon?"

"Forget it. I'm tired. Let's follow this road and see where it comes out."

They had barely gone twenty meters when an old wooden footbridge came into view.

"At last, my luck's changing," said Elena, smiling and clapping her hands together.

"Let's get across it before making any pronouncements," said Grant. He let go of Elena's arm and unslung his MP7. If someone was waiting for them, the bridge made the perfect spot for an ambush.

Nadia must have sensed the danger as well. She stopped and drew her pistol before placing a foot on the old bridge. As she walked across, the wood creaked and moaned, but didn't give way.

"Now you," said Grant to Elena. He waited for a couple of seconds to see if there was anyone lying in wait for them. When nothing happened, he started for the bridge. No sooner had he stepped onto the bridge, when a loud snort came from the woods next to him. A primal fear in the back of his subconscious gripped Grant.

The bear was back.

"Run!" hollered Grant.

With lightning-fast speed, the mutated bear, with its massive slobbering jaws wide open, burst from the forest and charged at the people on the bridge. Grant turned and ran as fast as his feet could move. The far end of the bridge seemed an impossible distance away. He could hear the bear's breath growing louder as it closed in on him from behind.

Elena heard Grant yell and turned her head. Her eyes widened, and her feet turned to lead when she saw the bear. She tried to scream but found her throat had turned dry with fear.

"Get out of the way, woman," yelled Nadia as she tried to get a shot at the creature.

What happened next seemed to be in slow motion to Elena. First, the bear smashed into Grant, sending him tumbling through the air. She lost sight of him the second he hit the dark, bubbling water. Next, she felt Nadia pull her back and out of the way of the charging beast. The alien brought up her weapon to fire, but the weight of the bear caused the wooden bridge to move up and down like a boat on the waves. A bright orange flash of light shot from Nadia's pistol and flew right over the head of the bear, striking the top of several trees on the other side of the river, incinerating them.

The bear was so close that Elena could see the drool cascading like a waterfall from its mouth. Before Nadia could get off another shot, it swatted her, sending her flying onto her back. The bear stopped in its tracks, easily dwarfing the two women. It sniffed the air and got up on its hind feet before letting out a thunderous roar.

Elena saw Nadia's pistol lying next to her feet. She had never held a firearm in her life, but fear and the instinct to survive made her scoop it up and aim it at the belly of the beast towering above her. Elena placed her finger on what she took to be the trigger and pulled back. There was no noise or recoil, only a bright flash of orange light. The bear's body seemed to glow for a second before the light faded away, and the bear was gone. Elena stood there for a few seconds trying to catch her breath and to let what had just occurred sink in. Her stomach turned. Elena ran to the side of the bridge and threw up everything she had in her stomach. She dropped to all fours and retched until there was only foul-tasting bile coming out of her mouth.

A weak moan from behind her reminded Elena that she wasn't alone. She wiped the spittle from her face with the back of her hand and crawled over to Nadia's side. The alien was trying to get up. By the pained look on her face, she was in great discomfort.

"Take it easy," said Elena as she helped Nadia to sit up.

"Where's the monster?" asked Nadia.

"Gone. I killed it," said Elena, handing back the pistol.

Nadia looked around. "Where's Dave?"

Elena looked away. "The bear knocked him into the river, and that's the last I saw of him."

"Get me to my feet."

"Wait, I need to see how bad your injuries are before we try and move you."

"There's no time for that," responded Nadia through clenched teeth. "We have to keep moving. The very survival of your species is on the line."

Elena grabbed hold of Nadia's arm and helped pull her to her feet.

"I think the animal broke my left arm and shattered some of my ribs," said Nadia. "If I hadn't been wearing my body armor, it surely would have torn me in two."

Nadia was putting on a brave face, and Elena knew it. She didn't doubt for one instant that Nadia had suffered internal injuries far worse than the young alien was letting on. "Well, you're taller and far heavier than I am, so the best we can do is for you to use my shoulder as a rest. Together, we should be able to help keep you on your feet."

Nadia moved around until she was resting her right hand on

Elena's shoulder. "Okay, this should work."

"I thought all the mutated animals were heading for the town," said Elena. "I wonder why this one was still hanging around up here."

"Once it had a taste for human flesh, that's all its mind wanted. It's probably been following us ever since we ran into the general."

With that, Nadia and Elena began to hobble to the other side of the bridge. When they were across, Nadia pointed at a track leading through the woods. "That should take us to the mine."

"If you say so," said Elena, wishing that her colleague was still there to help protect them. Nadia's warning of not making it to the end now seemed eerily prophetic.

42

Sheriff Black cringed when she heard the gears of the bus grinding as it came to a halt in the parking lot behind the school. The front door swung open, and the Munroe family got off the bus.

Harold and Trudy Munroe saw Black and walked to her side. "Sheriff, I hope this isn't some big misunderstanding," said Harold. "We've got plenty of livestock and horses back on the farm that need us to feed and look after them."

"Sir, trust me, there is a very real threat out there," replied Black. "You know me; I wouldn't have asked you to come into town if I didn't believe it was the right thing to do."

"Sheriff, two of your people went into the woods behind our place to look for two of our grandchildren, who had gone camping," said Trudy.

Black could see Hayes standing next to the bus. She was at a loss to understand which two people Trudy had meant. "Sorry, who did you say went to look for your grandchildren?"

"Officer Tibeluk and that Australian sergeant you deputized went to look for them."

"Damn," said Black under her breath. She couldn't comprehend why Tibeluk hadn't carried on to Valdez as ordered. Something had clearly gone wrong. She cursed again, feeling helpless at their inability to call for help.

Officer Kyle Harrison hobbled out of the open gymnasium doors on a pair of crutches and waved for the Munroes to join him inside the building.

"Sheriff, is there anything I can do to help?" asked Hayes.

"I don't know," she replied. "Can you shoot a rifle?"

"Sorry, no. But I believe I can assist those who can shoot."

"How?"

"I have a small drone in the back of my car. We can use it to monitor the area around the school."

Black smiled. "Great idea. Do you need help getting this drone operational?"

"As a matter of fact, I do. Is there a kid here who is particularly good with video games?"

"Sam," hollered Black.

"Yes, Mom," replied a youth from the roof of the school.

"Get down here, and bring Reba with you. I've got a job for the two of you."

"Thanks, Sheriff. Tell the kids to meet me at my car," said Hayes. "It's parked out front of the hotel."

Black watched Hayes leave. She looked over at the pinkish hue on the horizon and prayed that she and her son would live to see the sunset twelve hours from now. Black was surprised how many people had decided to come to the school for protection. With the Munroes, there were now close to sixty people in the gymnasium. Most had come from the town's clinic, while a fair number had come from the trailer park and were elderly or couples with young children. There were still plenty of people around the town who had grown up with weapons in their hands since they were kids and had decided to stay where they were and defend their homes.

Sam and a tall, red-haired, teenage girl ran outside to join Sheriff Black. "I found Reba," said Sam. "What is it you'd like us to do?"

"There's a redheaded Englishman wearing a bowtie walking to the hotel. Head over there and give him a hand retrieving whatever he's after. When you get back here, I want the three of you on the roof. Got it?"

"Sure do, Mom," said Sam with an eager nod.

"Go on then. Get a move on, you two, and run, don't walk!"

The two youths spun around and sprinted out of the school's parking lot in the direction of the hotel.

"Sheriff, a lot of people are asking why we can't talk with anyone inside or outside of the town," said Harrison as he took a seat on an old wooden crate to rest his injured leg.

"Tell them it's some kind of atmospheric anomaly that should pass later in the day," replied Black.

"I'll give it a try, but some of them aren't going to buy your explanation."

"Then ignore them and tell them you have work to do."

"I can do that."

Black looked down at Harrison's bandaged foot. "How's your ankle treating you?"

"Not bad at all. Mrs. Norton, bless her heart, pumped me full of painkillers before we left the clinic. She said I shouldn't feel a thing for hours. If I do, she brought along some more drugs with her to keep me on my feet until this blows over."

"Kyle, I hate to be the bearer of bad news, but you may be on your feet a lot longer than you think. It doesn't look like Tracey made it to Valdez."

Harrison sat straight up. "Is she okay?"

"I don't know. For whatever reason, Tracey turned around and ended up at the Munroes' farm, where she and Sergeant Maclean met up. I was told that they went in search of two missing kids."

"So, you're telling me that the state authorities are still in the dark as to what's happening here."

"Looks that way. I guess we're on our own for now."

"Sheriff, I wasn't there when you had your conversation with those UFO people. Do you honestly believe everything they said to you?"

"Kyle, we can't afford not to. I'd rather lose my job for overreacting than lose another person to the animals these scientific experts say are coming our way." Black had told

Harrison about the meeting but not her close encounter with an alien ship. She didn't want him to think she was becoming unhinged over the recent spate of disappearances.

"Have you heard from Bill and Sean lately?"

"Yes. They were here not fifteen minutes ago. I asked them to continue patrolling the roads to the north of the town, and to help anyone who wanted to come here but couldn't do so without assistance."

"I just wish we could make one phone call to Valdez."

Black patted her officer on the shoulder. "So do I, Kyle. So do I."

43

The world was dark, cold, and wet.

David Grant struggled to come back to the land of the living. He felt as if he were walking up a long, dark tunnel, which seemed to stretch on forever. A sharp, stabbing pain in his side shot him back into reality. He opened his eyes and saw he was jammed between two branches hanging just above the water. The pain he felt was from a fast-moving log which had hit his ribs, bounced off him, and carried on downriver. Grant took in a deep breath through his nostrils as he struggled to clear the fog in his mind. The last thing he could remember was a loud snort coming from the woods. After that, there was the image of a large shape coming for him, and then darkness.

The bear! There was a bear coming after them.

Grant turned his head in desperation and tried to see the women, but they weren't there. He reached over with his right hand, grabbed hold of one of the branches he was hung up on, and pulled himself toward shore. The moment his feet touched solid ground, he stood up and staggered out of the icy cold water. Steam rose from Grant's damp clothes. He took a seat on a rock and tried to collect his thoughts. Grant had expected to feel a lot worse than he did. The only pain he had was on his left side. He undid his jacket, pulled up his shirt, and removed his liquid body armor. It had hardened at the point of impact with the log. Grant ran his hand along the armor and knew if he hadn't been wearing it, the log would have pierced his side, perhaps even killing him. He grimaced when he saw a large purple-and-yellow bruise beginning to spread up his side. The pain would be a lot worse in a matter of hours, when his body and mind finally relaxed.

He reached for his submachine gun but found it was missing, having slid off his back when he hit the water. Thankfully, his pistol and a couple of spare magazines were still firmly attached to his belt. Grant stood up, removed his jacket and shirt, and wrung them out as best he could, before replacing the body armor and getting dressed again. The last thing he needed right now was to fall victim to hypothermia. Grant looked around, trying to get his bearings. He had no idea if he had floated right past the mine or was still a kilometer or more from it. There was only one way to find out. Grant picked a tall fir tree nearby and started to climb it. Each time he raised his left arm above his head, his side hurt, as if he had been kicked by an angry mule. Grant slowed down to ease the discomfort. When he was about fifty meters in the air, he stopped and looked around. He nodded when he spotted a cluster of aged wooden shacks marking the entrance to the old mine. He judged it to be less than a ten minute walk from where he was. Grant made his way down the tree and began to jog. In an instant, the pain in his left side told him to slow down and take it easy. Grant gritted his teeth and carried on at a fast walk instead. He could worry about his wounds when it was all said and done, and the general was dead.

44

Maclean smiled when the two boys ran to join their parents. At least something good had come out of all the misery.

"I'm going to check in with the sheriff," announced Tibeluk. "Want to come with me?"

"Sure. Why not."

Inside the gym, mats were laid out on the floor as makeshift beds and several people were getting some sleep, while others sat around talking quietly to one another. They found Black sitting on a bench with Harrison, drinking a cup of coffee.

"Sheriff, I'm sorry I couldn't make it all the way to Valdez," said Tibeluk. "Trust me, I have a good reason for it. But before I say anything, I'd like to report that Sergeant Maclean and I found the two missing Munroe kids and brought them back here safely."

"That's good news, Tracey," responded Black. "Now, please tell me what happened and why you're not still on your way to Valdez?"

"I know this is going to sound crazy, but I was making good time when, at about sixty kilometers out of town, the vehicle went dead. It wasn't just the Suburban, either. The batteries in my flashlight stopped working as well. Since my vehicle had been working fine only a few seconds earlier, I decided to push it back down the road to see if the power would come back on. And what do you know, it did."

"Something very similar happened to us in the Iraqi desert," added Maclean.

Black stood and patted Tibeluk on the shoulder. "Today, I'll believe anything. I hate to say it but we're more cut off from the outside than I had originally imagined."

"Ma'am, Sergeant Maclean and I ran into things out at the Munroe farm that I've never seen before. Huge, flightless birds tried to kill us. Thankfully, the sergeant took care of them."

"It wasn't just me," said Maclean. "Officer Tibeluk brought one down herself."

"Good shooting is what we may need shortly," said Black. "I'd like you two up on the roof to help keep the animals at bay, should they make their way into town."

"I'll grab my shotgun," said Tibeluk.

"Any word from my people?" Maclean asked Black.

"Professor Hayes is on the roof with my son and his girlfriend," said Black. "As for the other two, I haven't seen them since they left."

"Well, no news is good news, according to my late grandmother, so I'll go with the power of positive thinking for now."

On the roof, Hayes let out a whoop when he saw Maclean alive and ran to shake his hand.

"Sergeant, thank God you're alive. I was beginning to fear the worst."

"No need to worry about me, Doc," said Maclean, waving his MP7 in the air. "As long as you keep me supplied with the latest and greatest toys, I'll be all right. By the way, do you have any more ammo?"

"I brought what was left of the ammunition with me," replied Hayes, indicating to two black plastic containers stacked by his feet.

"Good call, Doc." Maclean looked around the roof and spotted two young people sitting down watching the feed from the UAV. It was flying in a tight circle above the school. He walked over and smiled at the youths. "See anything?"

"No, sir," replied the boy.

"Since we're going to be trapped up here for the foreseeable future, please call me James, or Jim if you like," said Maclean.

"My name is Sam, and this is my friend Reba." At the boy's feet was a Winchester hunting rifle with a telescopic sight mounted on it.

"Are you any good with that?" said Maclean, pointing to the rifle.

"Yes, sir. I mean, Jim. My mom taught me how to shoot. I can bring down a deer at three hundred meters."

Maclean nodded. "Three hundred meters, that's not too shabby."

"So, what's the plan?" asked Hayes.

"We wait it out until someone comes to rescue us," replied Maclean.

"That's not much of a plan."

"Yeah, but it's all we've got right now. Doc, you may wish to chat with Officer Tibeluk. She had car problems while driving to Valdez. I think there's a powerful invisible shield around the town stopping us from getting out, or anyone else from getting in."

"Yes, that does sound interesting." Hayes waved at Tibeluk and walked over to introduce himself.

"Sorry, Tracey," Maclean muttered to himself. He unslung his weapon and walked the perimeter of the roof. There were woods on three sides of the school, making it easy for a predator to get close without being observed. He glanced up at the UAV as it gracefully banked over in the air and hoped it would prove up to the task as their early-warning eye in the sky.

45

The size of the abandoned copper mine was staggering. There were at least a dozen red-painted wooden buildings on the side of a hill. The largest was the mill, which had once been used to extract the ore from the rocks. It stood ten stories high.

You could hide in there, and no one would ever find you, thought Grant as he left the wooded trail and walked to the closest building. He drew his pistol, made sure it was loaded, and peered through a smashed window. Broken glass, rust-covered tins, and old papers littered the floor. Grant was surprised to see that much of the old machinery was still there. Although the machines had long since been picked over and were covered in rust, it looked like the place could start up at any time and resume mining copper from the hills behind it.

Grant's stomach rumbled. He dug through his pockets, found a crushed granola bar, and wolfed it down. Nadia had said that she had hidden her ship inside the mine, so he reasoned checking out the mining camp would be pointless. Still, he wanted to be careful. He was outnumbered and outgunned by the opposition. Grant walked along, using the buildings for cover, until he came to a dirt road leading up to the mill. He was about to follow the road when he spotted his stolen car parked outside a three-story structure about sixty meters up the hill. Grant ducked back and waited to see if he had been spotted. When no one called out or took a shot in his direction, Grant nipped inside the building he was hiding behind and tiptoed through the maze of debris on the floor. Each step he took, Grant feared he would crush something underfoot, alerting the mercenaries to his presence. He barely breathed until he reached the far end of the building. Grant got down on one knee and peered through a crack in the wall. Outside, there was a dry riverbed, which ran past his location and the building the car was parked against.

"You've come this far," Grant said to himself. "There's no point in turning back now."

He placed his hand on a half-opened door and pushed it until it was wide enough to let him slide out. Grant hunched over and ran to the riverbed as fast as his injuries would allow. He scrambled down between the rocks and took the time to catch his breath. His wound was taking more out of him than he had expected. After a short pause, he rose, and wound his way through the rocks until he was next to the three-story building. He crawled up and took a quick look around. Apart from the car, there was no other sign of life. Grant hauled himself up and dashed to the side of the building. He moved down the side of the structure until he was at the back of the building. He spotted a door and tried opening it. The door creaked slightly, making him cringe. With his weapon held tight in his right hand, Grant slipped inside and dropped to one knee, ready to engage any targets.

He was alone.

Grant stood and looked around for any sign that someone had been there recently. When he didn't spot any footprints on the dust-covered floor, Grant pushed on deeper inside the old workshop. The place looked to be frozen in time. He walked past tables still covered in tools and a bandsaw with a piece of lumber lined up, waiting to be cut in half.

Up ahead, someone coughed.

His heart raced. Grant brought up his pistol, crept to one side of the room, and moved in the direction of the sound. Grant hugged an old furnace hidden in the shadows for cover as he edged forward. He froze when he spotted a stocky man with a black beard sitting on a box, wiping down his dissembled pistol. Grant paused to make sure there wasn't anyone else in the room with the mercenary. Certain the man was alone, Grant walked out from behind the furnace and strode straight at the killer.

The man saw Grant coming at him and panicked to put his pistol back together.

"Don't!" warned Grant, aiming his pistol at the man's head. "Drop it."

The mercenary gnashed his teeth and let his disassembled pistol fall to his feet.

Grant kicked the weapon's parts away with his foot. "I recognize you. Your name's Raoul. You're one of the goons who threatened to kill my family before a bear decided to make a late-night snack out of your friend."

Anger flashed in the killer's eyes. "Yeah, that was me."

"Where are the others?"

"What others?"

Grant took a step forward. "Don't play games with me. There were three of you left after the fight with the alien. Now where the hell are they?"

Raoul smiled. "If you kill me, my friends will hear the shot and come running. Besides, you're a soldier. You live by rules and regulations. You can't kill an unarmed man. You've got to take me prisoner." Raoul raised his hands in mock surrender.

"Not today," replied Grant coldly as he pulled the trigger. The sound of the pistol firing inside the room sounded like a cannon going off. Raoul fell straight back, with a hole in his forehead.

Grant had never killed a person in cold blood before. He felt a mix of shame and guilt for what he had done. It was something he knew he would never get used to. Shoving the feeling deep inside, Grant dropped to one knee and searched through the dead man's clothes for anything he could use.

"Hey, Raoul, are you all right?" called out a man's voice.

Grant stepped back from the corpse and melted back into the

shadows. He held his breath as a bald man entered the room with a gun in his hand.

"Damn," said the man, looking down at his dead comrade.

Grant went to raise to his gun when he heard a pistol's hammer being pulled back right next to his head.

"You're good, but not that good, Captain," said a man behind him with a slight German accent. "Toss your pistol on the floor right next to Carter, and then place your hands on your head."

Grant couldn't believe someone had been able to sneak up on him without making a single sound. He lowered his right arm, threw his pistol away, and slowly placed his hands on his head.

"You seem to know who I am," said Grant. "Care to let me know who you are, and who you work for?"

"My name is Max, and who we work far is beyond your comprehension. Now walk," said the man, jamming his pistol barrel hard against Grant's head.

Grant clenched his jaw and walked out of the darkness.

Carter saw Grant and let out an angered cry before smashing him across the face with his pistol.

Pain flashed through Grant's head as he tumbled to the ground.

"You're going to die, you son of a bitch!" screamed Carter, thrusting his pistol against Grant's temple.

"Wait," ordered Max. "We may yet need him."

"He'll kill us if he gets the chance," protested Carter.

"Then let's not give him one." Max looked around the old workshop. "Captain, where are your companions?"

"I honestly don't know," said Grant, rolling over and looking up at his captors. "We were crossing a bridge when a bear attacked us. I was knocked into the river and blacked out. The women could have gotten away, or they could be dead for all I know."

"He's lying," snarled Carter. "They're hidden somewhere nearby."

Blood trickled from a gash on Grant's cheek onto his jacket. "Tear this place apart if you want. But I guarantee you won't find them."

"I hope for your sake, Captain, that they're still alive," said Max. "If not, then you're of no value to me."

"Do what you must. I don't want to die, but I'm telling you the truth. I don't know where they are."

Max tapped his foot on the floor for a few seconds. "Captain, my gut tells me that they are both still alive. Like you, they will come here, and when they do I need you to convince the female alien to give me what I want."

Grant snickered. "You're fooling yourself. She'd rather die than let her technology fall into our hands."

"Then you're going to have to persuade her otherwise," said Max. "Your life depends on it."

"I hope whoever you work for has a good life insurance policy, because she doesn't expect any of us to come out of this alive."

"If this is a suicide mission, then why are you here, Captain?"

"Because it's my job. That's why."

Max tutted. "Your foolish Boy Scout mentality is admirable, but you should know that I never fail to get what I'm after."

Grant looked directly into his opponent's ice-blue eyes and smiled. "Well, as they say, there's always a first time for everything."

Max shook his head. "Carter, tie him up and bring him with us."

A pair of rough hands hauled Grant to his feet. For a brief second, he thought about trying to grab Carter's pistol. However, before he could act, the mercenary shot his fist into Grant's stomach, doubling him over. White light flashed in front of his eyes as he fought to breathe.

"Damn," said Carter, shaking his hand. "He must be wearing some kind of body armor under his clothes. I nearly broke my hand."

"Don't worry about that right now," said Max. "Tie him up, and let's get going."

"Did you hear that?" said Elena. "It sounded like a gunshot."

"It sounded like weapons' fire," agreed Nadia. "Come on; we can't stop now. We're almost there."

"Nadia, perhaps we should take a five-minute break, so I can check your wounds. You're bleeding pretty badly," said Elena, looking at the blood seeping out of the bottom of Nadia's boots.

"I doubt there's anything you can do for me. We have to push on and stop the general from getting away."

Elena nodded and helped her companion continue on the path leading up to the mine's entrance. "Nadia, where exactly did you leave your ship?"

"I found an old shaft and brought my ship to rest in a cavern near the bottom of the mine."

Elena thought of the fifty-meter-wide diameter of the first disc and tried to reconcile what Nadia was saying. "Your craft can't be that big if you were able to fly it down a shaft."

"It's not. It's a very slender, one-person ship, which is designed for speed and nothing else."

"Nadia, have you given any thought about what we're going to do when we catch up with this general?"

"If I can, I'll shoot him with my phase pistol. If that fails, I have a highly explosive charge on my belt that I will set off, hopefully, killing me and the general."

"Wonderful," said Elena. "Are there any plans floating around in your mind in which we all come out of this alive?"

"No. In the grand scheme of things, our deaths are unimportant. Stopping a genocide is all that matters to me right now. I'll deal with my sins in the afterlife."

"I, for one, don't share your pessimism. If that was gunfire, then it could mean that David is still alive. If he is here, I know he won't stop until he has killed your general and gotten us all to safety."

Nadia stopped in her tracks. She bent over, coughing, and then spit out a mouthful of blood. She gasped. "That animal must have hurt me far worse than I thought. I don't think I have long to live. Please, let us hurry."

At the mine's entrance, General Nagan lowered his binoculars and nodded. The government assassin looked to be hobbling along in a considerable amount of pain. He had no idea what had happened to her. As far as Nagan was concerned, the gods were smiling on him and his project, and had shifted the odds considerably in his favor. His handheld detector told him what he already knew—that the girl had flown her ship into the mine, as its plasma fuel signature still lingered in the air. Where it was, was still a mystery. He knew he'd find it given enough time, but he wanted to be away from this backwater planet with his findings before his deep-cover allies in the military lost their nerve and branded him as a renegade and a traitor.

Nagan spied three humans coming up the road to the mine. He flashed his razor-sharp teeth and let out a hiss. He didn't need anyone else trying to interfere in his mission. The general reached for his pistol and silently cursed his luck when he saw the power was almost drained. He had wasted too many shots killing the large animals so he could test his DNA regression chemicals on one of their young. Nagan turned around and walked inside the dimly lit mine. The darkness would be his ally while he dealt with the interlopers and searched for the assassin's ship.

46

"Like a coffee and donut?" asked Tracey Tibeluk as she sat down next to Maclean with a plastic tray covered with Styrofoam cups and assorted donuts.

"Thanks, and I promise not to make any cop jokes about what we're having for breakfast," he replied with a boyish grin, helping himself to a beverage and frosted donut.

"You had better not make any snide remarks since that's all there is for breakfast."

Maclean took a sip of coffee and glanced down at his watch. "You know, I thought the animals would be here by now."

"Perhaps they've bypassed the town completely and will never come our way?"

"I wish that were true. However, they're biological weapons designed with only one purpose in mind, to kill," said Hayes, sliding into the conversation. "I just hope we can hold them off. I only counted three civilians with firearms in the gym."

"We'll be okay, Doc," said Maclean. "All we need to do is keep them from getting too close to the school, and we'll come through this all right."

"Sergeant, Reba's got something on the monitor," said Sam. His voice did little to hide his nervous anticipation.

Maclean, Tibeluk, and Hayes walked to where Reba was sitting.

"What have you got?" Maclean asked.

"This," replied Reba, pointing at the screen. The display showed three terror birds standing on Main Street looking around. The tallest of the three predators lifted its head and sniffed the air. It let out a loud squawk. The three creatures turned and moved as one. Their heads bobbed back and forth as they walked.

"What the hell are those things?" asked Sam.

"It's complicated," said Maclean. "Just think of them as really big, pissed-off turkeys. They can't harm you or Reba if you kill them first."

Sam picked up his rifle, walked to the edge of the roof, and got down on his stomach.

"Everyone who isn't armed, inside, now!" said Maclean to Hayes. The professor nodded and ran to pass the word.

Maclean moved over next to Sam. "Nervous?"

"Yeah, you could say that."

"It's only natural to be scared. Just try to relax and watch your breathing."

"You sound just like my mom."

Maclean chuckled. "She's a smart person."

"Here they come," said Tibeluk, pointing down Main Street.

Sam brought his rifle up to his shoulder and took aim. A second later, he took up the slack on the trigger, held his breath, and fired. The sound of the weapon firing echoed down the deserted street. The lead bird staggered forward for a few paces before falling over on its side. Its two companions, startled by the gunfire, ran for cover behind the nearest building. The dying bird's legs kicked in the air before the animal finished convulsing and died

"Damn good shooting," said Maclean, patting Sam on the back.

"Thanks," he replied, ejecting the spent casing and loading a fresh bullet.

Maclean looked over his shoulder at Reba. "Can you see the other birds?"

"I have them on the screen," she responded. "They've taken cover behind the hardware store."

"If only we had a fully-armed predator drone under our command. We could blast those bastards to kingdom come without breaking out in a sweat."

"How's it going up here?" asked Black, sitting down next to her son.

"Your son's one hell of a shot," said Maclean.

"That's good, because I've got a gymnasium packed with frightened people."

"Here come the other two," announced Reba.

Warily, the two terror birds walked back out onto the road and made their way straight to their companion's dead body. They nudged it with their heads. When it didn't move, they ripped and tore at its flesh with their sharp beaks.

"Drop them," ordered Maclean.

Sam adjusted his body position slightly, took dead aim, and fired. One of the birds fell with a shot to its head. The other bird, oblivious to what had just happened, raised its blood-covered beak to look around when Sam shot it through the neck. The bird let out a wet cry as it fell in a heap next to the two other creatures.

"That's my boy," said Black, nodding at her son.

"Okay, that's three down, and who knows how many to go," said Maclean.

"Do you hear something?" said Tibeluk, staring straight ahead.

"Yeah, it sounds like a car, and it's heading our way," said Black.

A police Suburban came into view. It sped down the street, weaving from side to side, just missing the pile of dead birds

"My God, that's Bill and Sean's vehicle," said Black.

Before the SUV made it halfway to the school, the vehicle veered off the road and smashed into a parked car right outside the police station. The SUV came to a sudden, jarring halt. Steam rose from the engine like a genie escaping its bottle. Even from where they were, Maclean could see the men in the vehicle were in trouble. He spun on his heel and ran for the ladder leading down to the gym.

"Where are you going?" called out Tibeluk.

"Those men need help, said Maclean"

"Wait, I'm coming with you!"

Black placed a hand on her son's shoulder. "Cover them."

"Will do, Mom," responded Sam. He placed his weapon's sight on the wrecked vehicle and slowly moved around, looking for any animals.

In the school's parking lot, Tibeluk raced to open the door to her SUV. She jumped inside and started the vehicle as Maclean leaped in beside her.

"Step on it," said Maclean as he flipped off the safety on his MP7 with his thumb.

The Suburban's tires squealed as Tibeluk floored the accelerator. She spun the steering wheel around in her hands and drove like a bat out of hell straight down Main Street.

As they closed in, they could see the windshield on their compatriots' car was smashed, and blood was streaked across the glass. Tibeluk brought her vehicle to a screeching halt right next to the wrecked Suburban.

"Stay here in case we need to take off quickly," said Maclean. "I'll get your friends." He didn't wait for her reply. Maclean opened the door and jumped out. He ran to the other vehicle driver's side and yanked open the door. A man sat there, holding a hand to his blood-covered face. Maclean stuck his head inside and saw the other officer slumped over in his seat. His neck was torn open, and his uniform was drenched in blood. Maclean knew the man was dead. He unbuckled the driver.

A shot rang out.

Maclean forced himself to ignore the gunfire and scooped up the badly injured man into his arms. He ran back to the waiting Suburban, laid the officer down in passenger seat, and jumped up on the running board. With one hand gripping the open-door frame and the other his MP7, Maclean looked at Tibeluk and said, "Drive."

She nodded and slammed her foot down on the gas pedal as two birds broke from the cover of the trees and ran after the vehicle. Maclean lined up the closest one with his submachine gun and fired. The monster let out a cry before slowing down and giving up the chase. Maclean was positive that he had hit the bird, just not bad enough to kill it.

The second creature tore down the street, intent on pulling Maclean from the car to devour him. The bird snapped its beak and let out a loud cry. It was incredibly fast, but the SUV was faster. A gap between the bird and the police vehicle grew. On the roof of the school, Sam waited until he had a clear shot and fired his Winchester, dropping the predator with one shot.

Tibeluk jammed on the brakes and stopped her vehicle right outside of the doors that led to the school gymnasium. Black and Hayes were waiting there to help.

Maclean jumped down to the ground, slung his weapon, and reached into the SUV to take the wounded man in his arms.

Black let out a horrified gasp when she saw the bloodstained uniform. "That's Bill. Where's Sean?"

Maclean shook his head.

Mrs. Norton, the clinical nurse, ran to take charge of the badly injured man. "Take him inside. I need to check on the extent of this man's injuries."

Everyone ran inside the building before the door was closed and locked.

Maclean walked to an empty classroom, laid him down on a table, and stepped aside as Mrs. Norton got to work. A woman in the hallway let out a stifled cry when she saw the mangled body dripping blood onto the floor. Black ushered the bystanders away from the room, telling Harrison to keep the people in the gym.

"Did he say what happened to them?" Black asked.

"No, but by the look of the wounds he and the other officer sustained, there's no doubt in my mind that they had a run-in with some of the terror birds," said Maclean. "He's lucky to be alive."

"Sheriff, Bill wants to talk to you," said Mrs. Norton.

Black removed her hat and bent down until her ear was right above the officer's lips. Maclean couldn't hear what was being said, but he had the helpless feeling that the man was on his way out. It never got easier for Maclean to watch good men and women lose the fight to live. A few seconds later, Black raised her head. Tears filled her eyes. "Bill's gone."

"I'm sorry," said Maclean, placing a hand on the sheriff's arm.

Tibeluk turned away, hiding her tears.

"Was he able to tell you what happened?" asked Maclean.

"Yes. They stopped to help a couple who had driven off the road, and that's when the birds attacked," said Black. "He said they came out of nowhere. They killed the couple and injured both men before they could get back into their vehicle. Bill and Sean were two of the best men I've ever had the honor to serve with."

"Sheriff, this is only just beginning. We can mourn their loss when this is all behind us. Until then, the people in this school are scared and are looking for a leader, and you're it. I'm a sergeant in the Australian Army. I'll do my job, but you're the person they need right now."

Black took a deep breath and composed herself. "You're right, Sergeant, thanks for trying to save my men. But I think Sam needs you on the roof."

"Right you are, ma'am," replied Maclean.

"You too, Tracey."

"Yes, Sheriff," she replied, wiping the tears from her cheeks.

Maclean climbed the ladder in the back of the gym to the roof and sat down next to Sam and Reba. "Any more nasties on the screen?"

"No, sir," said Reba.

"Jim, was that Bill Scott and Sean McCartney's vehicle?" asked Sam.

"Yes, and before you ask, I'm sorry to say that they're both dead," said Maclean.

Sam's lower lip trembled. "I'd known them both for years. Bill used to take me fishing when my mom wasn't around. It's hard to believe they're gone."

Maclean placed an arm around Sam and pulled him in close. "Son, these things happen. How we deal with death helps define who we are. What I need you and Reba to do is stay sharp and keep an eye out. We can't afford for one of those things to get past us."

Sam stood and gripped his rifle tight in his hands, his expression cold. "I hope they try. I haven't killed enough of the feathered bastards yet."

47

The entrance to the mine grew closer. It soon took on the appearance of a gateway to hell.

Grant walked with his hands tied behind his back. He had the disconcerting feeling as if he were being marched to his execution. Max and Carter walked behind him with their weapons trained his back.

"I'm curious, how did you know to come here?" said Grant over his shoulder.

"We followed the big alien's tracks," explained Max. "After we hightailed it away from the fight at the old man's house, we hid in the woods and watched the creature run by us. We decided to screw you over and borrow your car. We used it to follow the alien. His tracks are hard not to miss."

Grant glanced down, and sure enough, a trail of large footprints headed toward the mine. "Aren't you worried that you're walking into a trap? The big bastard could be waiting in the shadows to kill us all the second he sees us."

"What I'd like you to do is shut your mouth," snapped Max. "No more talking."

Grant's mind was a whirl. He had to escape before it was too late. He just didn't know how he was going to pull it off without getting shot in the back.

At the opening to the mine, Grant stopped. There was a cold, unwelcoming feeling in the air. He turned to face Max. "You know, I've got a really bad feeling about this. Are you sure you still want to go in there?"

"Quit stalling," said Max. "We're not going to turn back now."

"Okay, but it looks pretty dark in there. I hope you were smart enough to bring along some flashlights."

"We're not a pair of idiots, Captain," replied Max.

Grant was pushed from behind into the mine. He had to watch his footing, as the ground slanted downward and there were several large rocks in his path. Grant came to a sliding halt right next to the narrow rail tracks, which had been used decades ago to bring the ore carts in and out of the mine. The ground was covered with shattered lanterns, old, broken tools, and wooden support beams for the roof from the time when the mine was still active.

"Carter, take the lead," ordered Max. "Captain, if you so much as look sideways I won't hesitate to blow your head off."

"I'm not here to tell you how to do your job, but don't you think it would be better to confirm if the women who were with me about thirty minutes ago are still alive?" said Grant. "The only tracks I see on the ground clearly belong to the general."

Max shone his light down the tunnel. There was only a single set of tracks leading deeper into the mine.

Grant could see a flicker of hesitation in Max's eyes.

"Boss, he could be right," said Carter. "Without the other alien to help us, we're going to come out of this empty-handed."

"They could already be here in the mine," said Max.

"The tracks say otherwise," countered Grant, playing for time. He was positive the deeper they went into the mine, the less chances he had to escape.

"Fine, we'll wait here for thirty minutes," said Max. "If they haven't shown up by then, we're pushing on. I'm sure there're things of great technological value we can retrieve from the big alien's body after we've killed him."

"Yeah, if he lets you…which I strongly doubt."

Carter jammed his pistol in Grant's face. "That's enough out of you. Take a seat, shut your mouth, and don't try any heroics."

Grant stepped back against the cool rock wall and slid to the ground. He sat silently watching the two mercenaries as they quietly discussed their next move. The instant he saw he wasn't being watched, Grant searched the ground behind him with his fingers. He was desperate to find something to cut his bonds. If Nadia and Elena were still alive and on their way to the mine, the last thing he wanted was for them to be killed or taken prisoner as well. His fingers touched something thin and smooth with a jagged edge. It felt like a piece of broken glass. Grant wrapped his fingers around the shard and moved it along until it was touching the rope binding his wrists together. With one eye on the killers, Grant began to saw at his bonds. He prayed he would be able to cut himself free before the women showed up, or his time ran out.

48

"Uh, guys, I think I've got something," said Reba.

Maclean, Tibeluk, and Hayes walked over and looked down at the monitor. "What did you see?" asked Maclean.

"In the woods, just to the west of us, I'm certain I saw some of those birds creeping toward the school."

"Use the thermal camera," suggested Hayes.

"I'm not sure where that is," replied Reba, looking confused at all the buttons on the controller.

Maclean placed a hand on Hayes' shoulder. "Why don't you take a seat right next to Reba and help her use your gadget to its fullest."

"Yes, of course," said Hayes, sitting down. He smiled at Reba and pointed at the button to switch the camera from normal to thermal imaging.

"Whoa," remarked Maclean when a large, white blob appeared on the screen. "There's got be a dozen or more of them down there."

"Sam, time to switch locations," said Tibeluk as she picked up her shotgun and ran to the western edge of the roof.

Maclean jogged over and saw that the distance from the edge of the woods to the school was less than thirty meters. He shook his head. If all the birds rushed at once, it would be near impossible to bring them all down before they reached the school.

"Sergeant, they're coming," shouted Hayes.

Maclean looked at his compatriots. "Don't get fancy. One shot, one kill. After you fire on one of the beasts, don't wait to see if you've dropped it. Switch targets and keep firing until they're all dead. Got it?"

"Got it," replied Sam. He licked his dry lips and brought up his rifle to his shoulder.

"Here they come," said Tibeluk, just as the horde of predators burst from the cover of the woods and ran toward the school. She pulled back on the trigger of her shotgun. With a loud boom, the shotgun slug flew straight into the chest of an onrushing terror bird, stopping it cold in its tracks.

Maclean flipped his MP7's selector switch to automatic and fired along the line of charging beasts. Like the Grim Reaper's scythe, the bullets tore through the flesh of the lead animals, killing or badly wounding them.

As fast as he could fire and reload, Sam selected his targets with ruthless efficiency and killed everything he aimed at.

Within seconds, there was a line of dead and dying creatures. None had made it closer than ten meters from the school. The smell of cordite hung in the air.

Maclean lowered his submachine gun, ejected the empty magazine, and inserted a full, forty-round clip.

Some of the birds tried standing but were finished off by Sam and Tibeluk. Silence descended on the horrific field of battle.

"Is that it?" said Tibeluk, lowering her shotgun.

"Doc, Reba, any more signals hidden in the woods?" asked Maclean.

"No, it looks like you killed them all," responded Hayes.

"Thank God for that," said Tibeluk, wiping the sweat from her glistening brow.

"Was that all of them, Jim?" asked Sam.

"I don't think so," Maclean replied. "I wish it were, but we saw dozens of destroyed cages at Sparks' home. I hate to say it, but we've probably only killed a third of what's out there." Maclean stepped back from the edge of the roof and turned around. He was about to take a walk around the entire perimeter of the roof when a shot cut through the air. Maclean spun around and rushed to bring his MP7 up to his shoulder.

One of the birds had been playing dead and waited for the right moment to strike. With a loud cry, it jumped to its feet and sprinted forward. Sam's shot struck the animal through its right shoulder. The beast didn't even flinch. Driven on by gut instinct and an insatiable hunger, it kept charging to where it could smell its prey.

Maclean rushed to get a shot off, but the animal ran headfirst into a window and smashed it with its head. In the blink of an eye, it was gone. "Stay here," said Maclean to his two companions. He had to get below before the creature found a way into the gymnasium and began to feast. With his heart pounding in his ears, Maclean placed his hands and feet on the outside of the ladder and slid all the way to the bottom. He ran through the gym, dodging people who tried to stop him to find out what was going on. Maclean kicked open a set of doors near where he had last seen the predator and rushed out into the hallway with his MP7 ready to fire.

The corridor was empty.

"What the hell's going on?" asked Black, running to catch up with him.

Maclean brought a finger up to his lips and pointed down the hallway.

Black removed her pistol from its holster.

With Maclean leading, they edged down the corridor. As they moved past the shattered door, they saw a trail of blood on the floor. A second later, a horrified scream filled the air. Maclean took off running. He turned the corner and saw a man on the floor with his arm clenched tightly in the beak of a terror bird, being thrown around as if he were a child's toy.

Black brought up her pistol but hesitated to fire. The terrified man held in the bird's beak blocked her from getting off a clear shot.

With a sickening, wet snap, the bird bit right through the man's arm. The man dropped to the ground, writhing in agony. Blood sprayed like a fountain all over the floor.

Maclean held his MP7 straight out like a pistol and let go with a sustained burst of fire. The rounds struck the bird in the stomach. Red patches of blood stained the animal's feathers. It stepped back, dropped the severed arm from its bloody maw, and turned to face its attackers. The creature lifted a leg to move but died a split second later when Sheriff Black fired her pistol, hitting it squarely between the eyes.

Maclean ran to the injured man's side and pulled him back from the bird. He looked back at Black and said, "Fetch Mrs. Norton before he bleeds out."

Black nodded and ran off.

Maclean yanked off the injured man's belt and wrapped it around his arm just below the bloody stump. He looked into the man's green eyes. "What's your name?"

"Doug, my name is Doug," he replied through gritted teeth. The injured man's face was already pale. He was minutes away from going into shock.

"Okay, Doug, my name's Jim, and I'm going to count to three and then pull this belt tight. It's going to hurt like hell, but it's going to save your life. Ready?"

Doug nodded.

"Three," said Maclean, yanking hard on the expedient tourniquet.

Doug let out a moan before blacking out.

"Pick him up and follow me," ordered Mrs. Norton as she gave the wound a quick check.

Maclean gathered Doug in his arms and followed Mrs. Norton back to the classroom she had set up as a temporary triage station. Several smaller children standing in the hallway screamed out in fright when they saw Doug's bloody stump hanging down by his side.

"Parents, round up your children, and please keep them in the gym from now on," said Black to the stunned people.

A red-haired woman bolted from the crowd. "Doug! Please God, please don't let him die."

Black grabbed hold of the frantic woman and held her. "It's okay, Kerry. He's lost an arm, but Doug's going to be all right."

Maclean gently placed the man's body on two tables that had been pushed together.

"Dear Lord, save my husband," cried Kerry. Tears ran like a river down her slender face.

"Kerry, what was Doug doing outside of the gym?" asked Black.

"He went in the hallway to have a smoke."

"That's it. No one leaves the gym from now on." Black let go of Kerry and let her walk to her husband's side before stepping out into the hallway.

Black steered the onlookers back inside the gymnasium. "Everyone, inside. No one is to come in or out from now on. Please. We're going to keep the doors closed for your safety."

Maclean looked at the blood on his hands and clothes. He turned to face Black. "I'm going to wash up. Do you happen to know if there are any former army engineers with us?"

Black nodded. "I think so. Let me find him."

A couple of minutes had passed before Maclean emerged from the bathroom looking somewhat better. Black was standing with an older African-American man with a sizable belly that hung over his belt.

"Sergeant," she said, indicating to the gentleman, "this is Tony. Tony, my friend here would like to talk with you."

"Sir, my name is Sergeant James Maclean. Were you by chance a combat engineer in the army?"

Tony shook his head. "No, sorry, I was a construction engineer."

"Close enough. One of those creatures got in and attacked a

man. Now we have to be prepared for the very real possibility that more of those animals will find their way in here. So, here's what I want you to do. Draft whoever you need and build me a redoubt in the far corner of the gym. Anything you don't use, I want to be piled up against the doors to help slow them down."

Tony glanced around. "I guess I could use the bleachers and some of the gymnastics equipment."

"That's what I wanted to hear."

"What are you going to do?" asked Black.

"I'm going to head back up to the roof and help your son and Tracey keep these creatures from getting too close to the school."

"James, what if you can't? Then what?"

"Then we'll join you down here and make our stand from behind the redoubt. Let's just hope it doesn't come to that."

"Take care of my son for me."

Maclean grinned darkly. "He's probably taking care of me."

49

Sweat trickled down Grant's face and into his eyes. He tried blowing the sweat away, but it didn't help. Grant wanted to shake his head, but that would have drawn unwanted attention from his captors. He resigned himself to the discomfort and kept on sawing away at the rope behind his back.

"How much time's left?" Carter asked his boss.

Max checked his watch. "Five minutes."

"Want me to walk back to the entrance and see if I can spot the women?"

"Good idea."

Max tapped Grant with the toe of his boot. "Don't even think about trying to escape while he's gone."

"Never crossed my mind," he replied without looking up. With only one mercenary left to guard him, his chance to escape would never be better. Grant furiously dug at the rope. Within seconds, he could feel the bonds in the rope breaking. The next thing he knew, his hands were free. Behind his back, he rubbed his aching wrists, trying to get the circulation flowing again. Grant watched Max pace and tried to determine his best chance to strike.

A light shone down the tunnel.

Grant silently cursed his luck. Carter was coming back.

"Well, did you see them?" Max asked Carter as he came into view.

Carter shook his head. He seemed to be having a hard time standing on his feet.

"You okay?" asked Max.

"Yeah, I wasn't looking at what I was doing and bumped my head on a low-hanging support beam," replied Carter.

The hair on the back of Grant's neck went up. Something about the way Carter was acting didn't seem right. He readied himself to fight or run, if he had to.

"Let me take a look at your head," said Max.

Grant saw he wasn't being watched and got up on one knee. The familiar mix of fear and adrenaline raced through his system.

Without warning, Carter lashed out and hit Max in the chest, sending him flying onto his back. Max hit the rocky ground and let out a muffled moan. His pistol landed farther down the dark tunnel.

Grant jumped to his feet and shot his right fist as hard as he could against Carter's head. Pain shot through Grant's hand when his opponent's head didn't budge a millimeter. It was like punching a granite statue.

Carter turned his head and smiled coldly before hitting Grant across the face with the back of his hand.

Stars flashed before Grant's eyes. His knees buckled. Before he could stop himself, Grant dropped back against the wall and slid to the ground. He took in a deep breath and shook his head to clear the fog. When Grant looked up, his heart skipped a beat. Carter was gone. General Nagan stood there, looking from man to man, apparently trying to decide whom to kill first.

Max moaned as he rolled over and crawled along the old train tracks, trying to find his pistol.

Nagan hissed and drew his pistol. He took a couple of steps toward his quarry and brought up his weapon to finish him off.

A sturdy-looking piece of wood lying on the ground near Grant's feet was the only practicable weapon he could see. He grabbed it, stood up, and hauled back on the wood like a baseball player.

"No! Please no!" begged Max as Nagan towered above him.

With all the strength he could muster, Grant sent the wood flying onto the side of the general's head. With a loud snap, the wood broke in two on contact with the alien's thick skull. Nagan let out a cry and reached up for his face. By pure luck, Grant had hit the general on his injured side. Before Nagan could recover, Grant brought what was left of his bat down onto the general's hand, knocking the phase pistol free.

Grant and Max saw the pistol fall and rushed to get it. Grant, however, was faster on his feet and scooped up the weapon. He moved back away from Nagan and Max. "Both of you, up against the wall."

"Don't be a fool," said Max. "You have his gun. We can make him take us to the other alien's ship. Think about it; the rewards you would receive would be beyond measure. A man like you would do well in my organization."

"I already have a job," replied Grant.

Nagan stood there, holding a hand to his face. Blood seeped through his gloved fingers and down his body armor.

A deep growl echoed down the tunnel.

Grant's guts dropped as a saber-toothed tiger walked out of the dark and strode toward the men, clearly looking for its next meal. It was as long as a modern-day Bengal Tiger, but had two razor-sharp teeth jutting down from its upper jaw.

"For God's sake, kill it," said Max.

Grant brought up his arm and aimed the phase pistol at the creature. He lined it up with the center of the animal's body and pulled back on the trigger.

Nothing happened.

Grant yanked back on the trigger three more times before yelling at the big cat and hurling the pistol at the animal's head.

The weapon went flying harmlessly over the top of the tiger's head. It stopped for a second and looked at its prey before opening its mouth wide and letting out a thunderous roar.

The sight of dozens of sharp teeth was all it took. All three men turned and ran for their lives down the tunnel. Fear drove them on. They had gone less than fifteen meters when the tiger struck. It dove at Nagan's back, scratching and clawing at his body armor, trying to grab hold of its victim and bring him down.

In the dim light of the tunnel, Grant saw Max struggling to keep up. All of a sudden, Grant felt the ground give way under his feet. He realized too late that he wasn't standing on the rocky floor, but instead on an old tarp that had been spread over a hole. He struggled to grab something—anything—which would stop his fall. It was no good. Grant was hit by Max as he fell into the hole. The two men fell into the dark. Above them, Nagan and the tiger tumbled into the opening and joined them.

Grant hit a pool of cold water and sank until his feet touched the bottom. He pushed up with his feet, broke the surface, and filled his lungs with air. The space was nearly pitch-black. Grant felt around with his hands and found that he was in a tunnel.

"Did anyone else fall in here with me?" he asked.

No one answered his call.

Grant slid along the wall and discovered an old ladder built into the wall almost directly under the hole he had fallen though. He scrambled up, grabbed hold of a wooden beam, and hauled himself out of the water. He crawled through the hole and sat down on the floor of the tunnel.

Light…he needed light. On all fours, Grant scoured the floor for something he could use as a torch. His fingers bumped into something hard. He picked it up and held it close to his face. In the dim light filtering down from above, Grant saw that it was an old miner's hat. The kerosene lamp on the front of the helmet looked to be in good shape. Grant unscrewed the reservoir and took a whiff. He smiled when he smelled kerosene. Now, all he had to do was find a way of relighting the lamp. Grant placed the lamp down and continued his search. He soon found some old canvas and the end of a shattered pickaxe. Grant poured a few drops of kerosene onto the canvas, picked up the pickaxe, and began chipping away at the metal with a sharp rock. It didn't take long for sparks to fly. Grant bent down and kept striking the metal in his hand until several sparks landed on the canvas and caught light. He blew gently on the flames until the cloth was fully alight, and then moved the burning canvas over to the lamp and lit the old wick. Right away, light spread through the tunnel. It wasn't as good as a flashlight, but it was better than nothing. Grant placed the old helmet on his head and looked around. He was standing in a tunnel that disappeared into darkness farther in. He looked up and saw the hole he had fallen through and was amazed to see how far he had fallen. Grant looked up and down the tunnel, but there was no sight of Max, the general, or the tiger.

He knew he had to stop Nagan from getting away. Nothing else mattered. Grant walked down the tunnel and into the never-ending darkness.

50

"What do you think?" Elena asked Nadia as she looked at the myriad of foot and paw prints leading into the mine.

"At some point today, three men, General Nagan, and a large animal of some kind went in there," replied Nadia. She was having a hard time staying on her feet.

"Those look like giant cat prints to me. As much as I don't want to, I guess we've got to go in there if we want to accomplish your mission."

Nadia nodded, removed a portable light from her belt, and handed it to Elena.

They walked inside the tunnel. It didn't take them long to find Carter's dead body. From the way he lay on the floor, it was easy to see that his neck had been snapped in half. Elena turned her head away when she noticed that the cat had taken a large bite out of the dead man's body before carrying on down the tunnel.

"Do you still have your pistol?" asked Elena.

Nadia patted the weapon on her belt.

"Okay, then, let's go."

They carefully skirted the massive hole in the floor and kept moving down the tunnel. When they came to the end, they found their plan to carry on into the depths of the mine had hit a dead end. Without power, there was no way to work the rusting elevator the miners had once used to take them to and from the bottom of the mine.

Elena shone her light down the elevator shaft. The wood-and-metal frame of the elevator shaft looked to be intact. Elena looked back at Nadia. She doubted the alien could make the climb to the bottom without falling. Elena wasn't certain she could make it, either.

"Let me take a seat for a minute," said Nadia. Her voice was growing weak.

Elena helped her sit down on an overturned ore cart. "Are you still reading your ship?"

Nadia held out her scanner and nodded. "It's in a cavern five floors below us."

"I still don't know how you flew it in here," said Elena, looking at the size of the elevator shaft.

"I didn't come in this way. There's an old airshaft on the other side of the mountain that I used."

"I'm not an aeronautical expert, but an airshaft surely isn't wide enough to allow a ship to fly down it."

"My ship is an experimental one. If need be, I can adjust its mass for a limited time. That is how I was able to make my way through the shaft and down into the mine."

"I'll take your word for it." Elena placed a hand on Nadia's arm. "Look, I've got to be honest here. In your condition, I'm not sure you're going to be able to climb all the way down the elevator shaft to the bottom."

Nadia opened a pouch and retrieved a slender silver tube. "I was saving this for the end."

"What are you doing?"

"I'm too badly hurt to carry on without dulling the pain. This injection contains a powerful narcotic and is only meant to be used as a last resort. Unfortunately, as it helps me deal with the pain, it also saps what little strength I have left from my body." Nadia placed the tube against her neck and pressed a button on its side, injecting the medicine into her bloodstream. She closed her eyes and sat silently for close to a minute before opening her eyes and standing. "Come, Elena, I don't have much time left. Let's climb down to my ship and rig it for detonation."

Elena hesitated. "Did you say detonation?"

"Yes. It's the only way to ensure it doesn't fall into the wrong hands."

"By that, I take it you mean General Nagan and us?"

"That is correct."

"At least you're still being straightforward with me. Since you seem to be in better spirits, and you're heavier than me, you can climb down first. I'll follow your lead."

Nadia got to her feet, walked straight to the elevator shaft, and placed her foot on one of the aged wooden beams. When she was sure it would take her weight, Nadia began to climb down into the bowels of the mine.

Elena waited until Nadia was on her way before making the sign of the cross and climbing down the shaft. She had never liked heights. Now, making her way down a mine shaft, with only Nadia's bobbing light below, Elena's mind saw things in the shadows that made her skin crawl. A broken piece of wood became a snake waiting to strike. A cobweb held a hairy spider bigger than her fist. Elena tried to block the discomforting images from her mind and hurried to catch up with Nadia. She couldn't wait to feel the hard ground under her feet.

51

The sound of three gunshots echoing in the distance caused Maclean to sit straight up. He jumped to his feet and ran to join Sam and Tibeluk, who were using the drone to look to the north. "Did you see anything?" he asked the youth.

"No. But I think the shots came from the trailer park. I didn't see Mr. Johnson with the rest of the people downstairs. I think he decided to stay where he was and defend his home."

"Is he a good shot?"

"When he's sober, he's not too bad," said Tibeluk. "Hopefully, he hasn't had a drop in a day or so."

Another shot rang out.

"Well, whatever's happening, he's not giving up without a fight." Maclean waved at Hayes. "Have Reba fly the drone over the trailer park."

"Will do," replied Hayes.

"Stay here and keep a lookout while I see what's happening," said Maclean to Sam.

Sam nodded, brought up a pair of binoculars, and surveyed the woods.

Maclean and Tibeluk looked over Hayes's shoulder. "Anything?"

"Regrettably, yes," said Hayes. He turned the screen so Maclean could get a better view.

A mobile home was being swarmed by at least a dozen birds, all smashing their heads against the flimsy walls and doors of the trailer, trying to break in. The front door buckled, and a bird stuck its head inside, only to fall backward with a hole in the side of its skull. It didn't matter. Driven by their insatiable desire to feed, the rest of the birds saw the opening and charged inside the trailer.

"Reba, why don't you keep Sam company for a few minutes while we have a quick chat with Professor Hayes," said Tibeluk.

The young girl knew she was being sent away to avoid seeing what was happening. She handed the controller to Hayes, stood, and ran to be with her boyfriend.

Thankfully, Johnson's death was hidden from sight inside his home.

"The bloody fool should have come to the school with the others. He'd still be alive," said Maclean.

"Some people will never leave their homes, no matter the threat facing them," said Tibeluk. "If they're going to die, they'd rather do it in their home."

"Jim, there are at least two dozen birds in that group," pointed out Hayes. "I know this is going to sound gruesome, but one man isn't going to satisfy their hunger. We've got minutes before they come our way."

"I guess we had best get ready for them, then." Maclean stood and looked over at Reba and Sam. They were holding hands and laughing at something. He envied them. They were able to find a moment of tenderness in a world that had been turned upside down.

"Sergeant, there's something you should see," said Hayes as he got up to his feet. His voice was somber.

"What is it?"

"They've split apart. One group has peeled off and is making its way through the woods to the west side of the school."

"Those bastards sure do learn fast," said Tibeluk.

"They want to divide our firepower," said Maclean. "So, they're going to come at us from two directions."

"What are we going to do?"

"I know you've never held a weapon before, but there's always a first time," said Maclean, handing him his pistol and spare magazines. "I've removed the safety. All you have to do is point and gently pull back the trigger. Aim for the bird's chest, and you can't miss."

Hayes' face had blanched. He struggled to speak, but his mouth was dry with fear.

Maclean patted the professor on the shoulder. "I'm going to take the northern wall with Sam, while you and Tracey defend the western wall. Listen to her, and you'll do okay."

"What about the people with guns in the gym?" asked Hayes.

"They have to stay where they are in case one of those bastards manages to sneak in without us seeing it. Someone has to protect the children."

Hayes placed the UAV controls down, slid the spare pistol magazines in his pockets, and walked beside Tibeluk to the edge of the roof.

"Sam, we've got company coming," said Maclean. "Reba, I want you to keep the drone high in the sky, and if the birds try anything fancy, call out and let us know what they're doing."

Reba nodded and kissed her boyfriend on the cheek before jogging back to pick up the controller.

"How many this time, Jim?" asked Sam.

"Probably thirty birds, split between the northern and western walls."

"Do you think we can stop them all before they get to the school?"

Maclean nodded. "The way you shoot? Why not?"

"Sir, we've got another problem," cried out Reba.

"What is it?" asked Maclean.

"I've got another group of animals coming at us from the south."

Maclean swore. "Call down below and get Sheriff Black to join Sam on the roof before it's too late."

A loud blast from Tibeluk's shotgun heralded the beginning of the fight. Maclean patted Sam on the shoulder, spun about, and sprinted for the southern wall. He came to a sliding halt and brought up his MP7 just as a group of terror birds let out a bone-chilling cry and rushed the school. Maclean placed his sights on the bird on the far left of the group and pulled the trigger. He never released the trigger as he moved down the line, trying to stop the charge in its tracks.

Behind him, he could hear his compatriots firing and reloading as fast as they could. The din of battle filled his ears. Although six of the birds had fallen, the rest had split apart to make it harder for him to hit them. Maclean cursed his cunning opponents, ejected his empty magazine, and rushed to place a full one in the housing.

The birds were less than twenty meters from the school and closing fast. Maclean fired off a couple of short bursts and dropped two more. But it was too late, two surviving creatures dove at the glass windows of a classroom, smashing them. His fight on the roof was over. Maclean had to get below to help keep the birds from reaching the people in the gym. He ran to Reba's side and took a quick look at the fight on the screen. The battle had mostly gone their way, dozens of bodies were strewn across the ground. But one bird, followed by another, made it to the edge of the school and began to force their way inside.

Maclean brought two fingers up to his mouth and let out a loud whistle. "Everyone down the ladder. We've got people to protect down below."

Maclean placed his hands and feet on the outside of the ladder and slid down to the gymnasium floor. He moved aside to let his comrades come down and nodded when he saw the redoubt Tony had built. The collapsible bleachers were stacked flush in a corner of the room, making it hard for the birds to climb. Almost all the people were hiding behind the fortification. On top stood three armed men and Officer Harrison. Chairs were strewn across the hardwood floor to impede the birds' movement.

"Okay, they've gotten inside the school again," called out Maclean. "They'll be coming for us."

"Sergeant," said Tony. "I had the men pile up all the spare equipment we could find in front of the gym doors. I think that should hold them for a while."

To Maclean, it looked like anything not nailed down had been thrust against the doors.

"Well done. Let's hope it holds."

"Where do you want us?" asked Black.

"On the top of the redoubt with the other armed men."

"Hey, I can still control the drone from in here," said Reba, holding the controller in her hands.

"Climb to the top of the redoubt and then bring the UAV around, so it can see the hallways leading to the gym," Maclean suggested.

Reba scooted off and took a seat on the top of the fortification.

Hayes handed back Maclean's pistol. His hands were shaking. He avoided eye contact with Maclean. "I'll help Reba, if that's all right with you."

"Yeah, you do that, Doc."

The far doors rattled. A hushed silence fell on the room.

They were here.

52

Grant brought a hand up to block the light coming from his helmet and froze. He was positive he had heard someone or something moving around just beyond the bend in the tunnel. He held his breath and listened. Sure enough, Grant could hear someone coming his way. He glanced at the ground and tried to find a weapon. The only thing of use he could find was a broken piece of wood. Still, he reasoned it was better than nothing. Grant brought the wood up behind his head and tensed. Each second that passed, the sound grew louder. He saw a light creep along the floor of the tunnel, getting brighter as it got closer. Grant leaped around the corner and prepared to strike.

"David, no!" cried out Elena, instinctively bringing up her hands to protect her face.

Grant stopped in mid-air and dropped his makeshift bat. "Jesus, Elena, I nearly bashed your head in. Where the hell did you come from?"

"Thank God you didn't. We climbed down from above."

"Where is the general?" asked Nadia.

"I have no idea," replied Grant. "We got separated when a saber-toothed tiger attacked us. I fell into a hole and ended up in a pool of water. I've been wandering around ever since. Some of the tunnels in here are dead ends, and others are blocked due to cave-ins."

"We had to stop climbing down the elevator shaft when we got to this floor. The way below is inaccessible. It looks like when they abandoned the mine, the owners dumped a lot of the old ore carts down the shaft."

"Or a bunch of bored kids did over the years."

"Enough talking," said Nadia, scanning the tunnel with her handheld device. "This tunnel bends down and eventually joins with the cavern where I left my ship."

"Nadia, what are we going to do when we reach your ship?" asked Grant.

"If I don't need your help, I'll send you on your way and set my ship for detonation."

"Aren't you going to try and make it home?"

"No. I'm dying. I'll never survive the trip. My mission ends here."

"You look fine to me."

"I'm not." Nadia lowered her light and started to walk down the blackened tunnel.

Elena touched Grant's arm. "She's drugged up. Nadia was badly injured when the bear attacked us. If we removed her body armor, I bet we'd see several deep gashes in her lower body. She's bleeding out, David."

Grant leaned his head over and whispered, "Let's just hope that she gives us enough time to make our escape. I'd rather not be entombed under thousands of tons of rock."

They walked along in silence until they came to the bend in the tunnel that led down into the cavern. A green glow emitted from the cave.

Grant tapped Nadia on the arm. "What's giving off the light?"

"That's coming from my engines. Nagan must have found my ship and is warming up the jump drive."

"How long until he can leave?"

"Five, maybe ten minutes. It depends on when he started the engines."

"Okay, now what?"

Nadia held up a slender rectangular device and pressed a series of buttons on it. An enraged cry burst from the cavern.

"I've just locked him out of my ship's main computer drive."

"Will he be able to break your code?"

"Knowing Nagan, yes. But it has at least bought us some time to stop him. Try sneaking around from the right, while I go around from the left."

"Nadia, you're the only one of us who has a gun. Make sure you don't miss."

"Give this to Elena," she said, giving Grant her light. "I won't need this anymore."

Grant watched Nadia move over to the shadows before disappearing down into the cave. He turned and looked into Elena's eyes. "Go back; there's nothing you can do here. I want you to make a run for the surface. Nadia and I can handle this."

"David, I can help. I know I can."

"You can help me by getting the hell out of here and living another day."

Elena hesitated, unsure what to say. She nodded, reached into a pocket, and pulled out her Taser, which she handed to Grant. "In case you need it."

He took the device and smiled. "Get going. I'll see you shortly."

Elena leaned forward and kissed Grant on the cheek. "For luck." With that, she picked up the light and began to run back down the tunnel.

Grant placed his helmet on the ground and slid down the tunnel on his backside. He came out in the cave right next to a tall rock, which he dove behind for cover. Grant took a quick look at Nadia's craft and was amazed. The ship was no longer than a pickup truck, but was slender and looked like a long icicle. In places, he could see the far wall through the ship. Nagan stood next to the craft with his back to Grant. The general seemed to be focused on affixing something on the side of Nadia's ship.

"Captain Grant, how nice of you to join me," said Nagan, turning to look in his direction. "Please don't pretend you didn't hear me. I can read your mind, remember?"

Grant swore as he stood up and came out from behind the rock, waving. "How long have you known I was here?"

"Only a few seconds. My telepathic ability with your species is limited to about thirty meters."

Grant walked slowly toward Nagan. "I take it you're trying to hotwire Nadia's ship, so you can jet off back home and tell your friends that your illegal mission was a success."

"That's correct. But that traitorous whore has locked me out of all her computer systems. Not to worry, my more-advanced computer will break her code, and I'll be out of here shortly."

Grant saw a black, triangular device attached to the side of the ship. Since it didn't match anything else on Nadia's craft, he surmised that was the general's code-cracking computer.

Nagan brought up his arm and pointed at Grant. "That's close enough. Now drop the stick you have hidden behind your back."

Grant stopped and tossed his weapon aside.

"I have to say that you have truly amazed me with your tenacity and your willingness to risk your life for others," said Nagan. "I honestly hadn't expected that from your species."

Grant shrugged. "I guess on both worlds you can't judge a book by its cover."

"Evidently not. Now where is that government agent hiding? I can read your mind but not hers."

A flash of orange light blinded Grant for a second as Nadia opened fire. The shot missed Nagan's head by millimeters and hit the wall, blasting a hole in the rock. Nagan ducked down and took cover behind Nadia's ship, turning his back to Grant.

Grant scooped up his stick and charged toward the alien. At the last possible moment, Nagan spun around, drew a knife from his belt, and prepared to slash Grant with it. With a guttural cry, Grant thrust the stick into Nagan's outstretched arm. The weapon penetrated a weak spot in the general's armor and came out the other side.

Nagan screamed in pain and smashed his left arm across Grant's chest, sending him flying back onto the rocky ground. He moaned in pain as he tried to take a breath. This time, Grant was sure he had broken a couple of ribs.

"Don't move, General," warned Nadia, as she slid out of the shadows. Her phase pistol was aimed at Nagan's head.

He stood, smiling at Nadia. "You may be brave, but you're as green as they come."

Nadia stopped moving and looked around. Fear gripped her. What had she missed? All of a sudden, a bright blue light from a sensor hidden among the rocks at the nose of the ship lit up. Before Nadia could move, a silver dart shot from the device, penetrating her armor.

Grant watched helplessly as Nadia reached for the dart protruding from her chest. She staggered forward a couple of paces before falling to the ground.

"Now it's your turn to die," said Nagan, striding over to pick up Grant. He grabbed the soldier by the collar of his jacket and hauled him to his feet. Nagan bared his teeth. "Goodbye, Captain."

Grant yanked the Taser from his pocket, switched it on, and jammed it into Nagan's mouth. In the blink of an eye, 1200 volts shot through Nagan's head. The general howled in pain, let go of Grant, and cradled his head with his hands. Grant saw his one opportunity to kill the alien and took it. He pulled the stick from Nagan's arm and thrust it into his left eye socket and twisted it. The general's body shook for a couple of seconds before falling backward to the ground.

Grant's heart was racing. He spotted Nagan's knife and picked it up. He placed the knife against the general's throat and was about to push it home when he realized the alien was no longer breathing. He sat back on his rear and shook his head. Grant was physically and emotionally drained. It hurt just to breathe. He looked around the cavern and saw Nadia struggling to sit upright. He got to his feet and stumbled to her side.

"Take it easy," said Grant, placing an arm around her shoulders.

"The general?"

"Dead."

Blood trickled from the corner of Nadia's mouth. "Thank you. When we first met, I doubted that you and your primitive comrades would be of any value to me. I guess I was wrong."

"It's not the first time someone judged me wrong. Now lie down, and I'll see what I can do for you."

"Dave, there is nothing you can do. I've only got a minute or two left. You have to go now and try to save yourself."

Grant glanced at the glow coming from the spaceship's engines. "How long do I have?"

"The ship will sense something is wrong when no one climbs into the cockpit and activates its jump engine. You have at best twenty minutes to get as far away from the mine as you can."

Grant lay Nadia down on the ground. "I'll never forget you."

She looked up at him through glassy eyes. "Dave, I did what I had to because it was my job. Your planet is one of several my species has taken a very keen interest in. The next person like me you come across may not be so friendly. Go now, while you can."

Grant looked for the way out and started to run. The pain in his side was far worse than before. Each step was followed by a white-hot shooting pain in his ribs. Grant clenched his teeth until his jaw hurt. Pain be damned; he had to get away. Grant came to the elevator shaft and began to climb. He was in a race against the clock, and his life hung in the balance.

53

The banging and clawing on the other side of the gymnasium doors was becoming frantic. Behind the makeshift redoubt, families huddled together and prayed that the doors would hold.

Maclean, sitting atop of the fortification, brought up his MP7 to his shoulder and let off a burst at the door. He heard squawking and clawed feet shuffling about. The attack stopped for a few seconds before fresh animals took over the assault.

"Sir, I've got them on my screen," yelled out Reba, trying to be heard over the racket.

Maclean looked over and counted seven predators still on their feet. Quite unexpectedly, the birds stopped what they were doing and turned their heads to look down the hallway. One by one, they ran away from the battered doors and disappeared from view.

"Bring the drone up over the top of school," suggested Hayes. "Perhaps something happened to draw them outside."

Maclean heard a mother soothing a terrified child in her arms, while another knelt, hand-in-hand with her four children and prayed for someone to come to their aid. When they finished, Maclean added a silent amen.

"Oh crap!" blurted out Hayes when the drone came to a stop and hovered over the school.

"What's wrong?" Maclean asked.

"That," he said, pointing at the screen.

Maclean's eyes widened when he saw another batch of terror birds come out of the woods to join the surviving creatures. One bird stood out among the others. It was at least a meter taller than the rest and had a frill of feathers around its head.

"Well, well, well," muttered Maclean. "Looks like the alpha male has arrived."

"Professor, it looks like they're talking to one another," said Reba. "Birds can't do that, can they?"

"Normally, no, but we know so little about these hybrid animals," replied Hayes.

"With the addition of the extra birds, I'd say there are almost twenty of them out there now," said Maclean.

"They're on the move again," said Reba.

"Where are they heading?"

"Looks like the back of the gymnasium."

Maclean looked over at the far side of the gym at the long, gray curtains. "Sheriff Black, what's behind those curtains?"

"That's the school's stage," she replied.

"Can you get to the stage from the outside?"

"Yes."

Maclean broke out in a cold sweat. He should have known they'd swing around the building. It was too late to do anything about barricading the stage doors now. There was a loud crash as the outside door was smashed open. The sound of birds crying out as their feet scrambled on the stage's polished wooden floor filled the air.

"Everyone down behind the redoubt!" ordered Maclean.

Reba, Hayes, and a couple of others ducked down, leaving Maclean, Black, Sam, Tibeluk, and three civilians standing on a slender parapet to repel the attack.

The curtains parted and four terror birds charged out, tumbling off the edge of the stage and onto the gym floor. The men with the rifles opened up.

Like a tidal wave of feathers, claws, and beaks, the rest of the birds tumbled down onto the floor, jumped back to their feet, and ran toward the redoubt.

The noise inside the gym was deafening. The defenders fired as quickly as they could to bring down the creatures before they could reach the fort. The birds dodged around the debris on the floor, shrieking and crying as they closed in. Maclean didn't bother to aim. He pointed his MP7 at the swarm and pulled back on the trigger. The birds in the lead took the brunt of the weapons' fire. Their bloodied bodies fell to the floor at the bottom of the redoubt. The rest of the horde slammed their bodies against the makeshift fortification, trying to find a way inside. Bird after bird died trying to claw its way up the side of the redoubt. Black and Sam kept up a hot fire, with Tibeluk calmly firing her shotgun at anything that moved.

One of the men's rifles jammed. As he struggled to eject the casing, one of the birds leaped up and clamped its beak around the man's right arm and pulled him down to the floor. Before anyone could swing their weapons over to fire, the starving bird thrust its beak into the man's exposed stomach and ripped him open. Blood gushed from the wound.

"Say goodbye, you son of a bitch," said Black as she shot the bird in the head, killing it.

The surviving birds snapped their beaks and squawked in anger and frustration. They clawed at the bleachers and smashed their beaks against the wooden fort. All of a sudden, the alpha male let out a cry, leaped up onto the top of the redoubt, and smashed Tibeluk with its head, sending her tumbling down onto the gym floor.

"No!" hollered Maclean. He jumped over the side of the redoubt and landed next to Tibeluk. He drew his pistol with his left hand, and with both hands held out, he opened fire on any bird which looked his way.

Sam saw the alpha bird about to jump down among the families. He brought his rifle over, took less than a second to aim, and fired. The bird, struck on the side of the head, let out a cry. It wobbled on its unsteady feet before falling back onto another bird trying to climb the redoubt.

Maclean switched targets as fast as he could. His submachine gun's action stayed back. He was out of rounds. Maclean dropped the weapon and switched his pistol from his left to his right hand and kept on firing.

The last couple of birds, sensing the fight was over, began to step back from the carpet of dead and dying animals.

"Don't let them escape," yelled Maclean, switching magazines on his pistol.

It wasn't an order he needed to give. With their blood up, Sam and his mother repeatedly fired until the last two birds lay motionless on the floor.

"Are you okay?" Maclean asked Tibeluk.

She looked up at him and nodded. "I am now."

The scene in the gymnasium was nauseating. Blood, bone, and tissue was everywhere.

Black and Sam climbed down from the redoubt and moved from bird to bird, firing a shot into each skull to make sure they were all dead.

"My God, we made it," said Hayes.

Maclean looked back and stared at his colleague. The man looked as if he had aged a decade in the past couple of days. His eyes were bloodshot, and his face was pale.

"Doc, can you please have Reba keep watch over the school until we know this is really over?" said Maclean.

"Yes, of course." Hayes waved the young girl to his side.

Maclean glanced over at Black, who was busy soothing and calming the terrified civilians.

"Now what?" asked Tibeluk.

"First, we fix the stage door so nothing else can get inside. Once that's done, we'll wait here until we know it's safe to go outside," replied Maclean. He placed an arm around Tracey's shoulders and gave her a hug. Maclean took in a deep breath to slow his racing heart. For the first time in hours, he wondered how his friends were doing, and if they were still alive.

54

Grant could see light coming down from above. He scrambled up the elevator shaft as fast as his exhausted muscles could move. His clothes were drenched with sweat, while the inside of his mouth felt like sandpaper. Grant had no idea how much time it had taken him to climb this far, all he knew was that he couldn't afford to slow down. He pushed on until his hands reached the rocky floor at the top of the shaft. With a pained grunt, Grant pulled himself up onto the floor. He got up on his knees, wiped the sweat away from his face, and stood. Grant peered down the tunnel for any sign of Elena. When he didn't see her, he smiled. *She must have made it*, he thought.

From the shadows, a light switched on, blinding Grant.

Max walked out of the dark, holding a pistol to Elena's head. "If you're carrying a gun, I suggest that you drop it down the elevator shaft, or I'll kill Ms. Leon."

Grant shook his head and held out his arms. "I'm unarmed, and for the love of God, man, give it up. If we don't leave now, we're all going to die when this whole mountain explodes."

"You're lying. Surely, you took something of value that belonged to them."

"I have nothing. I'm not like you. I just want to come out of this alive."

"Liar!" screamed Max. Spittle flew from his lips. The man's right eye twitched uncontrollably. "Empty your pockets. I want to see what you have."

Grant took a step toward Max. "Please listen to me. I have nothing; I never wanted anything from them. We have to go, or we're going to die."

"No. I can't go back to my brother without something to give him."

Grant kept walking, taking one slow, careful step after another. "Max, come with us. There's no need for you to die."

"Never. I'd rather die here than face the shame I will bring on my family's name for failing to accomplish my mission."

"Okay, have it your way. But please let Elena go."

"No. I think it best if we all go together."

Elena had heard enough. She balled up her right fist and sent it flying straight back into Max's crotch. The man let out a muffled moan as he doubled over and reached for his injured groin.

Grant leaped forward and hit Max in the jaw with his right fist. The mercenary staggered back on his feet. Max raised his arm to fire, but Grant saw the move coming, grabbed his opponent's right arm, and thrust his knee into Max's elbow, dislocating it.

The mercenary cried out. His pistol fell to the ground.

Grant kicked it away and pulled Max to him, flipping him over his hip. The killer landed hard on the ground. Before he could regain his strength, Grant grabbed him by the collar and dragged him toward the elevator shaft.

"Rot in hell," said Grant as he pushed Max out into the open air.

Max realized he was about to die and tried to grab hold of Grant's arms. It was too late; he cried out in fear as he fell back into the darkness.

Grant stood still. He stared down the shaft as he struggled to catch his breath.

Elena took him by the hand. "Come on, David; he's gone. Let's make a run for it."

Grant nodded and ran as best as he could beside Elena. Within a matter of seconds, they were out of the mine and under a clear blue sky.

"The car," said Grant, pointing at the vehicle the mercenaries had stolen from him.

"You don't believe they left the keys in the ignition, do you?" said Elena.

"If they didn't, we're dead."

Elena opened the driver's door and saw the keys were missing.

"Look behind the driver's visor," suggested Grant.

Elena flipped it down. The keys fell into her hand. She slid down onto the seat and started the car. As soon as Grant was inside, she placed the car in gear, thrust her foot down on the gas pedal, and spun the steering wheel around in her hands. The car's tires spun on the gravel, shooting rocks up into the air. The instant the car was facing downhill, Elena let out a whoop and drove the car as if she were a NASCAR driver. She sped around several long-abandoned trucks and made straight for the road leading back to town.

Max slowly opened his eyes and looked up. He could see the faint light at the top of the shaft. He tried to sit up but found that he couldn't move his arms or his legs. He let out a mournful cry when he realized that he had broken his back. Out of the corner of his eye, he saw something moving in the dark. It sniffed the air before letting out a throaty growl. Fear gripped Max's soul when he realized the saber-toothed tiger was only an arm's reach away from him. The creature placed a paw on his chest, digging its claws in. It swung its head over until its salivating mouth was right above Max's face. He tried to scream, but found he had no voice. For the next few horrible seconds, Max Roth found out what it was like to be eaten alive.

Grant glanced down at his watch. They were out of time. "Pull over," he said to Elena.

"Why?"

"Because we need to get out of the car and take cover in a ditch."

Elena saw a spot a few hundred meters ahead and brought the car to a sliding halt. They jumped out of the car and ran to a steel culvert on the side of the road. No sooner had they crawled inside when the ground beneath them seemed to vibrate and shake. Grant looked back at the mine. The whole mountain was rocking back and forth. A second later, a brilliant-white light shot from the top of the mountain, followed by an earsplitting explosion. The mountain disappeared behind a cloud of dust. Debris was thrown skyward before tumbling back to the ground. A boulder slammed into the hood of Grant's car, flattening it like a pancake.

He saw the wall of dust racing down the side of the mountain toward them and took Elena in his arms. He had to yell to be heard. "Cover your mouth and close your eyes!"

The world went dark as the dust surged over the top and then inside the culvert. The last thing Grant heard before blacking out was Elena screaming.

55

Two hours had passed since the attack on the gym, and not a single predator had been seen. Reba saw some of the townspeople walking down Main Street.

It was over.

The doors to the school opened, and the people were allowed to head home. A fine, gray dust covered everything in town. When Maclean had heard the explosion and felt the ground move, his gut told him Robertson's Mine was no longer there. He feared for his friends' lives.

"Should I grab the keys to one of our Suburbans?" said Tibeluk to Maclean.

"Yeah, I'd like to head up to the mine right away," he replied, silently praying his colleagues had somehow survived the blast.

"Can I come along?" asked Hayes.

"Of course you can. But I wouldn't hold out much hope for David and Elena."

"There's always hope, Sergeant."

"And I took you for the eternal pessimist."

The sound of helicopter blades cutting through the air made Maclean stop and look skyward. A half-dozen dark shapes flew over the top of a nearby hill, heading toward the town at treetop level.

"Are those Blackhawk helicopters?" asked Hayes.

"They sure are," replied Maclean. "Must be the National Guard. Better late than never, I suppose."

The helicopters flew over the town and broke into three pairs. Two turned about and came back down over Main Street. Maclean frowned when he realized the choppers were unmarked. He spotted two racks protruding from the side of the helicopters with rows of canisters attached to them. His jaw dropped when he saw a man in a biohazard suit looking down at them from an open side door. Maclean smelled an odd odor in the air. His vision began to blur. He reached out for something to grab hold of. He never felt his feet buckle underneath him.

The onrushing dust cloud filled the sky. The sound of the mountain coming apart deafened Grant. He held Elena tight in his arms and closed his eyes. Grant didn't want to die.

With a loud gasp, he opened his mouth wide and sat straight up, trying to get air into his lungs. Grant opened his eyes and saw he wasn't in the culvert anymore. Instead, he was lying in bed inside a brightly lit military tent. He looked around and saw he was alone. There was an IV in his arm. His breathing and heart rate were being monitored by a machine behind his bed. No matter how hard he tried, Grant had no recollection of being rescued.

A door on the side of the tent opened. Grant could have jumped for joy when Maclean and Hayes walked inside. They were wearing matching dark gray coveralls and sneakers.

"I'm glad to see that you've returned to the land of the living," said Maclean. "It was touch-and-go there for a while. Your lungs were caked with dust. If they hadn't found you when they did, you and Elena would both be dead."

"Where is Elena?" asked Grant. His voice was hoarse and barely audible.

"She's still in intensive care," said Hayes. "She's going to be all right, but the medics wanted to make sure her lungs were completely cleaned out and working as they should."

Grant ran a hand over his bristle-covered chin, "How long have

I been here?"

"Four days."

"Really?"

"Yeah, four long days," replied Maclean.

Grant tried getting out of bed. In an instant, his head began to swim. He sat back on the edge of his bed. Maclean poured him a glass of ice water. Grant smiled and took a swig to wet his parched mouth. "So, who's in charge of the cleanup?"

"Beats me," said Maclean. "But I can assure you it's not your army."

Grant looked at Hayes. "Do you know who they are?"

"I'm positive they're not from our partners in the DIA. The best I could get out of a colonel was to mind my own business," said Hayes. "If I hadn't had my Project Gauntlet ID on me, we'd be with the rest of the people of Robertson's Mine being reprogrammed."

"What the hell does reprogrammed mean?"

"David, these people are experts at covering things up. Within hours, all the animals were gone. They were flown out in the back of Chinook helicopters to who knows where. Next, all the people in the town were rounded up under the guise of administering first aid and trauma counseling. They were given a concoction of drugs that made their minds malleable to suggestion. Right now, they're being told that there were no prehistoric creatures on the loose. That what happened was a catastrophic volcanic eruption. All of the people who died over the past few days did so when the volcano blew."

"What about the Sheriff? She met us and knows all about the aliens."

"Come tomorrow, we'll be able to walk into her office and she won't recognize us, or ever recall meeting us."

"My God, this is all so unbelievable."

"I know, but it's happening as we speak," said Maclean.

"Have either of you heard from Colonel Andrews?"

"I have," said Hayes. "He's on his way up here. It seems he doesn't trust whoever our hosts are to see us home safely."

"Until he gets here, I'd like one of you to be by Elena's side night and day. If these people are as untrustworthy as they sound, I don't want them tinkering with her memory."

"We can do that," said Maclean. "Now, you need to put your head down for a little nap. I'll come by at suppertime to see how you're doing."

Grant lay back on his bed. Right away, his eyes grew heavy and sleep washed over him. In seconds, he was snoring loud enough to be head over the generators running outside of the medical tent.

56

Peterson Air Force Base

Colorado Springs, Colorado

David Grant took a seat in Project Gauntlet's briefing room and waited for his friends to arrive. It had been six weeks since the incident in Alaska. Since then, he and the rest of team had written a comprehensive report on their activities at Robertson's Mine, which was subsequently presented in absolute secrecy to the Secretary of Defense and the Chairman of the Joint Chiefs of Staff. This was followed by some more-than-welcome extended leave for most of the organization. Grant knew it was time to return to work when he could no longer take his father's incessant demands that he quit the army and return home. He loved his father, but he just wasn't ready to settle down. Grant left home in the middle of the night and went hiking in the Rockies for a few days by himself before coming back to Colorado.

Maclean strolled into the room with a smile on his face and a spring in his step. He sat down and handed his friend a cup of coffee from a nearby cafe.

"Thanks," said Grant.

"I knew you'd want one," said Maclean. "The stuff they have here is simply godawful."

"So, how was leave?"

"Not too bad. I got to see my kid sister and her husband for a few days before I took off and went surfing with some of my mates from the regiment. After that, I spent a week in Bali lying under the sun, drinking far too much alcohol, and enjoying my life. Almost being killed a few times gives you a new perspective on things."

"That it does. Did your friends ask you any questions about what happened in Iraq?"

"Yeah, but I told them I was knocked unconscious a second after the whole thing started and didn't see anything. After that, they stopped asking."

"My parents never asked me a single question. I think they were just happy to see me alive."

"Speaking of that, how was your leave?"

"My dad and I clashed over the family business from the day I arrived there until the day I left."

"Families. What are you going to do? You don't get to choose them, you just have to learn to live with them."

Elena, Hayes, and Colonel Andrews walked in and joined them at the table.

The two soldiers respectfully stood.

"I hope everyone had a good time on leave," said Andrews, waving for everyone to take a seat.

"It was okay," said Maclean. "But it could have been longer."

"I'll see what I can do next time around."

Hayes set a cup of tea on the table in front of him. "During my time off, I was given special access to the British Ministry of Defense's top secret World War Two archives. The whole time we were in Alaska, there was a nagging thought in the back of my mind that I couldn't shake. I was sure I'd once skimmed over a file a number of years back that alluded to an incident in Norway in 1942 that bore some striking similarities to the situation we recently found ourselves in."

"And did you rediscover this file?" asked Elena.

"Yes, I did. This time, I read the report from cover to cover. In the winter of 1942, a team of Allied commandos parachuted into Norway to investigate what was reported to be an advanced German fighter, which had crashed in the mountains. Captain Shaw, the team leader, wrote in his report that the alleged German plane was unlike any he had ever seen in his life. He even drew a picture of it for his report. I wasn't allowed to bring the file with me, but the image he drew was a large ball, not a plane."

"I'm surprised he wasn't locked up after submitting his report," said Grant.

"Wait, it gets better…or worse, depending on your point of view. Before long, people started to disappear. Shaw and his team were hunted down and eventually captured by the Germans, who took them as prisoners to a weather station. It's here that the report comes the closest to our experiences. Shaw described creatures that were not of this world attacking and killing people. He even claimed that the person behind it all was able to change his appearance at will."

"Good lord, that sounds too much like what happened to us in Alaska," said Elena. "Does he say what happened to this person?"

"Yes, he was killed by an Allied soldier during a fight. Shaw claimed that the body vanished before his eyes."

"Makes you wonder how many more reports there are like this sitting in top secret vaults around the world, collecting dust?" said Grant.

"Makes my time off gardening seem like a bit of a waste," said Elena.

"Nonsense; you, of all people, needed to take it easy," said Andrews. "You were in the hospital far longer than Captain Grant was. The last thing you needed to do was crawl around some musty basement reading seventy-year-old documents."

"Colonel, how did your recent trip to Washington go?" asked Grant.

"Productive, to say the least. The report you people wrote caused quite a stir among the President's National Security

Council."

"I sure as hell hope it did," said Grant. "People needlessly died in Alaska because of the actions of an extraterrestrial madman."

"Because of what happened up there, the Secretary of Defense was ordered by the President to reexamine our mandate and our budget. The unofficial word I was given before leaving to fly home was that we will no longer be tasked with finding and retrieving downed UAVs and planes. That was handed lock, stock, and barrel to the DIA. Our primary focus from now on will be on the investigation of UFOs and other unexplainable incidents."

"I take it that means we're going to get some new offices?" said Hayes.

"Most definitely. I just don't know where yet."

"Sir, does this mean that you no longer require Sergeant Maclean and me?" said Grant.

"On the contrary, Captain," said Andrews. "This organization needs the two of you more now than the first day you arrived."

Maclean nudged Grant in the arm. "Hey, what are you doing? I'm being paid my normal salary, plus a foreign-duty allowance for living here in the States, plus your army's highest levels of hazard and danger pay. I sure as hell didn't join the army for the money, but let's not screw around with a good thing."

"Sorry, I thought you'd want to head back home to Australia and resume your duties in the SAS."

"I do miss my mates, but my old job doesn't seem as relevant as it once did. We're facing a new and deadly challenge that must be met head-on. Let's not forget some of the people trying to kill us to get their hands on alien technology were from our own planet. Besides, I still want to meet the man who financed the attack on our camp, so I can tell him goodbye to his face."

"When you put it that way, a man would be a fool not to want to stick around."

"So, I take it that I can count on your continued service with Gauntlet?" said Andrews.

Grant looked over at his friend and saw him nod. "Sure, Colonel, why not?"

"Okay, I'm glad to hear that. General McLeod has asked me to submit my new proposed organizational structure to him in a week's time. So, that will be the focus of all our efforts for the next three days. We need to build a team that is capable of both scientific and military responses to any situation it finds itself facing."

"I sure as hell hope your defense budget is bottomless," said Maclean. "I don't want to go anywhere without an armored brigade backing me up from now on."

"I think we can scrub the first suggestion put forward as being financially unobtainable," said Andrews as he picked up a marker and walked to a blank whiteboard hanging on the wall. "Come on, people, you've seen what we're lacking, let's do some spitballing and come up with something we and our bosses can all live with."

Maclean leaned over and whispered to his friend, "I was being serious."

Grant smiled. "I know you were, and I bet Elena and Jeremy were thinking precisely the same thing, too. Unfortunately, we need to be pragmatic. Let's ask for a Ranger battalion on standby and see what that gets us."

"Come on, people, you have to have something on your minds you'd like to contribute?" said Andrews looking at Hayes and Elena.

"I kind of like the sergeant's suggestion," said Hayes. "After watching an apex predatory bird from the past kill and eat a man, there isn't enough firepower on the planet that will ever make me feel safe again."

Andrews shook his head and took a seat. "Please, people, we need to be realistic."

Grant peered over at the clock on the wall. It was just past nine-thirty in the morning. He groaned. It was going to be a long three days.

57

Robertson's Mine

Alaska

Tracey Tibeluk unlocked the door to her apartment, flicked on a light, and walked inside. She was tired after a long day of driving around one of the new police officers the town had just hired to replace Bill Scott and Sean McCartney. All she wanted to do was crawl into a hot bath and lay there under a blanket of bubbles, while she closed her eyes and relaxed. Her roommate, a nurse currently working nights, had picked up their mail and left it in a neat pile on the kitchen table. Tibeluk dug through the mail, tossing their junk mail into the recycling bin, until she found a small parcel addressed to her. She looked for a return address but saw that there was none.

How odd, she thought. Tibeluk carefully opened the parcel and looked inside. Wrapped in some tissue paper was a golden pin with a kangaroo holding an Australian flag on the end of it. She took out the pin and held it up to the light. Tibeluk was puzzled. She couldn't think of anyone she knew who could be on holiday in Australia at the moment. She was about to put it back in its box when she thought of a man she had been seeing on and off in her dreams for the past month. No matter how hard she tried, she could never remember the man's face or his name when she awoke.

Tibeluk smiled and decided to stick the pin on a board next to the fridge. For reasons she would never understand, every time she looked at the pin she would feel safe and less alone in the world.

END